The GLIMMER Girl

andy onyx

MICRODOT BOOKS

nd Edition: 18/05/ 2021

MICRODOT BOOKS

odot.books@gmail.com

/.andyonyx.co.uk

P catalogue record for this book is available from the
sh Library

ring Information:
ial discounts are available on quantity purchases by
orations, associations, educators, and others. For details,
act the publisher at the above listed address.

J: 9798638660710

For Assa

'It will not do to act without knowing the opponent's
condition…
and knowing the opponent's condition is impossible
without espionage.'

- Sun Tzu, *The Art of War*

Author's Note

What follows is a work of fiction containing some imagined dialogue from historic personalities of note. The events take place between the early 20th and 21st centuries.

In Ireland, where an element of our story is rooted, a separate stratum of species has long been acknowledged and defined by folklore, considered by some to be just as real as our own. A view easily and quite naturally dispelled by others as mere faery tales and superstition.

But one back-lit morning, we may wake to question how much reality and truth is looking back at us, as we wipe away the steam from our AI mirror …

Can I ask you to imagine two identical doors side-by-side, any design or colour you like, but both are ajar? One has a sign saying, '*This Way*,' and the other, '*Secret. Do not enter.*'

Now make your choice and step forth...

خف

PROLOGUE

October 1914.

Meaux, France.

'Damn you, sir. You are no Englishman!' cursed the lone driver in a scornful outburst at the invisible deity and deliverer of the faith-shredding tempest. It began with pebbles of rain carried on an eastern gust, before a sudden, low darkness dropped amidst a shell-burst of hail. The icy shrapnel could have stripped the driver to the bone, were it not for the Silver Shadow's glass and canvas shield. Another fork of white-hot venom streaked above, cleaving the blackened sky, as if a celestial anvil had been struck by Prussian artillery.

The screaming wind spewed a horizontal fountain over the windshield. He sensed the vehicle lifting and the steering lightening, as if he were about to be snatched up by the enemy typhoon and thrown back above the clouds, beyond Paris and down into the Channel like a catch of unwanted small fry. But still the driver pressed on, man and machine joined with intent against the elemental enemy.

The mission was all. His view of the road ahead was impeded by each sleet-filled blast that collided like the accumulated mass of a crashing wave. Knuckles white and body hunched over the polished wheel, his internal battle raged, aggression and frustration pitted against fear and caution. The former had the upper hand as his foot pressed on the accelerator, increasing the tempo of the assault of hailstones against the glass.

In the tunnel of darkness formed by the storm, the light at its end was imagined, but the destination real, if only he could stay on the road. His only ally was the Rolls. With this realisation, he straightened his arms and stamped down on the pedal, the pistons snarling in response, the sound reassuring him for a few fleeting seconds during his lone cavalry charge against the sky's onslaught.

The headlights caught a blur of green hedgerow. He pulled the wheel down hard left at the last moment, cursing once more under his breath as the road snaked from right to left. He fought the overwhelming urge to brake. The rear end of the Rolls drifted with understeer, causing the car to aquaplane uncontrollably. All was lost, but suddenly the tyres gripped the road again with a shudder, whipping his head to the side. He revved hard, the engine now moaning its disapproval against deceleration as the Rolls climbed the hill. He dropped the gears down to second and struggled to the peak. Once the Rolls had crested the hill, he opened up again, eager to make up time.

The mission was all.

WILMA would be waiting at the rendezvous, and the drop was crucial. It would, the driver hoped, fill the void of information relating to the enemy's airship capabilities as the nascent conflict gained momentum.

The roll and slide of the car in the deluge stirred nauseous memories of his time at sea; a shameful stain on the performance of the naval officer which the stewardship of the Secret Service Bureau had all but cleansed.

At the bottom of the hill, he hit a torrent of rainfall.

The Rolls' engine stalled and threw up a veil of steam. The driver reached back for the oilskin, then out he leapt, cranking her back to life and setting off again. He was close; he could see the lights of the inn on the near horizon, its roof backlit by a volley of lightning. He sighed with relief, but his eyes caught a shape moving across the road yards ahead, quickly, upright, oblivious to the onrushing vehicle. Options flashed through the driver's mind: Left? Right? Brake? Accelerate? Left it was, as impact with the figure seemed inevitable. *Thump!* There, on the rear left wing. *Brake!* The vehicle aquaplaned horizontally to the road, then spun to a stop at forty-five degrees to the reverse.

'Damn, damn, *damn*!' screamed the driver,

striking the wheel with each word. He stepped out into the deluge and pushed along the length of the car, clawing at the bonnet's Silver Lady in desperation. He could see the outline of a figure ten yards ahead, lying prone and unmoving in the verge. The shape, defined by the headlamps, reflected off the stone walls on either side of the road and the glistening track. The driver ran over, almost lifted again by the gale at his back, and knelt, speechless, before the figure. The body lay twisted and face down, and despite the near pitch-dark, he could see it was a male, barefoot, virtually in rags, with hair that was long, matted and burning red.

Decisions now. Evaluations made as fast as the white forks from above. A crisis, or just a fly in the ointment? Possibly an escaped prisoner, or even a lunatic?

He reached down and grasped a shoulder to turn the body over. Should he put him in the back? He paused to consider the road death of a nobody, especially on a night like this. There was a war on, after all. He released his grip, sparing himself the lifeless eyes and the features of the unfortunate.

A streak of electricity struck a tree beyond the wall, expanding its trapped vapour in a millisecond with an ear-splitting crack. It was followed by the rumble of thunder above, akin in volume to detonating munitions. The storm was right on top. He looked left to the beckoning lights down the road, refocusing on his objective—WILMA, the mission—then back at the body. Shaking his head, he rose to his feet and said under his breath, 'Sorry, old boy.' He crossed himself—forehead, then shoulder to shoulder— even though he shuffled his morality, faith and atheism like a deck of dog-eared playing cards.

Bent double, he faced the wind and battled his way back toward the vehicle. The elements seemed to be pushing him back toward his victim, deafening him with howling accusations born of his conscience, but he fought on, advancing step by laboured step. He opened the car door, and with one foot inside, looked back over his shoulder.

The body was gone.

Chapter 1

MONUS

In the time it took Commander Mansfield Smith-Cumming to cover the final three miles to the inn, the storm had blown over to the west. The night air became fresh and clear, and the gale dialled down to a mild breeze. The clouds receded, allowing the full bomber's moon to illuminate the surrounding fields. Further down the track into the valley, he could see the houses of Chambry stretched out before him. He threw the oilskin on the rear seats and checked his weapon, then stowed it in the shoulder holster under his jacket. The funds for the exchange were safely strapped to the other side of his chest.

The combined impact of warmth, noise and gaslight hit him as he crossed the threshold. The inhabitants, held captive by the storm, were having a good time of it. There was a rabble of vernacular voices and laughter wrapped in tobacco smoke, accompanied by the high wheeze of a lone accordion.

The Commander entered with a finely balanced

demeanour of confidence and crumpled posture, one that would have drawn consternation and sharp words from his superior, Captain 'Blinker' Hall, back at the Admiralty, due to an absence of poise distinctly unbefitting an English naval officer.

He neither avoided nor sought eye contact with the clientele as he moved forward, making sure not to peer too closely, as he knew this would provoke an equal response. At the bar, he spotted the red shawl gathered around the neck of a blonde woman in the corner, and their eyes met. On the table before her was a glass of sherry, a lonely tankard set before the place opposite.

The first two stages were all clear. So far, so good. As he made his way over to the table, he bumped a patron's shoulder, causing a slight spillage of ale. Damn it. He uttered a hurried apology. The man turned side-on and fixed him with a penetrating gaze. Most unusual irises: one brown, the other green. Red and gold hair poked out from beneath the man's flat cap. The man said nothing and turned away.

The Commander reached the table and gestured as to whether he would be allowed to sit. The woman nodded. He lifted the tankard and shared a silent toast with her, metal clinking against her glass, followed by a mutual sip of their drinks and an unblinking glance above their rims.

The woman was first to set her glass down on the table. Stage three: all clear. He took her hand and exchanged the recognition code, an abstract phrase and response relating to French harvest.

Step four: all clear. This woman was indeed WILMA.

She nudged his leg under the table. There, his free hand open palm upwards, he felt the folded paper, taking it and making the exchange. Done. Now for the outro.

WILMA placed a room key in his left hand, then cursed loudly enough to be heard above the din and threw the remainder of her sherry at his chest. Those sitting nearest looked around as she rose, gathered her things and, in tears, made her exit. The Commander feigned shock and shrugged, smiling to his observers, who laughed and raised their glasses. He followed suit in response.

He placed the folded square of paper in the left side of his jacket and began to rise. As he did so, a figure sidled into WILMA's vacant chair opposite him. It was Mr Strange Eyes from a few minutes earlier. The Commander froze for a second, then sat back down. He smiled at the man and indicated another apology, thanking God for the presence of the service revolver next to his ribs. The man held his tankard in his right hand and took his cap off with his left, his eyes locked with the Commander's. Then the stony face cracked, revealing an impossibly broad smile of gleaming, crooked, sharkish teeth, punctuated by a single gold incisor that glinted in the candlelight. The Commander said nothing, but behind his forced apologetic smile, his mind screamed, Who the hell are you?

The man closed his mouth and wheezed a laugh, followed by a short, guttural cackle like a magpie's call, then settled himself down.

'Tis a good question, with many more to follow,' said the man, in plain English laced with a Celtic brogue and a sing-song cadence. 'And *what,* and *where,* and *how*'s maybe next, eh?'

The words, spoken in answer to his silent thought, shocked the Commander like the stab of a rapier. His palms curled involuntarily into fists before he gripped the edge of the table with his left and took hold of his own tankard with his right. He was poised to weaponise the pot, imagining a split second whereby he would bring the edge down hard on the bridge of the blackguard's roman nose in order to make his escape.

'We've met before, eh?' the man asked.

'I don't think so,' growled the Commander, through the wreckage of his smile. He stiffened and examined the man's attire and appearance: hair neatly cut, his shirt, tie, jacket and hat all shades of green, clean-shaven, but with fingernails that were unnaturally long and claw-like.

With an index finger, the man traced a small sign of the cross in front of his chest. The Commander's blood ran cold, and the colour drained from his face. He suddenly felt sicker than he had on any maritime adventure. He couldn't possibly have been seen back there on the road. He had barely been able to see his own hand in front of his face in the darkness and the rain.

'Is this some kind of trick?' asked the Commander.

'No.' The man came straight back, tapping his ear. 'But *this* may be!'

The accordion spontaneously began to play *God Save the King,* the other drinkers completely oblivious to the change. Sweat poured out of the spy, and he felt faint.

'Well,' said the man as he folded his hands. 'I'll help you out now, won't I? My name is Monus. I'm a king, a Willow King, and I'm so very pleased to meet ya.'

Smith-Cumming tried to talk, but Monus waved a finger. 'Now, I doesn't need your name to know who, and *what*, y'are.'

'But you,' whispered the Commander. 'Where are you from ,sir?'

'Way over there.' Monus nodded his head north-west, in the direction of the Channel. 'Across waters deep, mountains high, deserts wide … I upset me Ma, so she sent me walking.' He demonstrated with his two forefingers, their talon-like nails tapping along the table. 'Walking, walking, walking. And I haven't eaten, slept, or drank for a long time until … something stopped me.' The last words were a blend of accusation and celebration. 'Freed me. My Ma tied the knot, and it's you that's loosened it, out there this night when our paths crossed. And thus, by your careless driving, we are bound,' Monus concluded, before looking down into the tankard and then back up at his terrified companion.

With the storm having passed and the hour getting late, the place began to thin out until Monus and the Commander were alone with only the innkeeper, who was cleaning glasses behind the bar, and the accordion player, who continued with his patriotic English tune.

'So … what do you want?' stammered Smith-Cumming.

Monus mimicked the Commander's voice. Annoying in children of a certain age, thought Smith-Cumming, but unbearable in adults, especially this … thing in front of me. He strained to gather his thoughts and focus. Come on, man! The mission!

'Fair is … fair is, fairies,' mused Monus, 'or fair *isn't!*' He spat the last word out with contempt. 'What I want is a wager. If I prove all this to be real, you'll allow me to do your bidding. If it's all just a terrible dream, you need not worry. Now, how's that?'

The Commander, thinking that this dream could not become any stranger, was being proved wrong as he descended further into the nightmare.

'You would do my bidding? In what way … At what cost?'

'Ahhh, the cost.' Monus became even more animated. 'Let me see, something … priceless, but … only what you can afford.'

The intensity of the exchange was taking its toll on Smith-Cumming. 'Please,' he implored, 'stop with your riddles.'

Monus sat bolt upright and slapped the table, a sharp *crack* that silenced the accordion player, who blankly sauntered out. Smith-Cumming and Monus were left alone with the innkeeper, who continued, oblivious, with the rhythm of his work.

Monus nodded suggestively and stared in turn at the hidden gun on one side of the Commander's chest and the stashed documents concealed on the other.

'For what is … afoot, I will do your bidding. Three times,' he concluded with a fixed certainty. He uncurled the long-nailed fingers from his fist one at a time, three in all, then struck them down on the tabletop.

Oh God, the mission; Ally; tomorrow; the War! The realisation was like a cannon sounding in Smith-Cumming's brain. He longed to awaken in sodden bedclothes, but, alas, it didn't happen.

'For something … priceless and what you can … afford. That is my wager to you, as Monus, the Willow King. Do you accept?'

This was only a dream; what was there to lose? The Commander was deep in thought, trying to rationalise the proceedings to himself. He raised his tankard and Monus followed suit. When the metals clinked together, the spy thought, for an instant, that he heard every shot and desperate scream from the carnage unfolding on the Western Front. Through squinted eyes, he observed Monus draining his tankard before snatching the one from his own hand and repeating the gesture.

'As I say, I've been awfully thirsty,' said Monus with a wink. He got up, doffed his cap to the innkeeper and left. The Commander rubbed his eyes and temples, gaining little relief, and then rose.

'Monsieur Gabot, your room is prepared. I hope it is to your satisfaction,' said the innkeeper, without looking up from polishing his glass.

Once inside the room, the Commander locked the door and closed the curtains, then threw his revolver and the folded papers down onto the bed. They were blank, but of foul odour; the inconvenience of using man-fat as invisible ink.

Such was the importance of this mission that he had undertaken it himself. He increased the flame on the bracketed wall lamp and held the pages up to the lamplight. It was all there: sketches, figures, facts and locations, all in the most beautiful copperplate writing.

Smith-Cumming placed the papers under his pillow, made the room as secure as possible by wedging the dresser chair against the door and retired into a deep slumber, his loveless loaded companion by his side.

He dreamt lurid dreams recounting the singular events of the evening, tumbling over and over, like a sensory kaleidoscope: WILMA, the storm, the accident, the storm, Monus, the accordion, the gun-blast toast, the accident... Now in twilight—dawn or dusk, he couldn't discern—he was standing before a tree within a forest clearing, surrounded by three standing stones. He reached out, the bark warm to the touch. There was a presence beyond the other side of the tree, hiding from view. Try as he might, he couldn't catch a full glimpse, neither this way nor that, chasing the wheeze and magpie-cackle that came from the blind spot.

He awoke with a start to the cock's crow, mingled with the sounds of a carriage engine and the rasp of tyres on the gravel of the courtyard. Doors slammed, and he made out voices raised in concern. He checked under the pillow: his prized possession was still there. With haste, he dressed and left the room, finding the innkeeper in the parlour with two men, huddled in concern. The innkeeper gestured in the Commander's direction as he approached and walked to meet him in the centre of the room.

'I am so sorry, Monsieur Gabot,' the innkeeper said apologetically. 'It is your friend.'

He took Smith-Cumming by the arm and led him out into the yard, toward the carriage. He opened the rear door, and there, on the seat, was a shrouded figure. He pulled the material to one side enough to reveal blonde trails of hair and a charred red neckerchief. There was also the pungent scent of a dowsed fire.

It was WILMA.

'She must have been struck by lightning in the storm when she left, Monsieur,' said the innkeeper. 'They found her there, further down the track.' He pointed in the direction the Commander had approached from the previous night.

His mouth devoid of moisture, the Commander was silent.

'When she left last night,' the innkeeper said, 'she asked me to give you this.' He handed over an envelope.

Turning the envelope over in his hands, Smith-Cumming watched, non-committal, as the innkeeper respectfully closed the door on the dead. Smith-Cumming returned to the inn. Back in the room, he hurriedly opened the envelope and stared at the single sheet of blank paper within. He locked the door, drew the curtain and rushed to light the lamp.

Written in the same hand as before—large but beautiful copperplate writing—was a single phrase of three words:

Sorry, old boy.

On the drive to GHQ in Paris, the Commander's mind wrestled the fantastical events of the previous night. He was trying in vain to thresh apart dream, reality and tragedy. The events dominated his mind, and he fought in vain to push them back, like drunken queue-jumpers, behind his primary mission objective: to transcribe the intelligence report, transmit and return.

Unavoidably, the incident had required extra funds for the innkeeper to look after WILMA; after all, the Commander couldn't drive around Paris with a scorched corpse on the back seat. Full of remorse, he'd told the innkeeper that he must break the news of her death to the relatives of his 'friend', and they would return later in the evening to collect the body.

The importance of the mission had been the reason he had undertaken it solo, without so much as a driver, but to complete the transcription, he would need cover and security from the one serving officer in France he could trust absolutely: his only son.

Upon joining his father, the young man noted how pale and tired the Commander looked and insisted that he take the wheel. A leisurely lunch was out of the question, as time was constricted; the incident needed to be attended to.

Over a thirty-mile round trip, funds were collected and exchanged, the transcript copied and the blood money paid to the 'relatives' to collect WILMA from the innkeeper and get her back to her actual family, assuming she had one. Smith-Cumming now had two hours to get to the ferry and have the Rolls lifted aboard. He would be back behind the wheel as soon as he was able to drop his son off at GHQ. How proud he was to have undertaken the day's business with his son, a newly commissioned officer, as driver and security. The boy's mother hadn't forgiven him for facilitating her son's posting with the British Expeditionary Force at the outbreak of war in July, and he doubted she ever would. He would only be able to tell her that they'd met and that all was well, and for that, he felt a little guilty and selfish.

Despite the roar of the engine as the young driver threw them in and out of the corners, his adrenaline waning, Smith-Cumming soon began to nod off.

'Sorry, old boy!' was suddenly spat into his right ear, followed by the magpie-like cackle. His eyes snapped open, and he fixed his stare on the driver. The grinning man with a glinting gold tooth and flaming hair was at the wheel, wearing Ally's uniform.

Another nightmare. Wake up, he urged himself.

'Jesus Christ!' Smith-Cumming said as his senses fully returned to him.

The driver took his eyes off the road. 'Father, are you OK?' he asked.

The hedges flashed by as Smith-Cumming pulled his gaze from his son's concerned eyes back to the road. Out of the corner of his eye, he saw –

'Look out!'

There was a figure in the road. The driver pulled the wheel one way then the other, amid the squeal of tyres as one side of the carriage lifted from the surface. They slammed back down and the car flipped, the track replacing the sky above them. A moment's silence. Then, the impact, resulting in the carriage being wrapped around the trunk of a tree like an iron girdle. The wheels spun silently, the smell of fuel blooming in the air. Steam hissed from the ruptured radiator, water dripping from it in slow-motion. Time was marked by the ticking of cooling metal.

Smith-Cumming was face down. He raised his head, looking right and then left. He could see his son across the road, lying on his back as if resting, exhausted. He called out until he was hoarse, but there was no response. Both his legs were trapped; he managed to free one, but the other wouldn't budge, as if the willow they had struck held the car and himself fast within its strangulating grip.

He heard a whistle in the distance, indistinct at first from the birdsong above. As it drew closer, he recognised the tune of *God Save the King*, its tone and delivery mocking him with each note. Brown brogues shone like mirrors below green tweed bags and stopped a foot away, but the whistling continued. Smith-Cumming could see his pain and desperation reflected in the gleaming leather of the shoes.

'Please.' He coughed. 'Please. My son, over there. Please help!'

The whistling stopped. The man squatted, resting his chin on his palm and gazing across at the figure lying stock-still across the road. Smith-Cumming forced himself onto his elbow to see the man's face, which was side-on to his own. Then he heard the voice, and the familiar tone was unmistakable. He'd heard it for the first time only twenty hours before—and the words, too, but this time they were spoken much more slowly, with menace and gravitas.

'Something priceless, but … only what … you can afford.'

'No!' was the despairing response.

Monus turned his head from the boy to face him. The broad, glinting grin was gone, his mouth now closed in a modest half-smile. He looked over Smith-Cumming's shoulder at his trapped limb and winced.

Smith-Cumming collapsed face down again, exhausted. His tormentor laid down beside him to maintain eye contact, reached into his breast pocket and placed a long metal-headed object on the ground between them.

'All payments are taken in advance,' he quipped. 'Let's get it done, then.'

His tormentor got up and rested the axe on his shoulder, then, cackling, raised it above his head. The repeated scream of '*No,*' from the Englishman reverberated down the lanes and fields beyond.

Down came the axe.

His palms and forehead rested on the bark, soft and warm. The warmth was equal to the comfort of a lover, a mother, or a son. Smith-Cumming opened his eyes, his feet amongst the rich green grass at the base of the tree trunk. He discerned the comforting scents of woodsmoke and grilled meat and heard the crackle of a fire and a rasp of corvidian laughter. He looked around the tree and saw Monus, squatting before a spit suspended above a stone firepit. Monus beckoned to him to approach, and Smith-Cumming stood before him, his stare locked on the strange eyes.

'I won the wager, but as agreed, it's now I that owes you,' said Monus as he turned the spit. 'Three times, I said I would do your bidding, and that I'll do.'

'How … how will it be done?'

Monus stood up and spoke. 'On the morning after the night we met, you received a note.'

Smith-Cumming nodded his affirmation.

'Three words. The first thing you said to me that night.' Monus mimed a demonstration in thin air. 'Light a candle, tear off one word, and feed the flame. Think of them and say their name … I'll hear … and it will be done.'

Monus squatted back down to tend to the spit, and the Commander's gaze followed to take in the bubbling, charred remains of what looked to be a foot, toes and ankle.

There were hands on each arm, their fingers digging into his shoulders. There was the crack and sting of slaps against his cheeks as he came round, his own shouts ringing in his ears. The nurses reassured him and mopped his brow. Sweat, tears, pain and confusion reigned. Beneath the right knee was a void. The doctor sent the nurses away while he stayed with the patient. Finally, the patient tried to ask, but the words wouldn't come out. They didn't need to; the doctor understood.

'Your driver, Monsieur. I'm so sorry.'

A sedative injection took effect, and two days

later, Commander Mansfield Smith-Cumming woke to face an immeasurably changed world.

Chapter 2

SHEV

11/08/202?

0742 hrs, Caledonian Road & Barnsbury Station

London, UK.

In the beginning, they'd promised it would be harder to stay than to enter. Five minutes. That was how long it felt, but eighteen months were now behind her.

Every day, she would stand on Platform Three waiting for the Overground. Once she was at Shadwell, she'd vary her route. One day, she'd walk through Watney Market; another, she'd cross over and take the DLR to Limehouse or go on foot via Cable Street. All roads led to where the 'pleasures' of the Hive were waiting to test, adapt and improve.

Today, she wore a denim jacket, monochrome

flag tee-shirt, black leggings and lightweight DeWalt steel-toe-capped boots. Her hair would do whatever she wanted, but she settled on natural volume that day; auburn corkscrews traced with natural streaks of gold and red. Tiny freckles either side of her Kikuyu nose peppered her olive glow. Granny B had never stopped reminding her of the advantages of a mixed heritage: 'You've picked nought but the best from both bags, my love,' she'd say at regular intervals, ensuring the child would know her worth from the very day she arrived in her care.

The forecast had promised thunder and rain to banish the drought from the parched slab of London. She hoped the prediction was more accurate than the one offered by the orange dots of the digital matrix above her head: "HIGHBURY & ISLINGTON 2 MINS."

The regular passengers were all in their allotted places for the 06:45 arrival: Bhangra Man, with the jangly row seeping from his ear buds; Vape Girl, gifting her fruity fog to all and sundry on the rank hairdryer breeze; the double-shift unwashed labourer, suckling his rocket-fuel caffeine as it dissolved his tooth enamel and nerve endings; and, of course, the secret admirer, Herbert the Herbert, the nebby City Boy with the milk bottle lenses.

The ad had popped up on her phone screen eighteen months earlier. She'd clicked, read the blurb. Why not give it a whirl? she'd thought. The breaks hadn't come; at least, not the kind she was looking for. The future seemed vanilla, but at least she had a toe-hold proper job at M-City College, a zero-hours post teaching entry-level carpentry and joinery three full days and one evening a week.

Five years before, as a school leaver, her GCSEs had given her decent options: two Bs in English and Maths, and two As for French and woodwork. This opened the door to the local joiner and all-round Cally estate character, to take her on as an apprentice carpenter. By eighteen, she'd completed the framework and had a gold CSCS card. Soon after, she was running jobs, but the boss had some bad habits, all of which seemed to revolve around someone called *Charlie*. He spent more time moving between the pubs and bookies of Caledonian Road than watching the firm's accounts, so the firm soon died a death, shortly followed by his own When the global pandemic took hold, he preferred lock-in rather than lockdown, and, like his hero Elvis, Joe passed away loved tender, slumped on the throne in "trap one" of his local with a fiver glued up his nose. Before the drift, the boss had laid down the law when he handed over the reins on-site: 'Her word is as good as mine. You don't like it? Fuck off. There's the door.'

There'd been no problems back then, leaving the boss free to spend even more time in "the office". But since his passing and having to embrace the "new normal", she was out in the cold, just another agency chippie on the big lousy development sites of

London, another drop in the ocean of high-vis vests and hardhats.

Despite all the Equality and Diversity stuff at the induction and the posters in the canteen, the "silliness" at work had been getting too regular. On the final site, all the "-isms" had escalated from graffiti to verbal slights, to which she offered no reaction; as her sensei had always told her, in their age-old clichés: '*No emotional response, walk away, count to ten.*' She had played the game as required, but the bullies had misread this as timidity, and so it had started to get physical: a shove here, an elbow there.

The main offenders were the Trogs: Oleg and Dessie, an unlikely Ulster/Ukrainian double act. They called themselves chippies but, in actual fact, were nothing more than a pair of 'wood butchers'; jumped-up labourers who resented her skills and knowledge of the trade that easily dwarfed their own. They didn't know about her thirteen years of training, never mind the extras with Mr Snow. She didn't talk about it—she rarely talked at all—but the mugs clearly hadn't heard that you don't mess with the quiet ones and that thirteen may be unlucky for some. They'd put her physique, which they openly leered over, down to healthy eating and a bit of Zumba.

The whole site was going to White Bear on Friday for a drink after work, and Irma, one of Clifton's French Polishers, had insisted that she go along. It would've been rude to decline, and besides …

By the time they got there, the Friday feeling buzz had already taken hold. At one end of the beer garden at the rear of the pub, a DJ was attempting—and failing—to scratch *YMCA* into *Club Tropicana.* Along the edges, the bench tables were packed. There were multicoloured lights strung above—sad reminders of a Christmas long since passed—and, down the centre, pedestal tables crowned with red electric heaters were surrounded by clustered drinkers. At the opposite end of the garden to the DJ, one of the bar staff was continuing that most stressful of English traditions; struggling to light a barbecue.

Some faces were familiar from the site canteen, interspersed with local office workers and a few customary older locals, with their cheap-to-keep dogs and roll-ups to match. Oleg and Dessie were already half-cut. They'd sneaked off-site an hour early and were on a power-drinking mission, downing bottled lagers in two hits as if it were a race. They were drifting nearer, then Dessie suggested a visit to the gents for a 'livener'. They came back bolder than ever, their noses suitably white, and elbowed their way straight back into the girls' air space. She and Irma had been joking, dreaming about starting their own little cabinet-making and finishing firm and what they would call it, giggling about variations on a double act. They'd finally settled on either "Shape and Polish" or "Chisel and Shine" when she glanced over Irma's shoulder and caught sight of the two coked-up labourers.

'Speaking of the chisel, The Trogs are bang on the gear.'

'Then we should go,' said Irma. 'They're looking for trouble.' Her eyes became suddenly fearful as they, too, locked onto the approaching thugs.

'I know. You can go if you want, mate. But if you're staying, keep clear. OK?' She glanced up and saw they were within touching distance again. 'Maybe they've come to the right place, eh?'

Ever since Granny B had taken her to the dojo as an eight-year-old, she'd completed over ten thousand hours of training, and that was without counting the happy accident of additional Krav Maga instruction from Mr Snow from the flat next door. The sessions were blindfold, with no dialogue beyond 'Hello,' and the lesson subject, followed by, 'Goodbye. Take care now,' at the close. Mr Snow's accent had been so quiet and soft, almost a whisper, that everything else was purely physical. But Mr Snow had suddenly disappeared in a moonlight flit, as if by magic. The Ivanov family had moved into his place straight away, and it was as though he'd never existed. No goodbye or a lift with the furniture to the removal van. Nothing. Gone. But the skills and knowledge he'd passed on remained banked for time.

In the crowded beer garden, she played a determined game. Whenever she and Irma moved to a comfortable distance, Oleg and Dessie followed, time after time, as if attached by an elastic rope. Then it came: the grab for her backside. The fingertips of her right hand were already running down from Oleg's left elbow as the grubby palm hit the back pocket of her denim jeans. A millisecond later, as light as a feather, she located his fingers, separated them, gripped, turned, twisted and then lifted her 'prize' to shoulder height. *SNAP!* There was an intake of breath, then Oleg let out a squeal as he was introduced to a whole new world of blinding, unimaginable pain. Pint glasses crashed to the floor from a pedestal table as he tried to swing at her with his free right hand, but he was now a fourteen stone puppet; his fingers were holding the strings and control was hers. She flipped her grip over one-hundred-and-eighty degrees and brought him down to his knees amid the broken glass and lager, eliciting another shriek.

In her peripheral vision, she could see Dessie's shaven head approaching at speed, reflecting the coloured light bulbs from above. His right hand wound back like a spin bowler's, then wind-milled a bottle towards her head. She yanked on the strings, and her marionette duly danced into the arc of the swing as she withdrew. The bottle shattered, its stem raking through his scalp as it completed its route. Dessie's oncoming mass was defected into the pedestal off her shoulder, bringing a cheer from the rest of the drinkers as he hit the deck. She released the strings, and gravity did the rest for Oleg. There was a stunned silence, peppered thereafter with muted sniggers from the onlookers backing off as they scrambled to capture the moment on their phones.

Save All Your Kisses For Me came through the speakers as the big man wept on his knees in the centre of the action. There was no sickening axe-kick crashing down onto Oleg's crown and shattering his vertebrae, even though she felt like administering one. She knew such a technique would lead to a sure fatality, destroying more than one future in the process. She had been trained well and knew she was far better than that. Oleg was broken and defenceless, and that was enough.

Dessie scrambled to his feet and looked down at the quivering island of deathly pale meat coiled in a sea of beer, broken glass and ketchup. He still held the broken remnant of the bottle he'd unintentionally scythed across his pal's scalp. His eyes flicked back up to her, the bloodied shard aimed at her throat as he hissed, 'You fuck … you …' Unable to get the words out, he drew the stem back for the attack, his knees bent to propel him forwards. Calling upon another aspect of her training, she recalled struggling to hear Mr Snow's final lesson intro:

'*Physical psychology … We must now plant the opponent's moves* … heyeh'—he'd tapped his forehead—'*in* yeaction *to your own* …'

'More?' she asked Dessie, sliding back a metre and maintaining a stance of equal weight. Her assailant's blinking eyes were drawn back once more to his whimpering friend, then flickered back and forth between them for a couple of seconds. The seed of doubt that she'd planted in Dessie's tiny mind began to germinate. There was a commotion near the entrance; the towering door staff were approaching through the melee, drawn by the dog whistle of screaming and smashing glass. Precisely as she wished, Dessie enacted the move she had planted in his mind. He threw the weapon to one side and dragged Oleg to his feet. They staggered into the black-clad wall of doormen, who immediately head-locked the pair, assuming they were fighting each other. Dessie slurred threats as he was dragged out on his heels, involving the predictable words *black*, *bitch* and *dead*.

She was on-site at 07:00 on Saturday to collect her tools. The events of the previous night would soon be spreading like wildfire, and she didn't need the reverence or the requests to break breeze blocks with her bare hands or to 'teach us some'.

All she wanted to do was work so that the rent was paid and that she and Granny B could get by.

M-City College was an easy-ish option, located in a deprived and predominantly Asian borough which was easy to get to from Islington. Most of the kids were eager to learn, and teaching construction, she thought she could have a hand in reshaping the likes of potential Olegs and Dessies of the future before it was too late. The more wayward boys connoted her name on introduction with the ominous 'Shiv', a street term for a short blade used for no wholesome use. Word had spread through the grapevine, from

HR to the teaching staff and down to the kids, about her aptitude for martial arts, so discipline was no problem. Her stats for punctuality and attendance were the best in the college. A couple of days into a new class, she'd write her real full name on the whiteboard, much to the kids' amusement, and the first to pronounce it correctly could be the first to pack up and leave for break. No one ever did, not first time, but it was a good laugh. Everyone always left the class of Ms. Siobhan Uhuru-Behan together.

Home for as long as she could remember was a two-bed flat within a brick estate of tiered balconies draped haphazardly with laundry, just off Caledonian Road. On her return each day, Shev compared the college kids with the estate's baby ferals who'd always greet her on arrival from work. They seemed to circle around the entrance and central courtyard at all hours on their bikes, like little hooded sharks; a dadless pack looking for targets of opportunity. But the ferals knew she could handle herself and seemed to compete for her attention. Shev was one of the few positive role models showing light in vain against the dark corners, and they delighted when she answered with their nicknames.

She knew that the estate's premier dealer had them employed in his own academy of depravity, distributing packets of ruin, from megaponic weed to *pink*, the latest moreish variation of the Inca's Revenge to come onto the market. It was all plain as day, but she didn't preach or interfere. She could see the three-tier route of progression in the dealer's Academy. Entry-level was drop-offs on bikes. Next would come investment in Kugoo scooters as rewards for phone snatches around Archway and Camden, before sending them further out to service the suburban clientele. Graduation to the third tier was county lines: a train travel card, a new SIM, and trips out to where the air was fresh and customers were plenty; towns and villages where more naïve and vulnerable users would have their hovels cuckooed and their souls destroyed.

Across the courtyard, she'd spot the dealer, all 'roided up, chatting to his "students" by his detailed BMW with a weapon-dog at his feet on Kung Fu chunky chain. He'd nod, and she'd reciprocate. She could feel his letching eyes follow her as they had done since school, even though he knew he had no chance; she was way beyond his grooming net. An inflatable drug-dealing materialist corrupter and God-knows-what-else didn't float her boat.

She had Biff, anyway. He and his uncle had done all Joey P's French polishing since back in the day. Biff always made her laugh on site, when he wasn't off work with a bad back. That ability was the ultimate charm for Shev, and an aphrodisiac beyond aesthetic considerations. Which was lucky for Biff; in the shallow areas of looks and physique, Biff wasn't really at the races.

Shev told no-one about the application and progress, not even Granny B. As far back as she could remember, it had always been just them, plus friends and neighbours. Her parents had met an unfortunate end and were something of a taboo subject. Grandad's picture was still there on the wall, but he, too, was long gone. If Shev ever asked, Granny B would say nothing more than, 'It's the cost of loving, Siobhan,' and add, in her soft Dublin brogue, 'but they've all led to you. The beautiful gift that you are.'

They never went without, and no one ever seemed to have any truck with Granny B. She was a lady of classic beauty; a Sixties hippy-trail survivor who looked at least twenty-five years younger than her age. She was more like an elder of the estate and gave an ear to everyone's problems, and all who knew her always left their flat feeling better for confiding in her.

The positive response and phased selection process for the civil service that followed had all gone well.

Nobody in her small circle noticed any difference. The training was way beyond arduous, both physically and mentally, but she'd spent every moment of training during the last 'five minute' year feeling truly alive. She was wanted, had objectives and a meaning to life. She was no longer just getting by.

'Two minutes, my arse,' said Shev to herself as the train pulled in late, bringing her back to the present. She entered the cool air-conned carriage and chose, as always, an end-terrace starboard spot, opposite the priority seating. Day after day, she would study the scenic staples that marked the route: the purple gorgon on the white virus train, the grey nose of the giant bullet, the sunflower allotments thriving in the drought, and Man Artik daubed big and loud across that gable end. Same as, same as.

Shev wondered what they would have in store for her that day at The Hive.

It would be much more than she could ever have imagined.

Chapter 3

THE INVISIBLE STORM

1000 hrs, August 8th 202?

SIS Chief, Admiral Charlotte Dewhurst

London, SW8.

Why? asked the high pitched vocal, both accusatory and paranoid, as it cut through the jagged, two-tone beat. It was the icing on the bitter cake of crisis. Not precisely comfort food for the soul, but a life raft of sanity, setting her a course to re-focus on her roots and remind her how far she'd come to deal with such blows. Ska played at a normally unacceptable level was one luxury of being the queen of her cream and green castle.

The office's modern/classic concept design was a simulated Ray Adam brief. The entry door and seating were upholstered in deep burgundy leather. Furnishings of chrome Perspex and glass co-existed with the flared mahogany wall panelling. In its centre hung a portrait of a red-scarfed Mary Seacole; a tasteful distance to her left was an original Jamie Reid *God Save the Queen* print, and to the right, a Morgan Howell supersize reproduction of The Clash's *London Calling* LP. But above and behind the crescent ebony desk was an original oil in a shabby gilded frame. Sir Francis Walsingham glared down from a nest of pitch-black, his sideways stare penetrating all who stood before the Chief. Elizabeth I's spymaster literally had her back, watching over her shoulder without relent.

She rose from the G Plan chair and went over to the crescent bay windows. The slate grey clouds rolling out to the north-west were blackening by the second, and she imagined the relentless electrical torrent streaming in through the stratosphere, like formless vapour trails from all global stations. Intelligence: secrets, lies, warnings, and the threat that had filled her with a dread to match the leaden pregnant sky.

She nodded to the beat, and her thoughts drifted, sending her back, way back to her bedroom at 27, Corrs Street, Coventry, on December 12th, 1979…

Stretched out the bed and staring at the ceiling, she

was not alone. Twenty others gazed down from curly-edged posters: Madness, The Beat, The Clash, and local heroes The Specials, who owned the airtime and residency on her Dansette turntable. The tone had become fuzzy from hundreds of repeat plays, blunting the stylus. A close second to Jerry Dammers and Co. were the other two-tone favourites, The Selecter. Pauline Black had pride of place on the chimney breast wall; she was a lifetime of five years older, a style icon who would leave a permanent mark on the blank canvas of fourteen-year-old Charlie Dewhurst. The look was copied piece-by-piece, from whatever she could afford or inherit. Penny loafers, turn-ups, a collection of Fred Perrys and red braces were already in place. A burgundy Harrington, two sizes too big, was handed down by older brother Derek when he left for the Paras, and she topped the look off with one of Grandad's trilbies. She'd worn it outdoors and got a mixed reception at school, getting thumbs-ups from the mods and the usual '*Sieg Hiel*s' from the skinheads.

The Nazi salutes tended to stop whenever they heard Derek was back on leave, usually signalled by Charlie fronting the tormentors up instead of keeping her head down. Their leader, known as Topper, was a twenty-five-year-old ex-biker. He was a big lad who'd been very busy with Indian ink, confirming his commitment to the Third Reich on most parts of his body, including his face. He thought he'd give it a go a year before in the Wimpy when he'd taken exception to the red laces in Derek's dockers and explained why his and his gang's laces were white, in accordance with his eugenic theories. He'd felt Derek's left hand clamp around his throat and his feet leave the floor for three seconds that felt like a lifetime. Topper had been dumped on his back in front of the counter, choking for life, and through his tears, he had seen Derek bearing down upon him. His knees had pinned Topper's shoulders down as he'd peeled away his shirt sleeve, exposing a ripped, cannon-ball shoulder. It had an extensive professional tattoo across its expanse.

'What's that say?' Derek had snarled through gritted teeth and received no answer.

Slap!

'What's that say, eh?' he'd repeated. Topper had mumbled, the tears from the choke and fear trickling behind his ears. He was warm, wet, then cold at the other end, too.

'*Eh*?' Derek had shouted, drawing his fist back.

'It says T … T … Two Para,' Topper had whimpered. Derek's fist had wound back further. 'TWO PARA!' he yelped in surrender.

'Do you wanna fuckin' argue with that?' Derek had said, arms folded.

Topper had shaken his head, almost in spasm. 'No … no I don't.'

'Right, well you and your shit better stay out of my way.' He'd addressed the disappointed audience of boot boys whose eyes had hit the ground. 'And don't even *look* at my kid sister. Got it, cunt?'

Topper had nodded, holding his throat as he'd scrambled to his feet and sloped off with his followers to crawl back under the stone from whence they'd came.

In her room, Charlie had adjusted to skanking on her back while lying on her bed, dying fly style due to complaints from Grandad. Overall, he accepted the music, saying that it brought back lovely bluebeat memories, 'but not that bloody thumping!'

Lost in music, she opened her eyes to see blue light pulsing through the curtains. In a split second, she was at the window. Two police officers were closing their jam sandwich car doors; the female looked up first. Charlie's eyes locked with the WPC's, and she saw concern and apprehension held there, with a hint of the news they were bearing.

In hers, the officers saw abject fear.

The music faded with the awful memory in toe as the intercom sounded. Over at the desk, she opened the holographic channel.

'Mr Bradley is here, ma'am. He has been fully briefed,' said the flickering image of the bespectacled Chief of Staff.

'OK, Bring him in.' The Chief sank into the chair behind the large crescent desk.

The door opened to admit the rotund form of the CoS, followed by another man, a shade under six feet tall, fit, rangy and very dapper.

'One-to-one will be fines,'said Dewhurst, beckoning to the other man. The CoS nodded to both, then left the room, the door clicking shut behind him.

The dapper man took the ten paces to the desk, walking with a hardly discernible limp. The Chief rose and reached over the desktop, delivering a handshake befitting of a Naval Rear Admiral.

Small talk wasn't her style, but she had long understood it was a mandatory icebreaker.

'BREAKSPEAR.' The use of his codename forewarned ominous tidings. 'Good to see you again at such short notice, especially in these circumstances. Sit down. A drink?'

'No problem, ma'am,' Bradley replied. 'And yes, please, to the drink. You know my pour.'

The Chief moved to service the request: a Fentiman's D&B on the rocks. Her mouth donated a half-smile to her guest, but her eyes said, Cheeky bugger. Don't push it … yet.

Dewhurst and Bradley had several things in common that would elicit mutual respect, maybe even friendship, were it not for their vocation, division in rank and his age of a decade older than her. Both were Northerners and had a love of a culture retained from their youth.

The Chief handed him the glass. No clinking. Best not to get too familiar. She pushed back in her seat, crossing her legs and linking her hands on her lap, her eyes on Bradley. 'Well?'

Bradley took a swig from his tumbler and swallowed. 'You're no doubt off at a gallop, ma'am, and you've already dug deep on the surface theories. Coincidence, hoax etcetera or our own Soon Army?'

This was a sore point. Dewhurst's secretly funded and home grown eco-fascist group had bit the hand that created it, leading to civil unrest in Britain's cities throughout that seering summer. Her response contained a touch of venom. 'The Soon

Army's nativity problem has been neutralised, for the time being. It took the Riots to draw out the poison, but the sacrifice was worth it. We have three separate verbal outbursts linked by their content. When pieced together they give clear, accurate information about a specific area of defence: a hack. It was a reveal. A warning to us.

'The general public and the media are not aware of this, and the subjects seemed to be entirely disparate. The Others are on the deep trawl,' she said, referring to the domestic security service, MI5. 'So far, it's the usual sludge: debts, naughtiness, some nastiness which they'll bank … but no direct link. Conspiracy sites are asleep on it. The vital ingredient for that is missing: a spectacular, something big for global prime time coverage.'

'If I may, ma'am?' asked Bradley.

The Chief smiled and added with another slow and deliberate nod, 'You may, Bradley. Your vast knowledge and experience are in play. That's why you're here.'

She added the last two words like an electric fence. Best not let him get carried away.

'The Listeners will have put the rest of the info on catch net for all comms. This one, though cryptic, was clear enough to detect, whoever is behind this may try to communicate via cypher next time. We can then establish how much they have.'

'All in process, Mr Bradley, but the one connecting factor in the alert is compelling.'

'The three subjects appear to be devotees of the Eighth Day movement.'

'Indeed. A seemingly benign but opaque group.' The Chief summoned various holographic images and video clips relating to the pop-up wellness cult and its global outreach.

Bradley added his commentary to the glorious show reel: 'The Eighth Day are defined as a global self-help initiative. They've grown like lightning. What's their tag line, again? "Reaching out to all strata of society to heal a broken world." Post-Corona, of course.'

'And the rest,' said the Chief. 'There's no definable corporate ownership, and the IP addresses flip like a fruit machine. The international element puts this under our remit.'

'No negative doctrine, or uniform beyond the badge,' said Bradley as he studied the footage. 'It's all smiles and wellness. Total inclusivity. Beggars, thieves *and* bankers—apply within.'

'So, it seemed until the reveal,' added the Chief. 'We flip it, scratch the surface and what do we find? Insidious geo-reach, dark money, cryptocurrencies and their own Cloud. Suddenly we're blinded by red flags.'

'The mention of the Eighth Day gives us a possible time boundary but not its relevance, except concerning the movement's actual name,' said Bradley. 'Eight days seems far too obvious, but it's all we've got. Unless …'

'Go on,' urged the Chief.

'You said *insidious*. Maybe *that* is the spectacular. That it's amongst us, all around us. Not pinpointed to one hyper-event.'

The Chief gave a slow and deliberate nod. 'Great. Another invisible storm. A storm, if we've interpreted things correctly, that will grow to a new level of intensity eight days from now.'

They mulled over the concept in silence for a moment.

The Chief reverted back to his codename. 'BREAKSPEAR. What if I were to re-activate

BARBELL?'

'I'm happy to advise on someone to lead, but it's hypothetical in the time we have. Re-activation of BARBELL would require clearance at the highest level. That could take …' Bradley trailed off, noticing the unblinking stare matched with a knowing smile.

On the desk to the left was a charcoal grey trilby hat with a matching silk band, and beneath it was a thin green file. The Chief took the file, revolved it and pushed it toward her guest. He lifted and examined the document. It was the original directive from 1977 authorising the research cell's inception, complete with the signatures of men long deceased. Below those were the fresh squiggles of the current Chief and those of the Joint Intelligence Committee.

Bradley's face—tanned, lined and littered with the faded scars from sand and fire—was now like chalk as the colour drained from his cheeks. The talking, theory and research of forty years were over.

'Done.' Her blunt certainty was like taking a knee to the solar plexus straight after a deep breath.

'All signed off …' he responded, deadpan.

'Off or on, depending on your point of view.'

The Chief took back the document and closed the file. 'I'll give you a moment to consider your chosen cell.'

Bradley placed his glass on the Chief's desk and then gripped his hands together, mirroring hers. 'You know there's only one that's come close for psych. A new recruit. 808. The only find in decades.'

'Hmm. And for Ultra Tasker?'

'I'd like UT4 as analyst. Non-negotiable. The pair of them.' He'd parried her attack off-line and landed a counter punch.

The atmosphere of dread lifted. The Chief had got what she wanted: progress. She summoned a life-size rotating hologram of recruit Siobhan Uhuru-Behan on the training range and simultaneously ran the CCTV footage of her bar fight at the White Bear two years previously. The pair studied both intently.

'Ahhh, 808. Our likkle ragamuffin psych-op,' drawled the Chief.

Her brief adoption of Jamaican patois and description of the recruit was no surprise. She'd made it known that political correctness was one of her bug-bears and was pressing his buttons, probing for a reaction. She got one in his disapproving expression and wrongly judged it as sentimentality; a weakness.

The Chief reverted to her normal voice. 'She's a find as far as you can tell, but she is, as yet, untested … So why her?' After all, the recruit had no military experience; she was a tradeswoman and teacher. The pluses were that she was extremely bright, met the minimum requirements on languages, and her tradecraft, signals and combat stats were above average.

'No spoon-bending or furniture flying across the room, but I'm confident in what the controlled test results revealed, ma'am. 808 possesses stronger-than-average intuition.'

'I've seen the file,' the Chief responded. 'But I'd like you to explain your conclusions.'

'I examined the personal screening file, as with all candidates, looking for an "in". Nothing malicious, but areas where I can find reaction. The unusual thing about this candidate was the activity. She is a blogger, ma'am—a travel blogger, to be exact. It's called the *Shevalogue*. Novel, but not that unusual. Hardly any followers. But it was the content.'

Dewhurst gestured for him to continue.

'The personal file revealed that, barring a yearlong spell in Nairobi as a small child, Uhuru-Behan does not travel; has not travelled. She admitted the blog was a scam, just a bit of fun, dreaming of 'palm trees by the sea' and so on. There were scammed images framing the text, but there were two posts on the *Shevalogue* of particular interest. The first, the *Wonders of Seoul*, describes, light-heartedly, the pleasures and dangers of hot-tubbing. May I?' asked Bradley, removing his phone and projecting a holographic image. 'This is indeed Seoul, lifted as a screenshot from phone footage. On the periphery, among the crowd, I've circled a face. A year after the original film was posted online, the body of that man would be dumped in the DMZ.' He zoomed in. 'Do you recognise him, ma'am?'

The Chief nodded sadly. 'A good man, from HK station. My first loss. The autopsy confirmed he'd been boiled alive. A message from Utopia,' she said, referring to The Democratic People's Republic of North Korea.

Bradley continued, affecting the air of a barrister stating his watertight case. 'In the second post of interest, *Wonders of Iceland,* the text describes, in detail, the lunar landscape and activities available beyond the bars of Reykjavik, lifted as before from phone footage, this time captured a decade ago.' Again, he zoomed in on a face in the crowd.

The Chief understood the relevance. The face belonged to a classified astronaut, who had undertaken the fatal ARK 1 British Space Agency lunar mission, a catastrophe veiled in complete secrecy.

'Are there others?' asked the Chief.

'There are many more posts, but none of interest to us. 808's devices, all other links and contacts, are absolutely secure; nothing suspect. One hell of a coincidence. That's how I reached my objective conclusion,' Bradley slowed, a little exasperated at the rehash.

Dewhurst had read the report, but there was nothing like a first-hand verbal account. She rested her chin on the backs of her hands and swivelled back and forth in her chair.

'Let me get this straight. You're linking her Icelandic blog post to the moonshot via one scammed photo, and the one about the hot tub, to our man being boiled alive by the Utopians? What about imagination? Research? Or good old fashioned bullshit?'

'They are considered, ma'am,' Bradley responded. 'As I've said, we checked all search records on every device she's touched. Nothing corresponded. She *thinks* the text was imagination, with no bearing on real events. Just a lark, that's all.'

Dewhurst was far from convinced.

Bradley continued to make his case. 'After looking into all this, I observed the post entry intuition tests with the hidden symbols as usual, and the results were outstanding. I decided to dismiss the conduit, which was a first. I took over directly, face-to-face.' The Chief's eyebrows arched as Bradley continued. 'I feigned interest in the *Shevalogue* and presented her with a photograph. I asked her to imagine and present a report that I could taste and smell, including, most importantly, the weather.'

'Can I see it?' asked the Chief.

Bradley passed her his phone. On the screen was a soldier in desert fatigues sitting cross-legged by a campfire, giving a thumbs up, his head and face partially wrapped in a shamag. 'Who is it?'

'Look closer …' said Bradley. Dewhurst pinched

the screen and zoomed in. 'That's me in Tunisia, March 1976, six hours before the sandstorm. Six hours before …' Bradley trailed off.

'808 described it accurately?' Transfixed by the image, she'd bitten at last.

'Oh, yes. She didn't understand it, of course, but she described the conditions, in detail as requested, as a visual observation up to my blackout. It was challenging for me to hear it, as you can imagine, but she made no connection between me and the image. There is no beginning, aftermath, cause or rationale; just the facts. She could not have known. That's a personal Polaroid of mine, and the only evidence of the operation. It's not in circulation online or anywhere else.'

Dewhurst was satisfied with the jousting session, and she'd got Bradley where she wanted him: at the tip of her lance.

The swivelling in the chair stopped, and Dewhurst rested her head on one hand as she processed the information and evaluated it against the current external threat.

'This is unprecedented,' said the Chief. 'What are your suggestions for mentoring development? Assessment of risk? Supposing for one moment that her capability is credible …' The Chief threw her hands in the air. 'Real!'

'What is real, ma'am? Every BARBELL report I've submitted in forty years was objective. All the things I've witnessed, or think I've witnessed … each of them intangible. But what option do we have in the face of this threat but to go forward?' said Bradley. Receiving no answer, he continued. 'I'll mentor her as with any other neophyte. We'll put her selection down initially to her strong intuition because, in reality, that's all we have. If, or when, a capability manifests, the strength of our relationship will be a decisive factor. She's young, and her psychometrics are great.'

The Chief studied the small print in the holo-file. 'Parentage?'

'You'll find her parents were … unreliable, ma'am. With nasty habits.'

The Chief raised an eyebrow.

'They met as students on the late '90s rave scene,' explained Bradley. 'Mother: Sian Behan. Irish, student nurse. Father: Kensington Uhuru, medical student drop-out, son of a Kenyan diplomat. Whirlwind romance followed by a shotgun wedding. They visited Kenya when the child was eighteen months old, and the paternal grandparents later died in blowback related to the Goldenberg Scandal. The Uhuru-Behans descended into heroin addiction, later overdosing, the father, Kensington, fatally. The child, filthy and unfed, was found toddling around in the squalor of a Brighton crack house in 2002. She was placed in hospital care for a spell until Social Services located the maternal grandmother in Islington. 808 has lived with her—happily, I believe—ever since.'

'What of the mother?'

'Off-grid, presumed dead. She bugged out of the hospital and linked up with Spiral Tribe travellers. There's been no trace of her at all since '05.'

The Chief did a quick search. 'Hmm. The Others have had nothing on her for twenty years … That's an awful lot of camping.'

Bradley shrugged. 'The psych-map for 808 states, "She has a balanced level of patriotism and is duty-driven, with a strong moral compass." All this will be a factor in these … uncharted waters. As ever, when we get going, we'll know …'

The Chief nodded silently with pursed lips. 'Indeed, BREAKSPEAR. So we must begin.'

She stood, reached for her glass and raised it. 'To BARBELL.'

Bradley inclined his glass. The toast was sober, not celebratory. As they drained their glasses, their thoughts raced around two words that seemed as unassailable as Mount Everest. One of them had to say them.

It was the Chief who finally did. 'Eight Days.'

'Thank you, ma'am.' Bradley gave her a polite nod and headed for the door.

'Oh, Bradley?' the Chief called out as the old spy reached the panelled door. 'What is the codename assigned to Miss Uhuru-Behan?'

Bradley paused for a moment, as if reaching a decision. 'GLIMMER,' said Bradley as he passed through the door. 'Her codename shall be GLIMMER, ma'am.'

Dewhurst opened a channel on her desk, projecting a hologram before her.

'Yes, C.'

'BARBELL is activated. The intervention is underway. The files on the three subjects are complete.'

'What of the fourth, Subject X?'

'Subject X cannot be part of our direct investigations, sir. That is all I can say, as we both understand.'

'Excellent. I anticipate your updates on all eventualities and findings, C. God Save the King.'

'Yes, sir. God Save the King.'

The hologram beam flickered off. The Chief rose to her feet, donned the charcoal trilby and clicked both fingers. *Gangster* resumed at volume and, this time, she skanked, hard.

Chapter 4

ALBATROSS

0645 hrs, March 24th, 1976

St John Bradley

Nafusa Mountains, Libya

In the lamp black dome of the sky, a waxing crescent teased from behind wisps of gunmetal clouds, and the whitetails of shooters, usually hidden by ambient light, came and went in a blink. A warm north-eastern breeze blew constantly, all the way to the salt air of the Mediterranean, two hundred kilometres to the west.

The four's approach across the desert and into the mountains had been fast, silent and stealthy. They'd reached the rendezvous within six-and-a-half hours, each bearing massive loads balanced between destruction and survival, and made good on the plan to be in place and fully concealed by first light.

Dawn appeared as a stripe of fire across the horizon, gradually revealing the jagged medley of ridges and crests that made up the surrounding terracotta mountain range as it crackled its way down into tawny stone wadis and out to the Hamada stone desert. There was still little detail visible to Bradley's naked eye from the track two hundred metres down the slope and the clearing in the distance. The prone positions were at two points on the hill, amongst rocks and scrub vegetation of tamarisk and acacia.

They lay, cramped, silent and still; the surrounding rock could be home for them for the next three days. As commander, it was Bradley's stag—sentry duty—for the next hour, which he spent amid the mixed odours of canvas, gun oil, hessian and the testosterone permeating from the big sweaty lump in very close proximity. He could hear a faint call to prayer in the village beyond, which provoked mild nostalgia for the Jebel.

Cautiously satisfied with the operation so far, Bradley used his starlight scope to view the outlying clearing at the foot of the valley, then across the track either way and to the brows and greenery of an oasis spring. He scanned south up to the road crossing the horizon, beyond which lay the village from where the devotional voice came.

The four-man cell had been primed for the possibility of a reception committee with every step they'd taken as they crossed the border. Since the sickening revelation of Philby's and Blake's betrayal and its cost in Western agents' blood on foreign soil, this had to be the way.

From the other direction, he could hear goats and some human activity at the edge of the clearing. He fixed on that without blinking. No fear; just a heightened awareness of threat. But where there should have been anxiety, there was peace, clarity and time on the wild edge of desert.

It formed the strangest of circumstances in which to reflect…

The journey had been a colourful one for St John Bradley, born 1954 in Singapore, the first child of a British rubber trader, and an Austrian nurse. He'd been a hyperactive child, and a curious nature conversely made him a bookworm, too. This offset the general disapproval of his parents to their son's wilder inclinations. They'd lost count of the scrapes he'd got into for the first ten years of his life.

The family's sudden relocation back to the family seat of Tideswell in the heart of the UK's Peak District had been a shock to the system. A massive adjustment for all the family was required. St John and his sister Hester, his junior by eighteen months, knew nothing of England, its traditions or inclement weather. Once he was acclimatised, his mother and father couldn't keep the boy indoors out of school time. He was always amongst the green and grey of the peaks, climbing, walking, running and swimming in all seasons. As his schoolwork was top-notch, he'd eased through to exit Lady Manners school with four A levels, one of which was in Theology to further satisfy his folks. But, in truth, he remained, as ever, a heathen.

By the age of eighteen, there were daily rows in the Bradley household about his parents' want for him to go to University against his own preference for the Armed Forces. His mother made it her duty to 'disappear' return correspondence from her son's applications to the Royal Marines and the Parachute Regiment, the fledgling unit in which his father had served with as a Chaplain in Europe during the Second World War. The time he didn't speak about. The time in which he'd jumped from an aircraft and spiralled down through the charcoal clouds of night into Arnhem with thirteen other clergymen into the midst of a ferocious battle. Faced with evil intent, his father had picked up a weapon from a fallen comrade to protect the wounded and the civilian villagers held at the mercy of an enraged SS Panzer unit. Overwhelmed with the need to preserve life, give comfort and medical aid to his men, he surrendered himself after three days in order to do so, and that's how he met the woman would restore his faith in both humanity and God.

When he returned to extend the family business into post-war Europe, he spent every spare moment of the first five years in the shattered Occupied Germany searching for that special nurse . He'd visited countless hospitals and presented the small, tattered photo he kept close to his heart. Its fading likeness couldn't match his vivid memory of her Nordic beauty. He repeatedly saw pity and sympathy in the eyes of his former enemies, those who dutifully examined the picture only to shake their heads, pat his shoulder and say, '*Viel Gluck*.'

In the end, he found her in West Berlin, and, with relief, discovered that she, too, carried a torch for him, smitten by his zeal and devotion to his quest on the strength of the memory of their meeting. As newlyweds, they went to London and then to Tanglin, Singapore, to open the first Far East office, finally start a family twelve years after meeting in the carnage of Arnhem.

Eighteen years later, in the battle of wills for her grown son's future, the distraught mother turned to an unlikely source for guidance and mediation: his godfather, Maurice.

Maurice had been a member of the British ex-pat

community who had been the occasional organist for the Church back in Tanglin. Mr. Bradley had bonded with him over their shared Derbyshire roots. They'd been at Lady Manners school together, though separated by four years. Maurice had revealed that he'd been an Intelligence Corps officer during the War and was remaining in Singapore for a spell with the Foreign Office. He'd become a close and supportive friend to the couple and was moved when called to ask him to stand in absentia as godfather to their newborn son, St John.

The christening had been a hurried affair, as the child had developed pneumonia soon after birth and, at one stage, things were touch-and-go. By the time Maurice returned to Singapore two years later, little St John was long over it and was now a toddling ball of energy and noise. Maurice, as a religious—though non-pious—man with no children of his own, took the honour of godparent seriously, and though he had left Singapore again when St John and Hester were two and five years old respectively, he had never missed a Christmas, birthday or Easter since, either with gifts or his own presence.

It was for this reason that Mrs. Bradley had chosen to call on him all those years later. Perhaps the young man would listen to him, if no one else. They collectively agreed that Maurice would take the eighteen-year-old force of nature to the local pub, an area off-limits to his father, to discuss all the options. Through several pints and a solid lunch, they talked—or rather St John did, with Maurice mostly listening intently and nodding his understanding. He sent the young man wobbling home with a reminder that he'd told his parents they must all sleep on their thoughts, including him, and he'd speak to the family the following day.

True to his word, he was at the door at six pm. The family were all present as Maurice sat at the head of the table. He summed up all positions with supporting arguments for each and then asked Hester what she thought. Hester said she didn't want her brother to go away or to hurt anyone, but she also wanted him to be happy. The atmosphere had lightened and warmed due to her input. Maurice had made it clear to St John that his parent's position was one of love and concern more than religious dogma and then, as agreed, Maurice gave his side. He closed by saying they'd done well to listen to the different positions, and the love in the family was very apparent from all.

His gaze met that of the father as he said, 'Ultimately, St John is a man now.' Then to the mother, he said, 'And love may turn to bitterness if he follows the will of others and neglects his own, however disappointing that may be.'

He turned to St John. 'But the decision is his. It *has* to be his, and, with due consideration, his alone.' He opened his arms as if to embrace. 'Lastly, look at me. Remember how we met thousands of miles away and years ago? If I'd not done one thing, we may never have met. Imagine how empty my life would have been without knowing all of you?'

Maurice's eyes finally rested on Hester, who'd spoken last. 'And what a harmless old buffer I am, eh?'

There were tears, some visible, some dammed by stiff upper lips that allowed only pained smiles. St John had already made his decision.

Sandhurst was endured with a commission into the Intelligence Corps. A year in Dhofar was followed, unbeknownst to all but Hester, by Special Forces Selection. Selection had been secured due to a bet placed with the squadron commander, one that Bradley needed to win before the conversation on Selection would even be considered: traversing from the Eagle's Nest on the crown of the Jebel Samhan, down through the heat shimmered crags and back, three times, point-to-point with a full bergen and his SLR rifle. It took time, dedication and a bloody mind, with shoulders and feet to match, but in the end the bet was won.

It marked the beginning of an almost vertical learning curve entering the final two years of the secret Dhofar War with the Regiment. The squadron was tasked with training and commanding the *Furquat*, defected rebel units, assisting in clearing the remaining *Adoo*, the communist-backed enemy guerrillas, from the caves of Jebel Qamar and winning the "hearts and minds" of the villages by offering medical aid in exchange for loyalty to the young reformist Sultan. The villagers had their own name for Bradley: *Sama' alsabii*—Sky Boy. They were fascinated by his eyes and touched his blond locks during medical treatment, believing it brought them luck. This amused the rest of the grunts, who misheard *Sama' alsabii* as "Kimo-Sabi", the Native American Tonto's name for his partner, the Lone Ranger.

Hester had always been a bridge between him and their folks. Unlike her brother, she bought the 'God' ticket but also took to the hills and rivers of Derbyshire with equal passion. After college, she gained a position as a student nurse at Hereford, in part to keep an eye on St John as much as was possible. The unaccounted-for event was him hooking up on leave with her Jamaican colleague and best mate, Janice. The three would do most stuff together on his bi-annual leave.

He'd found twenty-two tougher than he could imagine—both his age and the Regiment— and not just physically. The first cohort of officers and NCOs from *Operation Storm* ruled the roost, and if your face didn't fit … With a name like St John, which was alternated between "Singe" and "Sinbad" in the officer's mess and coming from the Green Slime—the Intelligence Corps—he was up against it. He was often referred to with a condescending "Sir" by the battle-hardened NCO's more than ten years his senior. The respected term "Boss" would have to be earned, possibly with blood. Regular skirmishes on the Jebel didn't count in comparison with the heroism of the Mirbat engagement the previous year.

Sweat was a given. It wasn't about capability or potential; those were false summits once you were in the Regiment. The chief currency was *experience* at the sharp end—and the sharper, the better. Following Oman, Bradley had had two months of low intensity car patrols on the Northern Irish border, with no change in sight. The lull in pace had led him and three other virtual strangers to volunteer for the Inc. when the opportunity was suggested.

Spoken of in hushed terms even by the *Storm* vets, the Inc. was the ultimate Russian roulette, like a tightrope over Niagara Falls, with no safety net, which had been lit at one end. Enlistment comprised of officially leaving the Army and completing a deniable operation beyond the use of proxies in order to return with financial benefit and, finally, kudos. For Bradley, the commissioned rank of SAS acting captain, which hung on him like a baggy and undeserved hand-me-down, would become an acceptable tailormade fit. The final year of his three-year tour would be on another level and would warrant a return to the Regiment someday down the line, and hopefully soon.

The requirements for the Inc. were straight A grades in all test areas; to be single; to have no dependents; preferably to be orphaned; and to actually be deemed suitable. Given the risk of an op going wrong and seeing out your final seconds as a civvie punctured by a smoking hole in the "arse end of nowhere", the Inc. wasn't high on too many wish lists; applicants weren't queuing around the block to volunteer. No medals or promotion were on the table, just heavy coin and even heavier prestige, it was the latter that drove Bradley.

At Sennybridge Camp, they'd trained in concert to build trust and respect in preparation for the task, but "getting to know you" stuff was off the table. The operation was all. Each participant maintained anonymity as virtual strangers from different squadrons, and it was to be kept that way. The extreme fitness and skills of all four men surpassed the stratospheric levels demanded by the Regiment but the cell's specific tasks were divided between sniping and demolition with Bradley also serving as medic. The others were at least three years his senior. Bill, was a blond six-foot-six Viking throwback and missing a front incisor tooth, which gave his Scouse accent a slight whistle and was second-in-command and signaller. The others were Chas, a sandy-haired, stocky Geordie and Kal, a barrel-chested Fijian, who said very little. Each man witnessed the capabilities of the others, and they were soon working well in all aspects of the task drills.

They were under the command and instruction of Gantry, a former Regiment senior NCO in his early forties, who was bald and bearded. The man reeked of experience: Korea, Malaya, *Operation Jaguar* and the rest. The furrows that surrounded his watchful eyes signalled a life spent in harm's way. He was the human embodiment of the campaign banner back at Bradbury, a forehead crease for each skirmish and kill. But now his options were limited to bank jobs, the Sultan or the Inc., as the top brass had found him guilty on all charges, banged to rights, of being unable to avoid the most invincible of enemies: old age and time.

During the operation briefing, they sat behind desks in the briefing room, reclining like bored schoolboys, as Gantry stood at the lectern with maps taped to the board behind him. He tapped his pointing stick on his palm as he began.

'At 1230 hours today, a joint US/British film crew will be flying sets out from RAF Lyneham aboard a DC10 into Djerba, Tunisia. We will be embedded with them. Our cover is to act as their security detail.'

'Whether they like it or not,' Bill cut in.

Gantry paid no attention to the interruption and distributed the maps.

'We will link up with the film unit in Tozuer,' he said, tapping the map with his pointer. 'Then we go on to Matmata to prep. For the operation itself, we'll drive south cross-country by this route to the drop point three kilometres northeast of Dehiba.' He gave the six-figure grid reference, which the team located using their silver compasses. 'There is one-and-a-half kilometres of visibility in both directions from this metalled road. At 0000 hours, you will cross the porous border into Libya on foot, traverse the metalled road and continue for twenty kilometres to the R'a al Mihah ridge near the village of Amazigh, also known as *Albatross,* where you will establish two Observation Posts.'

Gantry gave the RV[i] grid reference and

continued. 'The Gaddafi regime, which is hostile to the West and on friendly terms with our enemies, has purchased and has in its possession a significant quantity of Chinese Semtex H. Intelligence has confirmed that, in its infinite generosity, the regime has donated *another* eight tonnes of it, along with other goodies, to revolutionary terrorists operating in the UK. That ordnance is concealed in this location: Hasy al Mihah, five hundred metres from the metalled road. The regime… with the *provisionals* plan to transport the ordnance along here'—he pointed to a track leading directly to the coast—'two hundred kilometres to the seaport of Zuwara, where, under a flag of convenience, it will be shipped to its intended destination.' He walked over to the map of Europe and used the pointer to strike, with considerable force, the area of Northern Ireland. 'Here!'

Gantry then sat on the edge of his desk, his arms folded. He looked into the eyes of the four men and continued, each word now being delivered with measured force.

'The last lot got lifted at sea. But the Libyans are still at it, so a knuckle wrapping is required, and we're the big stick. The transport must *not* reach Zuwara. You are to observe and record any activity on the target and subsequently attach timed charges while in transit. On clear out or night fall, bug out and cross back through the border to the entry point for exfil. No offensive action.

'*Do not* engage with fire unless compromised. In that event, escape and evade via the same route. There will be no air support. We are not at war with Libya.' Gantry repeated the orders verbatim in the same manner. The team began to discuss the route across the mountains to the RV.

'Twenty kilometres from drop to the RV,' said

Bradley.

'A straight trot across the desert,' added Chas, the Geordie.

'Which of us pricks is gonna say the famous last word beginning with "E", then?' said Bill, the Scouser, nodding at Kal, who, as usual, said nothing.

Gantry then handed out satellite photographs revealing scattered farmland and dwellings twelve kilometres in, beyond the desert plain to the foot of the mountains. The team scanned with their magnifiers. Kal's look of anger hit Bill dead centre, who grinned toothlessly and raised his hands in surrender.

Gantry cracked his knuckles and went on. 'The ammunition has been ferried and stored under the marked escarpment. The window for this operation, once you're in position, is five days. If it's a no-show four days in, further orders will follow regarding the relief cell.'

Bill raised his hand. 'Question. Where is the relief cell now?'

'Waiting,' Gantry answered flatly, without batting an eye.

*

Twelve hours later the tailgate of the DC10 dropped, letting in a deluge of warm, dry Tunisian air and crisp dawn light. The long flight, strapped in the back of a cargo plane, had been rough but uneventful for the cell and the film crew.

The cell unstrapped and dragged their bergens and metal strong boxes off. Their orders had been clear: as always, contact with "others", be them civvies or none-attached units, was limited to no small talk, conversation or eye contact. They clocked two men approaching across the landing strip in an angry strut, one skinny and fair in a flannel suit, the other dark and bearded and wearing shorts and a peaked cap.

'What the fuck is this?' they shouted almost in unison.

Gantry turned from the cell when they saw his eyes; they instinctively stepped back, their shakes changing from anger to fear. He reached into his jacket pocket and produced two letters. 'Please, gentlemen— step this way, and I'll explain. Which of you is the director?'

The man in the cap gulped and nodded.

'This is a copy of your agreement for the production of said film, er, Star Beast, at Elstree Studios, Great Britain, with an amendment that refers to your filming here. Are you familiar with the contract? Good. It's signed by the Minister for Trade and Industry as well as yourselves. What it doesn't say is that the cost of this DC10 has been reimbursed by my employer, FTL.'

The two men were dumbstruck. Gantry continued and presented the second letter.

'This explains that we, vis-à-vis FTL, are your security detail, again at no cost. There are contact details there to verify, if you must. OK?'

The man in the peaked cap looked at the two strong boxes and the four bergens now being loaded into one of two pink Land Rovers that had met the flight along with an articulated lorry. He peered at the five long-haired, handlebar-moustached gents talking to one of the road crew.

'B … but…' stammered the director.

'I have a third letter,' said Gantry, producing and handing another envelope to the director, who opened and read it along with his colleague over his shoulder, his hands shaking as he did so. In so many words, it stated the cancellation of contracts due to a breach in clause blah, blah, blah in the small print.

'Finished?' asked Gantry. The director nodded. 'So, do you want a lift home on this thing, or shall I tear that letter up?' He slapped the two men on their backs in a friendly gesture, knocking half the wind out of them, and left to join the cell.

While this was going on, the crew roadie came over to the five men, who did as they'd been trained to and looked down, arms folded and unresponsive.

'Hi, I'm Chuck. I'm with the road crew for the shoot. Who *are* you guys?' asked the American. He got no response. Bradley looked over to Gantry, who was pointing the finger and waving letters at the two men.

'You're big guys. We could use a hand. How about it?' the American continued.

Bill looked up and snapped in broadest Scouse, 'Look! I'm Brian, he's Barry, he's Bilbo, that's Bruce, and him'—he pointed at Bradley—'he's … fucking Tarquin. We've all pulled our backs with this lot, so fuck off and leave us alone. Got it?'

Which Chuck duly did, to the first side-splitting laugh the cell had shared together. They were all straightened up by the time Gantry came back, and they then jumped aboard the Land Rover to follow the convoy to Tozuer to set up camp.

In a blink Bradley's reminiscences was over, he was back in the present. From the hide he watched as the rising sun pushed the sky through a changing palette of purple, mauve, magenta and, finally, powder blue. He spotted movement from the clearing in front of the rise to the metalled road. It was a whole tribe of Bedouin—or Amazigh, as they were described in the intelligence report—nomadic Berbers herding their goats.

There was stirring beside him. His hour of stag was up, and so was Bill. He looked to the side and met Kal's and Chas's eye, to receive a wink and a wave from fifty metres away.

Another hour of nothing passed, except for goats traversing the terrain and chatter in the distance.

Then it came. The clack and chop of rotors—faint and distant at first—increased over thirty seconds until it reached a deafening maximum. Bradley checked his watch: 0718 hours, local time. Each member of the cell shrank down into the rock. The chopper moved down the valley, then descended and hovered within line of sight. The machine, with its green DPM camouflage, had the threat of a giant crocodile emerging from a tropical swamp, rotating slowly as if scanning the area for its next meal.

'Well, that's a new one,' whispered Bill.

Bradley took out a long lens camera and got the first recon shots. It was like nothing they had ever seen. A chopper, yes—but with wings? And those wings were racked out with brisling instruments of death, multiple rockets and missiles. It had a bottle-like nose housing the pilot and navigator, from which protruded what could only be guns or cannons, offering more carnage. Thankfully, the rotors were far enough away not to affect the hides.

The aircraft swept up and down again, then came back into view to land one hundred metres away. The four members of the covert cell were in total sync, the red star on the side of the chopper a collective stab in the eye.

'Soviet,' said Bradley, stating the obvious.

Bill spoke the other OP – observation post, by radio 'Standby.' He then broadcast the developments to Gantry on the main set.

The helicopter's pilot and navigator stayed on board and kept the rotors turning. The tailgate dropped, and passengers began to emerge and look around.

Bradley zoomed in and snapped away with the camera. He focused on a man in combat fatigues whose shoulder insignia bore the rank of Major; a ridiculously high rank for a man who appeared to be in his mid-twenties. He was blond and had a high forehead and slanted eyes like an English Bull Terrier. He approached the escarpment facing the OP, which was hidden in shadow, then reboarded the chopper.

In the distance, silhouetted against the changing sky, were two four-ton lorries with green canvas backs hiding their contents. They slowed, stopped and then turned slowly off the road, navigating the uneven rock surface down into the valley, their headlights revealing illuminated marker routes.

'This is it,' said Bradley.

The men readied themselves for imminent contact against overwhelming odds. The chopper could obliterate them if they were detected, never mind the potential thirty or so infantry transported in the backs of the lorries. Bradley supposed that was why, before they had parted company, Gantry had told them, 'Should the op go tits-up, save a round for yourselves, eh?'

The lorries stopped alongside the escarpment at the base of the facing slope, where—if the intel was to be believed—there was enough hidden explosive to flatten Belfast. The other OP signalled that they maintained a full visual, with Kal using his own camera.

Three personnel emerged from each of the

vehicles' cabs, followed by six troops from the rear, and all but two began loading boxed materiel from the shadowed area to the rear of the trucks.

When the engines revved up ten minutes later, Chas got on the radio and transmitted the events back to Gantry. It was now clear that the two overseers were non-Libyans, conspicuous by their physiques and attire. One was tall, skinny and bearded, wearing a sheepskin coat, a black beret and aviators: Revolutionary chic. Bradley mentally nicknamed him Lurch. The other— short and fat with a moustache and wearing a too-small leather jacket and a tartan flat cap—was tagged Tubby. They were joined and greeted warmly by the young Soviet officer, who gestured towards the chopper. They approached the tailgate and viewed the contents with approval.

Lurch instructed the soldiers to take the four cases from the chopper. The other seven had become agitated with the Amazigh, who were observing the exchange from two-hundred-and-fifty metres away, Bradley grabbed his field glasses and said, 'Dragunov, two-hundred-and-fifty metres, past the chopper.'

'Got it,' Bill said, and he adjusted the sight on the sniper rifle accordingly. He gave the visual order to the other OP.

The regime troops were now pushing and shoving the Amazigh men. A slap here, a kick up the backside there, but their aggression was escalating. Bradley removed the field glasses and picked up the camera. The Soviet officer bade a fond farewell to Lurch and Tubby and boarded the chopper. *Click-click*. Gotcha, comrade, thought Bradley. The helicopter was airborne in seconds, ascending and heading west, its rotors echoing from distant to silence as it tore towards its aircraft carrier.

The first gunshot reported around the valley. There were screams, then a volley of automatic gunfire. The troops were rounding up the Amazigh, who had formed a dense circle. Lurch and Tubby attempted to remonstrate but were shoved in the chest with rifle butts. They shrugged, went back to their lorry and sat in the cab.

It was getting nasty down there, but the distraction provided cover.

'Bill, you and Chas deploy the charges. Kal can cover the 4Ts. I'm on the Libs,' said Bradley.

Bill signalled the order to the other OP and, ten seconds later, Bill and Chas emerged slowly from the hides with the demolition charges strapped over each shoulder, silenced pistols in holsters on their thighs as a last line of defence or exit. They'd practised the drill a thousand times back at Sennybridge.

Kal had the profiles of Lurch and Tubby in the sight of his sniper rifle. Sat in the cab, they nodded, smoked and laughed, ignoring the mayhem unfolding at their backs a couple of hundred metres away. 'When in Rome,' they were probably saying, as more automatic gunfire and screams sounded all around them. 'At least it's not the Falls Road.'

'Stay there, stay there,' whispered Kal under his breath as Lurch and Tubby interchanged in his crosshairs. Bill and Chas crawled the last few metres to their respective lorries, avoiding the wing mirrors, rolled onto their backs and shimmied underneath the vehicles like iguanas.

Through his binocs, Bradley could see that, around the packed circle, which now consisted only of women, there was an outer rim of at least twenty bodies. The ground surrounding them was a black pool. Unrelenting, the troops carried on with the slaughter, through reload after reload. What were they after? What were the women protecting?

Both men under the lorries had shimmied into position, attached the charges to the petrol tanks, armed and set the timers.

It had to happen. The passenger side door of the cab opened, and Lurch and Tubby stepped out on the escarpment side and went out of Kal's line of sight.

'Fuck!' uttered Kal as the demolitionists no doubt did the same.

Bill, yards away from two pairs of bell-bottomed jeans, drew his Welrod and took aim. He heard Ulster accents, coughs, multi-pitched farting and the sound of zips, then two streams of steaming yellow liquid hit the rock for ten seconds, giving strange relief against the sound of the carnage unfolding in the valley. Penny spent, the pair re-boarded and lit another fag.

They were safely back in Kal's crosshairs. The demolitionists carefully emerged, crawling back the way they came. Kal checked with Bradley and got the all clear. The regime troops were entirely occupied with committing mass murder. He signalled, 'Clear, go for it,' and Chas and Bill rose, tore back up the slope to the OPs and slipped inside.

'Sorted, missus,' said Bill, making himself comfy next to Bradley.

'This is fucking shocking, mate,' said Bradley.

Bill grabbed the field glasses and took a sharp intake of breath.

Bradley took up the Dragunov as Bill reached for the scope.

Four women broke from the rear of the ever-decreasing circle of Amazigh carrying a purple bundle, running in the direction of the OP for all they were worth, probably trying to get to the escarpment. They'd cleared fifty metres before the regime troops reacted. The soldiers took potshots at the running women dropping three before one gave chase.

It was soon apparent that the purple bundle was a child of six or so years old. The soldier caught up, coughing and spluttering, and the remaining woman tried to attack him in defence of the child. She was quickly downed with a pistol-whip and then dispatched without mercy, leaving the child stood still and alone.

'Two-hundred-and-seventy-five metres, wind: NE nine knots,' uttered Bill over Bradley's shoulder.

Grinning, the regime soldier took aim at the child before him. *Click!* The pistol jammed. He cursed, cleared, reloaded and took aim again.

A finger squeezed a trigger.

The subsonic round entered above the troop's right eye and exited leaving an ensemble of grey matter worthy of Jackson Pollock to his rear. The Dragunov had spoken. Bill confirmed the hit and made a typically comedic comment.

The target hit the ground, crumpling like a demolished brick tower. Time enough for every man in the cell to ponder what would happen now. Long enough for Bradley to ask himself why he'd done it and why Bill hadn't stopped him.

Bradley couldn't believe what he was saying as the next order passed his lips. 'Bill, Chas, on the other eight. Kal, cover the Provos. I'm getting the kid out.'

Suddenly he was heading down the slope. Getting the kid out to where exactly? he asked himself as he broke into the run. It was as if the wave of depravity before them had rippled like a stone cast into a pond and had immersed the cell in pure compulsion. Bill and Chas took aim at the murderers, adjusted their sights and did as they were ordered with their Russian weapons.

Gantry's orders were in tatters, his final words in the briefing nothing more than a banal echo.

The child, with bodies either side, raised its arms and began to scream. Bradley was fifty metres down the slope when the sheer volume and pitch seemed to shred his eardrums, like red-hot knitting needles being driven into the centre of his brain. In reflex, his hands covered his ears, his footing gone. He tumbled head over heels, then scrambled behind two rocks at the base of the slope and curled into a ball.

He looked up to the OPs, where he saw movement as Bill stood, then fell. Chas and Kal met the same fate, their faces contorted in pain. He peered around the rock, looking for the child. The child didn't take a breath, the scream was continuous and growing in volume and pitch.

From beneath the child's feet, heatwaves began to form a gyre until there was a shimmering, conical pyramid with a purple stone at its heart. As it grew, the pyramid detonated the grenade on the dead soldier's kit belt, which went off with a thud. Bradley shrank back down into the foetal position between the two large rocks as the shimmering cone reached the first four-ton lorry. Up it went, the shock blowing the men in the OPs halfway to the top of the ridge, before rolling halfway down like khaki ragdolls, suspended by their webbing as it snagged on the shale.

Bradley was shielded by the rocks as the second lorry was consumed by fire, the massed intensity of heat and flame dragging the air from his lungs. The wind and red-hot sand generated a typhoon around the shimmering cone and emanated outwards to vaporisation point.

The rocks provided no shelter this time. Under the barrage of pressure, they fractured, and the heat and sand shredded his clothes, then his skin, before lifting him off his feet and into unconsciousness.

Frankincense. Myrrh. Lineament. Voices. Bells. Goats.

His senses were awakening. Bradley was lying on his left side. When he tried to move, every part of him screamed. His mouth, throat and lungs burned, and his breath was a shallow rattle.

A perfumed presence was close. He could hear movement and a woman's gentle singing. Amazigh? After countless attempts, he was able to open an eye. He was in a tent. A crack of light through a curtain revealed a silhouetted small figure.

The crack reduced as they entered and approached. Once more, he tried unsuccessfully to speak. The child, all purple silk shamag and robes, was close.

A girl?

She drew closer and put her finger to her lips. He looked into the large charcoal eyes: curious, kind, wise and strangely old.

In them, he saw the explosions reflected once more. His leaden eyelid fell, and he was gone again.

Chapter 5

BARBELL

October 3rd 1921

1 Melbury Road, London W1.

From the old world burst the new, like a phoenix rising from the ashes of conflict. The fledgling Bureau had survived the Great War intact, had come of age and emerged healthy and independent. Its reason for being was proven and evidenced again by the red and white inferno that followed in the East. The intelligence challenge of revolutionary Russia pitted the Empire against a new stark ideology.

Now, there was trouble closer to home, across the water. The potential founding of the Irish Free State was blurring lines domestically, so the hot coals and ashes of another conflict were passed from Vernon Kell's MI5 into the lap of the newly anointed Secret Intelligence Service and its Chief, now known internally by his signatory prefix, C.

The Irish victory in the preceding Tan War of Independence had broken the British yoke of seven hundred years of oppression. The possibility of freedom was drawing close, and with it, a new threat to the Empire. The Dáil delegation for the Treaty negotiations was to be led by a Tall Man of legend.

British operations had been led by Colonel Winters, known as O, the White Worm, a man possessed of a heart as black as his shirt, but who found himself crushed beneath the green heel of the Tall Man and a new kind of revolutionary warfare. This culminated in a devasting attack that tore up most, but not all, of his Cairo Gang of spies from Dublin Castle like confetti, but the White Worm's final acts of reprisals and atrocities had appalled even the King himself.

The secrecy and finesse required for the next operation pointed to the direct control of one man who had not yet failed. The briefing to C had been given jointly and in person by Prime Minister Lloyd-George and Minister for the Colonies, Winston Churchill. The briefing outlined a secret mission overseas, following the identification and surveillance of the target in London. They had made it implicit that, following the outcome of the Treaty negotiations, a black letter may be delivered to him by hand.

A letter sanctioning the assassination on foreign soil of the person named within.

C's former deputy of the SIS, Freddie Browning , wasn't good at either stillness or silence in any waking hour or company and never had been. He radiated light, humour and energy that most people in his orbit found either contagious or exhausting, depending on their age and temperament. Though a Lieutenant Colonel, he shunned uniform within the office. His starched collar and cravat contrasted with C's impeccable gold braids and buttons.

Browning leapt from the seat opposite C and paced the room up and down, the tails of his frock coat splaying out as he turned. He sat down again for another attempt at static composure.

'One small point, Freddie, and I'll let you go, as you're making me dizzy, old man.' C laughed at his former deputy. 'I'm tailoring a plan that demands the finest cuts.'

'Pray, tell?'

'The plan requires two men, each with unique qualities. Indeed, I already have the individuals in mind. Both are known to you, though for quite different reasons.'

'I'm intrigued, sir. Which specific qualities do you seek?' Browning leant forward, his hands clasped.

As director of the Savoy, Browning's connections and knowledge of both High Society and the seething underworld of London—and, indeed, every European capital—were vast. His brain was a library of vice and capability, and the continued availability of its black books upon leaving was an invaluable aid to the Service.

'I will begin with the light. Firstly, young, handsome, with charm and intelligence as well as of impeccable appearance.' C placed his hand on the brass handle of his stick, rose stiffly and limped over to the decanter.

'Well, count me out, C,' Browning cut in. 'I'm afraid I'm rather busy, old boy!' Browning was a spritely fifty years of age. He passed his empty tumbler into C's outstretched hand.

The Chief continued, his pipe gripped between his teeth as he poured the brandy. 'A brave fellow, lucky, and familiar in our methods.' He passed the glass back and returned to his position behind the desk. 'Skilled and courageous, a capable fighter, but ultimately more inclined to *amour* than combat.'

Browning produced a silver cigarette case from his breast pocket, withdrew and ignited a Chesterfield, then reclined side-on, curling his moustache. 'Hmm. Lucky, pretty, brave but no ruffian—*and* a Bureau man? I'd say that's a fair description of SHAMSTONE, the Mimic. That Jewish son of Erin, Simons. He bagged the clincher in Mexico, after all. And the New York Von Rintelen affair. Worthy of his bauble, I do concede.'

Browning drew deeply on the Chesterfield and tapped off its tail of ash. 'But I still think he should have done for that blackguard before he left the States. Are Simons' nerves up to scratch?'

'Back to the point, Freddie. Your punt on

SHAMSTONE is spot on,' C said, deflecting Browning's put down of his man.

The correct guess pleased Browning, and he punched the air and laughed momentarily before jumping to his feet.

C continued, 'But that's a rough take on the man. Black Tom came later, and that would have sizzled anyone's whiskers, including yours. No? It suited Blinker to take The Dark Invader alive at any rate.'

Browning's cheeks glowed a little, as if struck by C's open hand as well as his tongue.

'Also, the man was raised a Catholic, Freddie, if that's any better in your book. We've no shortage of John Bulls. Simons' mixed blood has proven to be his asset, and ours.'

Browning's oblique reference to the subject's shellshock, as if it were a common cold, didn't dim C's enthusiasm. The clincher to which Browning referred was Simons' acquisition of the original Zimmerman Telegram in Mexico City, allowing Captain 'Blinker' Hall, the then Director of Naval Intelligence, to reveal its existence to the Americans. In so doing, this absolved the British of accusations of interference—of which they were, of course, guilty—and thereby brought the USA into the war. All this was achieved by the extreme skill, daring, charm and coercion of the officer. As for the bauble, C remained steadfast: if Sidney Reilly was worthy of the Military Cross for espionage, so was Finn Mallow Simons.

‘To be fair, I hear there’s been no sign of the jitters,’ conceded Browning, as he delved into his mental dossier of continental gossip. ‘Still killing them at the Parisian tables, always adorned with a couple of sparkling flappers on each shoulder. An effective assassin of the heart, if nothing else. Hence meeting your requirement of …’

‘The counterbalance of absolute darkness, my friend.’ C shuffled forward, his own smile gone, and he pointed the stalk of his pipe to add emphasis. ‘The second man I require …’ He paused and chose his words carefully, his gravity further cooling Browning’s mood. ‘… must be polar opposite to the first. One whose talents, skills and sensibility are for violence and destruction. A stone-hearted fellow, whose purpose in life is only to take that of others.’

C’s emphasis continued as if he were guiding Browning to the correct answer in a critical exam. ‘A professional warrior, again familiar with our methods, but a terrible weapon of a …’ He grew silent in his description. ‘A man.’

The room was silent and still but for the movement of the pendulum’s eternal clack. Browning was as severe and static as Smith-Cumming had ever seen him. Perched on the edge of the chair, he gulped the brandy, the tumbler cupped in both hands to disguise their tremor. Now deathly pale, his blinking eyes were fixed on the foot of the desk, where they remained as he spoke.

‘Are we agreed,’ uttered Browning quietly, ‘The man you speak of is … Lt. Jonah Spirewick?’

Upon receiving C's cable, Simons immediately packed and drove to Calais for the crossing. He arrived at the office early the following morning and was shown in by Ann, the secretary.

He had dressed for the occasion in a double-breasted tailored suit—brown with a grey stripe—and a claret tie. He removed his fedora and strode to the desk, where he stood at attention and saluted stiffly. This pleased and amused C, who gestured to him with his pipe to sit down. There appeared to be no outward signs of the nerviness raised, then discounted, by Browning that he could discern.

It had been three years since C had set eyes on the spy since he posted him to Paris Station, and time had been kind. Simons was still a touch shy of thirty, clean-shaven, with a shock of lamp black hair that defied control. He had an olive complexion, high hollow cheekbones above which were intense eyes of coal and a furrowing brow. His teeth were straight and white and set in a robust sculpted jaw.

Following the war, these attributes had paved the way for an easy posting dominated by Parisian nightlife in the employ of the SIS. Simons radiated an unforced charm and quiet charisma. His looks were inherited from his father, Abel.

In 1890, as a young English-speaking student, Abel Simons had travelled from Berlin to London to study at the Royal College of Surgeons, where in due course he'd met and fallen for Róisín an Irish girl. They'd eloped in reverse, with Abel converting in to marry for love. They then crossed the water to settle in Limerick, Róisín's hometown.

There was both acceptance and simmering resentment in both communities. Some years later, the hate came to the surface, instigated by a malevolent priest, which lead to physical attacks on Jewish businesses and the boycotting of goods and services. Some stayed and endured with support and protection of the brave and kind. Others, whose memories of similar behaviour in Europe were still fresh and feared another a pogrom, made tracks.

Abel and Róisín. with an eight-year-old Finn and his brother Garrett, decided to travel for a new start, upcountry in Dublin. Abel served the poorhouse infirmary and, in time, progressed to a GP partnership and work as a surgeon in St Vincent's Hospital.

The years passed with little event beyond petty scrapes and the usual prejudices. At eighteen, the young Finn travelled to London to study surgery at his father's Alma-Mater, accompanied by the son of his father's partner, Seamus Behan.

Three years later, the long-anticipated war broke out, and Finn was conscripted as a reservist officer into Naval Intelligence on account of his expertise in German and Gaelic-Irish and for his "exotic looks". From the Room 40 decryption/code-breaking unit, he was posted in turn to New York and Mexico, where he spent every moment a heartbeat away from capture and a firing squad.

All at the behest of Smith-Cumming and Captain

Hall, Simons' exploits were crucial to the victorious outcome of the conflict. So, the peacetime and pastures of Paris would be Finn Simons' to graze, and his erstwhile mentor, Shlomo Reilly, was cast into the cauldron of Russia.

'I find you no stouter, Simons,' said C warmly.

'I could eat four horses, sink a vineyard and gain not an ounce, sir.'

'Is that due to that damned demon influenza or the—what did you call it?' He scrambled through the paperwork on his desk for a particular report. 'Ah, yes—the jitterbugging?'

Simons' pristine smile was revealed. 'No ill effects from dancing or the influenza since my convalescence, sir.'

'Your work … these reports, Simons, I must say, have been excellent and so profound. How's the play?' asked C.

'Thank you, sir. The play's a fair term, if you don't mind my saying so. A good time in the name of work, if I'm perfectly honest. The network chugs along, sir.'

'Can one become so quickly jaded by peacetime and by the decadence of—how did you describe it? The Jazz age? Give me thirty years and a good leg, and I'd give you a damn good run, man!' C stabbed at the wood within his shoe.

'We must guard against our wishes, sir,' said Simons soberly.

C cleared his throat at the poignancy of the young man's comment. 'Indeed … There have been few truer words spoken, Simons. May I be frank and ask ...'

'Of course. As it is, sir, I am unattached, haven't found the right gal … and since the war …'

There it is, thought C, a slight flicker revealing the hurt and carnage the man had witnessed during the apocalypse of Lucifer's Fall: the Black Tom ammunitions explosion on the banks of the Hudson River.

Simons regained his thread. 'Since the war … the greatest of times aren't all good. Not in a *good,* good way. Less than wholesome sometimes, if that makes sense, sir?'

C smiled his understanding that Simons may lost his way a little amongst the hedonistic whirl of Parisian nightlife. The young man's dark eyes glistened as he searched to find the words.

'Finn Simons, my sybaritic spy. Too much of the soft life. I believe what you require is a challenge, Simons; a test of your vast capabilities.'

The young man instinctively stood to attention but said nothing.

C nodded. 'I am planning a surveillance and intelligence operation to commence here in London and roll out overseas, in all probability in the land of your birth. Which, as you know, is now its own dominion.'

'A dominion that may soon be garnished with civil war, sir,' said Simons. His comment was made with no edge or sarcasm. 'Seven centuries, to do what they will before a fork in the road.'

C 's eyes narrowed. 'Lest we forget, all is dependent on the Truce holding, Simons, but what of your position regarding Eire? The whole world is a different place since our covenant was so swiftly broken.'

Simons smiled. 'I returned on Christmas leave following the armistice, just before the pestilence. I haven't returned since posting to Paris, sir. I remember it being different and yet the same, like every rose and thorn. But I didn't venture beyond the city. No one starved in Dublin, as my mother used to say.'

'Well said. I see from your reports that you've been keeping poetic company in Paris. But regarding this mission it's best that I warn you, in all sobriety, that the principle subject of this proposal could be described as fantastical, so the operation will require an open, yet pragmatic military mind.'

The mistiness had left Simons' sharp eyes, and they now burned with intensity below the frowning brow.

C continued. 'Upon arrival overseas, the officer will be required to use all his personal skills and training to obtain intelligence on which we can act to … eliminate the principal subject. What say you?'

Simons thought for a moment before speaking. 'I have no objection to active service in the field again. Any field, sir. I'd be most willing to undertake this mission.'

C looked satisfied. 'Excellent, Simons. Your codename for this operation is SHEATH. This mission requires one other. There will be three of us in all, and you will be recalled shortly for a joint briefing. Colonel Browning at the Savoy is expecting you and will see to your immediate needs.'

He offered his hand to Simons, who delivered a reassuringly firm shake before saluting and making his exit, with a spring in his step that had been absent when he'd arrived.

Though buoyed by Lt. Finn Simons' induction to his scheme, C awaited the next arrival with a trepidation approaching dread.

Preceding the truce, Lt. Jonah Spirewick was the White Worm's most formidable weapon of the Tan War.

In Dublin on the morning of 21st November 1920, he had dispatched five would-be assassins single-handedly. Amongst the papers on C's desk sat two reports of the event, which he'd examined and compared in depth. The first included the officer's debrief, which described his actions in self-defence, killing three attackers on first contact and his pursuit through the terrace house and back gardens to the next street, where he dispatched another two. It was straightforward reading, and Spirewick had indeed been decorated for his courage.

The second report consisted mainly of statements and had been struck through and discarded. It was a far more graphic and unsettling read, the accounts including that of a priest.

Mrs. Kathleen O'Hanlon stated that she had left

her house, 20 Oxford Road, Dublin, at nine am, together with her three-month-old daughter in a pram and was closing the door when she heard a car approaching and gunshots. The next thing she knew, she was lifted off her feet. There was more shooting and shouting as she was carried forward, then thrown to the ground in the road. She saw the car drive on and turn left, and the large man pick up a gun on the street before kicking open the door to her house and entering.

The second witness was Mary Ann Carty, the mother of Kathleen O'Hanlon, who was in the ground floor kitchen and stated that she had heard the shooting outside and a crash as the large man entered the property. She saw her husband, Edmond Carty—the father of Kathleen—struck on the head by the large man with the gun; he fell to the ground with their three-year-old granddaughter in his arms and died later that day. Mrs Carty stated that when the brute reached the kitchen, she was kicked in the stomach, which sent her to the floor. She last saw the large man exiting the rear of the property into the garden, from where she heard further crashes, screams and gunfire.

On Swan Grove, Father Michael recalled hearing four gunshots and a crash from the car outside. He stated that he saw, from the top window, a large man approach the crashed car with a gun and gaze at the men slumped inside. He opened the car door and removed the injured driver, dragging him into the road by his hair. The large man then knelt over the driver and set about his head with the butt of the pistol, '… as if it were a hammer and the man, a nail.'

Numerous witnesses described the same scene on Swan Grove. They said they saw a priest exit No. 15 and approach the scene bearing a crucifix. The large man continued the attack until the priest grabbed him with his free hand. The priest stated the man cursed, laughed and took a second gun from the crashed car before walking off down the centre of the road in the direction of Dublin Castle. Father Michael added the man's face and clothes were red with blood from the attack of 'such savagery, he couldn't imagine.' Thirty others stated seeing 'the red man with two guns' upon his return to Dublin Castle. He was not challenged en route and was redeployed to Croke Park that evening to continue the carnage.

The investigation into the morning's incident dispelled the statements from the witnesses and portrayed them as suspects who had collaborated in identifying Lt. Jonah Spirewick and his whereabouts to the murder squad. It closed by adding that their arrests and charges for conspiracy in an attempted murder were under consideration.

Despite his preoccupation with the Great War and post-revolution Russia, the contrasting statements and outcomes gave C a much deeper understanding of ancient native grievances finding justification for violence across the water. C had also acquired numerous reports of Spirewick's valour during the war and the terror that unfolded when he reached and cleared the enemy positions in Palestine.

Though a commissioned officer, Spirewick was much more adept at dispatching men than leading them, and he'd reportedly wept when the armistice was announced. From there he was called to the War in Ireland. Maintaining his commission, he joined D Company of the Dublin District Special Branch, becoming O's preferred assassin, executioner and torturer. Spirewick was in his element as a member of the Cairo Gang of intelligence officers, brutalising natives at his master's request irrespective of age or gender. Following the reprisals for the Sunday morning massacre of his brethren, O sent him down-country to Queenstown to continue his unique brand of savagery.

When the truce was signed on 7th July, Spirewick wept again and was withdrawn for leave back to London. Freddy Browning had been reluctant to discuss Spirewick's activities over the last three months, leading C to ask himself if the next interviewee was simply a violent man or was perhaps the personification of the Hindu deity Shiva, the destroyer of worlds.

C checked the position of the hands on his pocket watch against those of the grandfather clock and took a deep breath. It was time.

Ann knocked and opened the door. 'Lt. Spirewick, sir,' she announced, with a slight tremble in her voice.

A huge man stepped forward in silhouette. Was

he blocking out the light or absorbing it? He was in shirtsleeves and waistcoat, his hands in front of him and covered by his jacket. He approached C's desk and stopped, looking straight ahead. He offered no salute.

The chair didn't look an adequate width to accommodate him. Silence reigned.

C cleared his throat. 'So, Spirewick, what have you been up to on your … leave?'

Of course, he knew the worst of it. The behemoth looked C in his monocled eye. His own were blue, dead and lashless, like those of a predatory animal; no warmth, just lethal intellect. He began to speak in a high, almost effeminate monotone with a slight lisp, which was a shock. Every word was measured in its delivery. 'Sport. A boxing booth first, sir.'

Maybe his voice contributed to the psychopathy, considered C.

'Then it went quiet,' Spirewick went on, 'so I toured the booths and … in turn, I quietened them also … so they paid me to stay away. Then I got started with the racecourses and reminding, sir.'

'Reminding?' asked C.

'Yes, sir. I was engaged by men of means to remind others of what is due … and what is expected.'

'What if they don't need reminding?'

'I remind them just the same, sir. Then …'

C wondered if Freddy Browning's reticence regarding Spirewick was due to him, as a man of means, having employed Spirewick's reminding service for his own enterprises.

'Well, Spirewick, I have a task that befits your talents much more than reminding. It will begin with surveillance, with a view to direct action overseas. In your old stomping ground, to be exact. The quarry is formidable, maybe even unworldly, and thus I have sought you out for your prowess, which I consider to be more than a match.' C patted the files of Spirewick's exploits on his desk, and his gaze dropped to the overcoat in front of Spirewick.

'If you are in agreement, you will be released under licence and with accommodation provided. Following the successful completion of the mission, a pardon will be issued, with adequate remuneration and a ticket to … New York. Where a man of your … talents … should be able to make a new start.'

Spirewick looked strangely emotional as he stared out of the Georgian window, as if nostalgic for carnage like a lost love. He was a man devoid of spirituality or superstition of any kind.

'America? Sir … if this mission and quarry are all that you say …' he paused, '… then it's I that should remunerate you.'

C pressed his desk bell, and two trilbied police officers entered and removed the overcoat under which were large brass handcuffs connecting his thick wrists. They released Spirewick, then left without saying a word.

Spirewick had, in fact, been escorted to the office under a blanket directly from Brixton Prison.

He had been sentenced to drop following a court-martial for the horrific murder of two women while on leave. The women were, in fact, members of his own family—or the nearest he'd ever got to one.

In some senses, Brixton was a homecoming for Jonah, as it was there that he had been born thirty-two years previously, to member of the "Forty Elephants", an adept gang of all-female shoplifters based in South East London, resulting of incest from the attentions of her father. Evie hadn't survived the birth, so baby Jonah had been placed in an orphanage, only to be lifted by one of the gang and brought up in their "care". As a boy, always twice the size of others his age, they instilled in him a knowledge and experience of violence and criminality, for which he was never caught or convicted.

That experience started, under the Forty's supervision, with the castration and disembowelment of his drunken father/grandfather with a rusty cut-throat razor, aged eight. Jonah was starved of affection and rewarded for injury. They less raised a child than knowingly created a weapon. The boy showed intellect as well as physical strength, so the gang paid for his schooling and the trappings of privilege.

An elaborate façade was bought and maintained. He was commissioned into the Essex Regiment at eighteen. Infiltration of London Society aided the gang's operations on all fronts. Hence came the years of carnage in the Middle East and Ireland.

The booths and racecourses Spirewick mentioned to C were in the service of the "Elephant & Castle Mob" and the "Forty Elephants" respectively. Before Spirewick's gunpoint arrest in a Limehouse opium den, the gang leaders had marked him for the murders of their own, but they hadn't a man or woman good enough—or brave enough—to complete the task. The law, ironically, had provided the noose and completed the circle. A circle C had given him a chance to smash.

The selection was complete, the cut acquired. C closed with the beast as he had done with the beauty. He assigned Spirewick the codename DIRK and advised him of the joint briefing. The behemoth stood to attention, saluted with a paddle-like hand and left.

Hearing the thumping steps downstairs and the door to the street slam shut, C released a massive sigh of relief. With his stick of sharpened steel, he tapped the deadwood below his knee while looking towards the portrait on the wall, whose gaze, out of shame, he could never quite meet.

It was now time to set the trap.

On two occasions since the incident seven years previous in Meaux, he had carried out the ritual, just as Monus had advised in the fevered dream. From the paper the innkeeper had passed him, he'd torn off the word 'Sorry,' only visible by candlelight, and uttered the word, followed by the name of an enemy and committed it to the flame. The paper had burned to his fingers and left a smattering of ash on the green leather desktop. There had been no flash of light or thunderclap.

The first, Stewart, chosen out of exasperation, had been a compromised spy whose recriminations had been proving costly, both financially and professionally.

It was revealed following enquiry that the man had predeceased the curse, dying a month earlier at the front. C had been somewhat relieved that the supernatural was dispelled.

The second, chosen out of necessity and performed with a chuckle, had been GRECO, a despicable double agent responsible for countless deaths of good men and women due to his duplicity. GRECO, his demands for funds and betrayals, were not seen or heard of again, but, after all, there was a war on, with deaths in all quarters, every second of every day. Smith-Cumming's mind had been teetering on a knife-edge between doubt and faith, madness and sanity.

With the date of the Dublin Treaty delegation's arrival set, the lodging address of the Tall Man was revealed. C took the remnant of the paper handed to him by the tearful innkeeper that morning in 1914, lit a candle and read out the word revealed: 'Boy.' As the paper burned, he uttered the name of the target through gritted teeth: '*Monus.*'

He heard Ann come up the stairs, do her double knock and enter.

'Captain Monaghan's here for you, sir.'

'What?'

She repeated what she'd said, only for the Chief to bat it away as nonsense. Ann entered the room, quietly closing the door so the guest didn't overhear, and reached for the diary.

'Look, it's sandwiched just here.' She drew her finger under the text and tapped twice. 'Entered last week for today, and all entries going forward into next week.'

He couldn't believe his eyes, but there it was: Captain Monaghan, 2.30 pm, written in Ann's hand.

'I'll send him up, sir,' she said, and she headed back downstairs.

Slow, deliberate steps came up the stairs. Two knocks, and the door opened. A uniformed British Army officer entered with his head down and approached the desk. He removed his cap and smiled a familiar and terrifying gold-glinted smile. 'Sorry, old boy!'

Smith-Cumming felt just as sick and disorientated in the blackguard's presence as he had been the first time they'd met on that night in Meaux. Now, the fantastical appeared rooted in reality. The grandfather clock stopped dead, its pendulum still and silent. The sickening possibility seeped into his mind like a leaking hull that Monus had indeed dispatched Stewart and GRECO as requested and, in doing so, had demonstrated manipulation of time itself.

'So,' said Monus, sitting down and placing his

booted feet on the desk in typical defiance. 'You want me to off meself, do ye? Well, nice try, but it doesn't work like that.'

As at their last acquaintance, the tone was sing-song, flitting between humour, warmth, ridicule and cruelty. Again, C's gaze moved towards the elegant portrait; a constant reminder that what had been taken from him was truly priceless. What he felt for the creature before him was a pure hostility way beyond hate or contempt. 'No. I just wanted to talk to you. To see you. I've a target in mind … The final of our … agreement.'

'Oh, have you now?' said Monus, with keen interest.

'Do you follow the affairs of men?' asked C.

'Only what's under me.' Monus leant forwards and tapped his roman nose. 'Do ye follow the affairs of …' He could not find the word but indicated with his long-nailed fingers scratching along the desk.

'Mice?' guessed C.

'Yes, that's it—mice? I think your answer's the same as mine.'

C nodded. He felt a little better; maybe he'd found a weakness or advantage over this being at last.

'With Bertrand Stewart and GRECO, I knew them, and due to our … connection, so, in turn, did you,' C explained. 'But this man's likeness is a mystery. However, I do know where he'll be and when. You take a good look, and when the time's right'—he produced a slither of paper he'd cut from the remnant—'I'll burn this.'

C's guile genuinely amused Monus. He leant back and clapped as the Chief continued. 'Then you'll dispatch the target, and our pact will be at an end.'

The guest then rose and put his finger to his lips, donned his cap and skipped through the door without a word, closing it behind him.

Doubting his sanity again, C checked the diary and, with both relief and dread, found the afternoon's entry for Captain Monaghan was still there, plain as day.

The following afternoon, the two men standing before C's desk contrasted in almost every way. They had entered together, with the most significant leading. There was the scantest of acknowledgement between them, indicating a distant previous encounter.

C began. 'Welcome, gentlemen. The operation is BARBELL. You will both report directly to me via ciphered telegram or telephone daily at the hours advised. There will be no communication between yourselves, only through me. You must remain separate. There is an Irish delegation arriving from Dublin to participate in the treaty negotiations. Their leader, who I will refer to as the Tall Man, will be at 15 Cadogan Gardens at dawn tomorrow. He will have a security detail, but you'll get a good look at him from separate vantage points. Incidentally, he'll also sit for the artist John Lavery in this period, so we'll also have a likeness taken. But he is not our target. I repeat: he is *not* our target. Our target is the one who will hunt him. The potential assassin of the Tall Man will be present for you to observe. *He* is our quarry. His hair is as red as a fox, and he's as wily as a pack of them, so we will refer to him as FREDDY.'

He fixed on Spirewick. 'You will pursue the Tall Man for the duration and wait. When the time is right, you'll be given a final brief to eliminate FREDDY—and not before."

'Yes, sir,' lisped Spirewick in affirmation.

It was Simons' turn. 'You will pursue Freddy from a distance to his lair, wherever that may be,' said C. 'You have the advantage of drawing on your heritage and upbringing and your knowledge of the native tongue, mindset and customs. You've utilised charm, deception and mimicry in war to devastating effect. You must gain intelligence to find the very heart of these beings.' He looked again at Spirewick, piercing him through his monocle. 'So DIRK may be drawn to strike the killing blow!'

Simons gave his affirmation with enthusiasm.

C took a breath; he hadn't planned such a dramatic delivery. The three men of BARBELL seemed to be in silent agreement that a pause was needed for a few seconds.

C now alternated his gaze between them. 'My codename for the operation is CATHAL. I will remind you of this most crucial information at this point: you must not engage verbally, physically, or have eye contact with FREDDY or his ilk. This must be avoided at all costs. It is imperative. Should this happen, the entire operation and yourselves will be immediately compromised … with no hope of survival.'

Chapter 6

EXFIL

July 5th, 1976

MoD ward, QEH Hospital

Birmingham, UK

The dream ran on a loop: the child's eyes mirroring the blast; the black swelling pool beneath the Amazigh; the scream; the cell blasted out from their hides, a three corpse sandy avalanche tumbling down the shale before being vaporised as the incandescent wave hit; the child's eyes mirroring the blast …

Wake up!

White room. Oxygen mask. Drip. Tags. Plaster cast on wrist and knee. Bandages. Wires.

Pain. Thirst. Hunger.

Bradley lay at a reclining angle. The bed's cage bars were up on both sides, an ECG to his left. He was alone. The change in his condition gave an alert, and a nurse entered the room in response. She checked the reading, then came into his line of sight, checking his pupils and pulse as she made gentle, reassuring noises.

'It's OK to rest; you've been through a lot. The doctor's coming.'

An Asian woman in her mid-thirties and with wedged hair in a side parting duly entered, introducing herself as Doctor Chandra. She lifted the flipchart at the end of the bed. 'And you are?' she asked him, like it was a trick question. The nurse began to work on the dressings. The doctor ignored her patient's stonewalling, stood side-on and changed tack. 'How's the pain?'

Bradley drew on the oxygen and said his first word in eight weeks. 'Incan … descant.'

'Well, you may not think so, but that's a very positive answer,' said Chandra.

From Bradley's examination while comatose, Chandra had deduced, based on his combined physiology of resting heart rate, low blood pressure, musculature and hard, calloused feet, exactly what kind of soldier she was dealing with. 'This'—she tapped her head—'seems to be OK.' She paused and gave him a look of concern. 'Mechanically, at any rate. The nurse will adjust your painkillers, but you've been asleep for a long time, deep healing, and we need to start bringing you back. Liquids and calories by mouth from now.'

Bradley blinked his approval and asked, 'How bad?'

The doctor took a deep breath.

'From the top-down, inside out: one cracked vertebra L3, cracked pelvis, broken right wrist, shattered right kneecap. Synonymous with a fall from height. Second degree burns to the back, the rear of the legs, and some facial areas. Synonymous with exposure to extreme heat and/or an abrasion from silica. It's as if you've been … shot-blasted.'

Bradley took it all in and began to process the information. The doctor continued. 'You'll live. You're young, and you just need time. But there'll be some mild scarring, no doubt.'

'Where … am I?' asked Bradley, resisting the urge to doze as the painkillers kicked in.

'You're in the military wing of Birmingham Hospital, QEH, and you're in very safe hands. Someone will be in to see you now that you're back in the land of the living, but not until I let them, so for now—rest!'

Within thirty-six hours, Bradley's sleeping pattern became regular and mobility was improving, as was the relationship with the doctor. He tried to pump her for more information about the circumstances and events to no avail. She seemed well-experienced in the ruses of the likes of him.

Then came the visit.

Two men arrived. He didn't know or recognise either of them. A nondescript suit entered first: kind eyes behind aviator spectacles, about ten years his senior, with shoulder-length hair; a man who looked like he knew all the words to Tiger Feet. He carried a briefcase in one hand and a brown paper bag brimming with fruit in the other. The second was an old school tie: red face with a white moustache, bowler-hatted with a brolly and a folded newspaper beneath his arm and smelling of Old Spice aftershave or something suitably more expensive.

What ensued was a mild good cop/bad cop routine, with a bit of cat and mouse thrown in for good measure.

'Good morning, Mr Bradley. They say you're coming along fine. How are you feeling?' said the younger man. He had a deep, soft voice, born of a West Yorkshire mill town, and spoke slowly with purpose. He placed the bag of fruit on the bedside table.

OK, let's play, thought Bradley. I'll give a little and draw you two plums in.

'St John Bradley, Captain, 24720042, 26/02/1954,' he snapped, looking straight ahead.

The men looked at each other expectantly. The older man unfolded the broadsheet newspaper and presented the front page for Bradley to scan. It was a Sunday.

'It pains me—us—to state that what you've just said is not entirely true, is it … anymore?' said the red face in perfect Etonian. He snatched the newspaper back, located the crossword, and produced a pen from his breast pocket. He circled the letters 'e' and 'x' and re-presented the paper, stabbing at the letters with the gold pen.

'As I said, it pains us, but it seems we must remind you as you've … been through such a lot, that you are no longer officially serving.'

The glances were exchanged again, and the younger man interjected.

'I'd better introduce us. I'm Jamie Wallace from the Foreign Office, and this is Colonel Allenby, retired … the former Director of your last employer, Ferrum Tenuem Ltd.'

Bradley's head sank back into the pillow. Here we go, he thought.

'May I continue, Mr Bradley?' asked the Colonel.

'Please do, Colonel. Please do.'

Too nice, too polite.

'Thank you. In February, you resigned your commission, bought yourself out of HM's Forces and undertook employment by my former company as a … security contractor.'

'Could you explain "former," please, sir?' cut in Bradley.

'I'll come to that very soon, Mr Bradley. In March, FTL undertook a security detail in Tunisia, of which you were a member. The detail was successful in its tasks. No incidents befell the crew or production, which returned to the UK to continue their project as planned and as required.'

The Colonel's manners and geniality gave way to a cold, burning stare as he paused. Here comes the sickener, thought Bradley as the old man continued.

'Regarding your circumstances, and that of your cell, I have to enter the realm of supposition and hypotheses, as it would appear you are the only survivor.'

With Bradley's full attention, the Colonel sat back and crossed his legs, speaking quickly and directly, on full-automatic.

'Let us suppose that you found yourself across the border in country X. A country which was in the process of doing great damage to the UK by arming the Provisional IRA, while being aided and abetted to do so by country Z. Let us suppose further that that mission was successful in its execution, despite things going hot.'

'Hot? That's a fucking understatement,' cut in Bradley with a sarcastic chuckle. 'Sir,' he added with a sideways glance.

'Well, hot it got. They heard the explosions in Malta, by the way. Now begins your debrief of this supposition. We need everything, in particular any interplay you witnessed between X, Z and—' the colonel's face approached purple and the volume of his voice went up a notch '—the Provisional fucking IRA!'

Bradley caught a touch of spittle on a blast of Allenby's breath; an unholy triumvirate of brandy, Hamlet cigars and halitosis.

Wallace shuffled uncomfortably in his seat and added in a softer tone, 'The biggest mystery of all, Mr Bradley, is how you survived, metres away from a blast comparable to a tactical nuclear weapon, and then, forty-eight hours later, were deposited—spirited, might be a better description—inside the British Embassy in Tunis, five hundred bloody miles away!'

Wallace's perplexity had the effect of increasing the pitch of his voice. He took a deep breath and continued in his previous measured tone. 'You'd received considerable, if indeed medieval, care for your injuries from whoever left you there … Once hospitalised, you received the best available care over there, you were identified by FT and brought back here … by me.'

Bradley stared straight ahead, saying nothing.

The Colonel snapped his fingers and pulled control of the exchange back to him. 'As for your query regarding Ferrum Tenuem, the company was liquidated, as is the process upon completion of all operations. It is wrapped. Over. Dead. Gone. A fate that awaits us all.' Allenby's eyes narrowed to fierce slits. 'Sooner or later.'

The last three words of the coded threat were barely veiled; almost explicitly presented on a platter of 9mm retirement plans and scribed bullets.

The Colonel continued. 'All accounts paid up and settled, but your co-operation, as a civilian—an ordinary Joe, in this matter—is greatly appreciated and a requirement of your agreed terms, as was ours in getting you here.'

'The others … Bill, Chas and Kal? And Gantry? What about Gantry?' asked Bradley.

He turned to study his inquisitors, pain shooting

through him like fire. Their resigned expressions said that his naivety didn't warrant a reply. He imagined the cell spiralling down into an abyss, their parachute canopies torn and burning and surrounded by the ash debris of an incinerated tightrope.

This was the Inc., and Allenby, if that was his real name, would have many shell companies opening and closing like phoenix eggs to do the government's bidding.

Wallace produced a tape-to-tape recorder and microphone, tested the apparatus, cleared his throat and then pressed Record. Bradley gave a full account of the border crossing, the prototype chopper, the Soviet officer, Lurch, Tubby, the placing of the charges and the massacre of the Amazigh. He left out the headshot, the attempted rescue, the scream and the tent.

There must have been a fault on the charges, he told them. 'Maybe they were meant to go off and waste us all,' he added for emotional effect, 'to tie up loose ends. Because that's what I am: a loose end, eh?'

The two men's faces said that wasn't the case.

'Surviving comatose air transport with those injuries is not a foregone conclusion, Bradley, and here you are, for better or worse,' said Allenby, his complexion paling slightly to magenta.

There was more warmth and reassurance from Wallace. 'A loose end that's just provided us with some priceless intelligence. Some loose end that is.'

Bradley feigned confusion and distress. 'As for

winding up at the Embassy, as you say, I've no idea. I remember we were all back in the OPs, the charges were set, Bill was about to signal Gantry and they went off. I was out. Then I was here. I don't know anything else.'

'That's the problem,' Wallace responded. 'Nobody does. There will be follow-ups as part of the debrief, Mr Bradley. I'm sure you understand.'

With that, the pair bade farewell and took the recording of the debrief away for transcription and analysis.

As predicted by Wallace, over the next three weeks, there were more interrogations by FO men, always in twos and in possession of the previous typescripts. The final pair brought the new toy of a polygraph on their last visit. 'Of course, I don't mind,' laughed Bradley, before they asked. They grilled him over and over, requiring an ever more forensic degree of detail.

Wallace and Allenby returned the following Monday, and Doctor Chandra joined them.

'As you may have gathered, Mr Bradley, the doctor here has considerable military experience in theatre,' said Allenby, pompous and stuffy as ever. He turned to the physician. 'Doctor Chandra, can you give Mr Bradley, Mr Wallace and myself a full verbal prognosis regarding his return to serve with HM's Armed Forces … as an elite airborne officer?'

The doctor did as she was asked, concealing her resentment of Allenby's weaponising of her recital.

'An excellent recovery is underway: the fractures and skin layers are healing, and the patient is fully engaged in physio. We hope to introduce the walking frame very soon. A full and normal life should ensue in due course.' She paused and stiffened. 'Regarding future service, due to spinal and pelvic damage, my prognosis is … successful completion of a medical to serve in the Armed Forces as an airborne soldier—or otherwise—with these historic injuries, will not possible.'

With that, the doctor turned on her heel and left the room.

Colonel Allenby rose to his feet. 'You've seen the news, m'boy.' He threw his usual prop of the broadsheet paper onto Bradley's lap. 'The country's on its bloody knees. Strikes, coons, the likes of her lot flooding in like there's no tomorrow.' He nodded in the direction Dr Chandra had gone. 'A new PM, more of the same. A whole new set-up is what's really needed. The boot, the fist.' He looked towards Bradley but avoided his gaze as he slowly said with contempt, 'We may have some bits and bobs for you, a bit of pub grub to pay the bills, but we cannot … endure … passengers.'

There was silence as he surveyed the impact of his barbs on his stricken listener, as one would a group of shots on a range target. Satisfied with the damage, he donned his bowler hat and left the room without a goodbye to either man, slamming the door shut on them just as Doctor Chandra had on Bradley's future.

'Jesus Christ! Tell me that they're not making them like that anymore.' Bradley laughed to Wallace as tears streaked his face.

Wallace's eyes, as usual, were full of apology. 'The doctor says you'll soon be ready for release to the civilian ward, which we will sanction now that the debrief is complete. There's another guest for you; it's the least we could do. Try and enjoy the rest of the summer; it's a bloody hot one. We'll be in touch soon. Good luck.'

Jamie Wallace opened the door to admit the guest and left as soon as they'd entered.

'Hester!'

There was joy and relief for both after four months without a word, but for Bradley, a day of sickening blows was not yet over. They got all the front-end stuff out the way, including the fact that he was now out of the army, which meant he'd need to move in temporarily.

Hester took his cast-encased right hand and addressed the question she'd just dodged. 'I need to tell you about Mum …'

Chapter 7

THE FINDING

May, 1976
Century House, 100 Westminster Bridge Road, London SE1.

Tucked away at the top of the grey concrete tower sat Maurice Oldfield, a spymaster of three years standing. He sneezed, produced a clean white handkerchief and blew the offending particles of assorted tobacco brands free from his tender sinuses.

'The remnants. Always the damned remnants,' he muttered as the door clicked shut behind the last of the donors. He considered asking them to leave the door open so their fumes would follow, but as usual, he reconsidered, as it would be impolite and would reveal his preferences. The less they considered any personal facet of their Chief, the better. Keep it grey, Maurice, he told himself. A gift lighter than black.

He'd been blessed with an appearance best

described as unremarkable; a pear-shaped physique topped with a head of slicked-back greying hair, typical for men of his era. Black, horn-rimmed spectacles framed a round friendly face; behind the lenses were bright, watchful eyes.

The open windows brought welcome relief. Oldfield sat at his desk, relatively satisfied with the latest operation's review; it was just one of hundreds of covert actions protecting British interests overseas that spread out like a pyramid beneath him. The entwined Soviet and Libyan tentacles that had been stirring up the hornet's nest that was Northern Ireland had been cleaved and cauterised, nullifying such tactics for a decade.

The Libyans had found trace metallic remains of Russian weapons and radio apparatus at the Semtex handover site in the Nafusa Mountains, sowing further discord between the Queen's enemies. There was no blowback, as required of Inc. operations. But the report stated that seventy-five percent of the operational cell had been lost in action and were missing, presumed dead. There was only one survivor, who had been fully debriefed and cleared by security upon his return to the UK.

Oldfield made abbreviated acknowledgement with his initial, signed in the usual manner, but before the green ink had dried, he pulled the file back from the out-tray. He drummed his stubby fingers on the desk as he went over it again. His sixth sense had kicked in. Following a third perusal, Oldfield lifted the black phone receiver and requested the names and units of the MPD—missing, presumed dead—cell and the debriefing transcripts from the survivor.

The files arrived thirty minutes later, and when his eyes fell on the last name, his heart broke like a frigate cleaved in two by a torpedo. The trauma was unanticipated, the destruction decisive. But his demeanour settled again in no time, just as the depths embrace a punctured vessel, leaving the surface still and unchanged.

Upon reading the transcripts, Oldfield requested the medical reports and audio recordings, which he received on cassette. They made for difficult listening due to the pain and suffering, both physical and mental, of a loved one. This had followed the shock sudden death within the same family. For the daughter, the funeral had been an even sadder affair, due to her brother being unreachable.

Regarding the Special Forces affair, Oldfield had read between the lines when Hester had gained a nursing position in Hereford. There was a mixture of pride and trepidation for his godson's advancement in his chosen vocation, but that was the kind of stuff St John was made of. A primer of Dhofar with the Intelligence Corps had whetted his appetite, and with that experience and capability, he would be an asset to the Regiment, despite his tender years. The lad was a flier, but then, so was Icarus. Oldfield's instinctive analysis was already in flow as he compared the unexplained exfil events with the finding he'd stumbled across, by pure chance, eighteen months earlier.

He decided to let the revelations marinate in his mind overnight, allowing his subconscious to connect the dots that might lead to the bridgehead of a decision.

The spymaster's occasional excursions across the river into the West End had become rarer since his promotion, but even the Chief still occasionally spared some much needed 'me' time for himself, usually shadowed by the formidable form of his driver and bodyguard. Among the destinations were the bookshops of Cecil Court, which was Central London's bazaar of literary antiquities.

The large shop windows stretched to the end of the passage. Each had a specific flavour; from the Arts and cartography to mysticism and the more arcane corners of the occult. He didn't often come away with anything but enjoyed browsing and always enquired after anything of an ecclesiastical nature.

Sometimes, there was a morsel worth having, and on this occasion, his favourite shopkeeper, disappeared out the back and came back with an M&S carrier bag.

'How about hieroglyphics, sir?' He pulled out a thick bound journal, covered in a crust of brick dust, plaster and assorted paint spatter, under which there was possibly a black leather dustjacket. Oldfield took it and examined the exterior with caution. It had a clasp lock on the side that had been crudely forced open, perhaps with a screwdriver. The leaves were warped with damp, their edges covered in mould spores and the contamination of age. 'It was dug out of a demolition. A builder dropped it in,' said the shop keeper. 'Take a look inside.'

Oldfield maintained a worthy poker face as he scanned the contents and flicked through at random. 'I think not,' he said, almost in apology, as he handed it back, then added with his kindest smile, 'Thank you for digging it out for me, though. Good day.' Oldfield turned to leave.

The shop bell rang as he opened the door. Then he stopped and turned to allow the bell-stop to tinkle to silence before stepping back in. 'Dare I say the cover might scrub up … for re-use … What do you think?'

'Oh … oh, right you are sir,' answered the shop keeper with surprise. 'How does twenty sound?' Oldfield raised his eyebrows and turned slightly back towards the door, and the chancer relented. 'OK, OK. Fifteen, and it's yours.'

Oldfield smiled and opened his wallet. 'This demolition, … any idea where it was? What about the builder?'

'The fellow brings me bits and bobs now and again,' said the shop keeper as Oldfield passed him a twenty-pound note and he handed over the journal, tied in a brown paper bag. 'I think he said it was old bomb damage, over Chelsea way.'

'Hmm. I'll tell you what,—keep the change,' said Oldfield, and he headed for the door.

As soon as Oldfield had opened the journal in

the shop, his heart had almost jumped out of his chest. He immediately recognised the hieroglyphics as Vigenère cypher code. It was handwritten in Lincoln green ink that was almost black. He was thankful it had meant nothing to either the builder or the shopkeeper.

Oldfield spent every spare moment of the next week working on the decryption. Following that, he obtained archived diaries of the presumed author and confirmed the handwriting of Operation BARBELL and my encounters with the diabolical 1914-1922 did indeed match that of Sir Mansfield Smith-Cumming, his original predecessor as Chief of the Secret Intelligence Service.

If the spymaster had been twenty years younger, he would no doubt have referred to the contents of the journal as mind-blowing. It read like some lurid ghost story, but there was no evidence of the Service's original C being of a literary bent, unlike his erstwhile colleagues Compton McKenzie or Valentine Williams. The journal referenced critical covert missions of the Great War, but the main content, centred on the operation that followed, was beyond imagination.

Oldfield's train of thought took him closer to the present: to Uruguay in 1970, where British diplomat Geoffrey Jackson had been kidnapped by Tupamaros guerrillas. Faced with a stone-cold trail and out of desperation, it had been decided to seek the use of mediums to uncover his location, but to no avail. In the end, the PM at the time, Edward

Heath, had agreed a covert $45,000 ransom payment and Jackson had been spirited to freedom. This was the nearest Oldfield had got to entertaining the paranormal.

Upon waking, he arrived at a decision: he would wait for an opportune moment within business as usual to discuss the finding at the highest level. This could not involve private or foreign secretaries, or the minister. It could involve no-one but the PM himself.

When the time came, he fed a little bait to the newly incumbent James Callaghan out of earshot of all. Each was familiar with the character of the other, as their paths had crossed often during their ascents. Callaghan was interested in the revelations of such an artefact and wanted to know more. A further one-to-one meeting was arranged. Once forgery, hoax and counterespionage were all dispelled, the sole question from the PM was, 'What now, C? Where on earth do you want to go with this?'

Oldfield paused, then said, 'Bearing in mind we've considered every option in the past … I'd like us to consider the paranormal angle for research. No rush, as we're frying bigger, badder fish that we can reach out and touch.' He glanced at the PM to read his expression, which, thankfully, seemed to be engaged rather than sceptical or incredulous. 'All I request, Prime Minister, is your active consideration for research going forward, sir.'

Callaghan laughed. 'If that's all you want, C, my active consideration for BARBELL is granted.'

July 26th, 1976
Tideswell, Derbyshire

Hester passed her brother the coroner's report at the hospital. It stated that their mother had succumbed to an aneurysm in the early morning of March 23rd, a date branded into Bradley's mind as simultaneous with the Albatross operation.

The added horror of that realisation had a strange effect on him when combined with the existing trauma: numbness. It was as if he'd crossed the emotional pain threshold into desensitisation. He'd learnt about such things in Resistance to Interrogation training with the Regiment; expert sadists break the rhythm of torture to prevent desensitisation, allowing their victims some recovery before inflicting more pain. Hester had buried both parents in the space of a year, and he'd done a Lazarus and come back from the dead. He was gutted, but now mentally numb; the tears were all Hester's; they just wouldn't come for him.

He stayed on the ward until the bones were healed, and he could manage the basic independent functions needed to restore and maintain his dignity. He progressed from the walking frame to just one crutch, and Dr Chandra soon felt that his nervous system could endure the drive home to Tideswell.

It was agreed that his return to the Hereford flat share was not a good idea. Hester arrived with her Jamaican nursing colleague Janice, whose smile and warmth gave Bradley some welcome movement of the heart and some stirrings elsewhere. They'd got hold of an orange VW camper, resplendent with a couple of flowers painted on the side. It was dubbed the The Mystery Machine and promised a late summer of fun, despite the circumstances. Hester took the wheel, and Bradley was helped into the rear by Janice and lay flat for the journey north.

Bradley was largely silent; heavily dosed with painkillers, he stared out of the window and winced every time they went over a bump.

Once in Tideswell and with the shopping done, the girls left Bradley at his parents' home on Sunday night and told him they wouldn't be back until the weekend. He took their calls each day, which were usually reduced to, 'Everything's OK. Really, yes. Yes, yes, thanks,' before he rang off.

Eventually, though, he lost it. 'For Christ's sake, Hester, I'm twenty-three years old, and in the–' He stopped himself from saying SAS, hearing the hectoring echo of Allenby's barb at his hospital bedside: 'Well, that's not exactly true, is it.' Bradley felt the prickly heat of instant embarrassment.

'St John? St John, are you there?' Hester's panic brought him back to the present.

'Yes, yes, of course, Hester. Sorry, Sis. Stop worrying, OK? See you on Friday.'

Bradley had explained to Hester that he wanted to go to the churchyard alone when he was ready and not before. He used his time pushing himself with physio, perhaps a little too hard, naturally, on the stairs and out in the garden.

Being alone in the family home for the first time dredged poignant memories for him: birthdays, get-togethers and Christmases. He pulled old books from the shelf and sorted out things previously stored away that tallied with the faded posters still affixed to his bedroom walls. The sounds of rhythm and rebellion boomed through the house: The Who, Small Faces, T-Rex and David Bowie assured him, 'Oh no, love, you're not alone.'

He dusted off his dad's jazz long-players—Sinatra, Billie Holiday, Tubby Hayes—and saw, in the echoes of his mind, his parents dancing in front of the grey stone fireplace in a laughing embrace, with him and Hester clamped to their legs.

By Thursday, he felt ready for a challenge and limped into the village. Midsummer had passed a month before, and all the torch festivals came back to him, the earliest of which he'd spent on his dad's shoulders, among balls of fire as far as he could see.

Bradley reached his destination, the one with the faded David Cassidy wannabes taped to plate glass and the stench of base cologne, talc and small talk bullshit that emanated out onto the baking street. He requested a trim and shave.

'What happened?' asked the barber, finally recognising the gaunt, sun-baked wildman he'd known as a youngster. 'You look like you need to add "the Baptist" to your name.'

Bradley managed to grin. 'Maybe you can help

with that,' he replied to the unfunny over-familiar comment. The barber took his crutch, and he eased himself into the red leather chair. 'I was on the hippy trail, up through Turkey, Afghanistan, and India. I came off my scooter in Kashmir. Bang. Thank Christ for travel insurance.'

'Army didn't suit you in the end, then?' asked the barber as he tied the bib around Bradley's neck.

'Nope. Not in the end … All that screaming and shouting? A fool's game, man.' He laid on the hippieism to good effect.

'Bought yourself out?' asked the barber as drenched Bradley's locks with the diffuser.

'Yep. Worth every penny. I only signed up for six. Seen Belfast?' He shuddered. 'Too much like hard work, if you ask me. I'll leave it to the real tough guys. I've no quarrel with any of the Paddies.' He screamed inside at the irony lost on the barber, who couldn't imagine where he'd been and what he'd done over the last three years.

Twenty minutes of small talk later, the barber announced, 'Welcome back to Tideswell, Michael York!' as he mirrored the back for inspection, Bradley's mane now just resting on his collar. The hot towels and razor made an appearance, and the beard growth and the regulation issue SAS Zapata moustache were history.

Bradley struggled from there to the florists, and then on to the parish churchyard.

Wincing as he crouched down to replace the powdery husks in the circular grave grates, he noticed the bouquet had lost petals in the maddening heat, and he knew how that felt. He studied the drought-cracked earth of the plots and the twin white marble headstones of his parents and stood for a time in sad reflection, but still his sunken eyes remained dry.

At 18.30 on Friday night, Bradley lay immersed in the perfect crescendo of *Wild is the Wind* as Hester and Janice burst through the door. The Thin White Duke's gifts couldn't compete with wrapped fish and chips, laughter, wine and human comfort.

The next morning, at nine am sharp, the phone rang. Hester took the call and was on the phone for half an hour before she came up and knocked on her brother's door.

'It's OK. We're decent,' called Janice.

Hester entered to see them both with the duvet pulled up under their chins.

'Speak for yourself,' laughed Bradley.

'It's Maurice on the phone,' said Hester. 'He wants to come and visit this afternoon.'

Bradley's expression was non-plussed. 'You know, Maurice? Mo-Mo Maurice?' She formed her fingers into rings imitating spectacles. Bradley nodded slowly in recognition, but his expression dropped once more.

'Well?' prompted Hester.

'What harm can it do?' He shrugged, with an entire absence of enthusiasm.

Janice pulled the duvet back over their heads,

and Hester tutted and went downstairs to close the call.

The man at the door was a familiar face in aviator spectacles. It was the young man from the debrief, the Foreign Office's answer to Alvin Stardust, Jamie Wallace.

The four of them stood in awkward silence in the dining room at the rear of the house, as eight men swept the building and garden.

Wallace checked his watch. 'Would you mind waiting upstairs?' he said to Janice in an apologetic manner. 'For security reasons. Nothing else.'

She looked to Bradley, who, though seething, nodded his approval. Hester insisted that Janice join her and was freaked out by the whole episode.

Bradley fixed Wallace with a stare while addressing his sister. 'Hester; it's all about me … You know I can't explain. When Maurice arrives, you and Janice should go for a drive. It'll all be okay.' He deepened his frown at Wallace, telling, not asking, 'Won't it, Jamie.'

Wallace nodded in endorsement with his painful smile. You'd never make a dentist, thought Bradley with a sideways look. The sweep meant that old Mo-Mo Maurice was a lot more important than he used to be.

'But …' Hester exclaimed, and his azure eyes moved to hers. He meant it.

The men melted away, and the doorbell rang. Wallace brought Maurice through and then went outside.

'It's better that I stand or lie down, Maurice. Sitting's no good, but I'm getting there.'

Oldfield approached but stayed a distance away as if held by an invisible cord, his hands wanting to reach out but held in check. His godfather had a way of communicating so much non-verbally, the large eyes so expressive behind the thick lenses that Bradley sensed the equivalent of, 'I'm so, so sorry. Is there anything I can do?'

That was the part about his parents. Bradley didn't answer the silent question but shook his head and lifted his crutch off the floor, waving the subject away. His own body language said, 'Don't go there.'

Bradley limped forward until he was within arm's reach and took a moment to look deep into Oldfield's eyes, like a teacher trying to detect a lie in an unruly schoolboy.

'Albatross. That's why you're here, isn't it?' he whispered, and he nodded towards the door in suspicion.

'Don't worry, St John—I'm as high as it goes. It's just you and me.'

Bradley drew back, stunned at the revelation. He tried to make the connections in his mind; could Maurice have been behind it all? 'Did … did you …'

'Know?' Maurice gave a small movement of his head that was neither a nod nor a shake. 'Not of your involvement, I'm sorry to say. Personnel in such matters is not usually my concern, I'm afraid. Ordinarily, I'm focused on the big picture.' His hands were now clasped together on top of his belly. He spoke softly. 'Something made me inquire past signing off the report, and there you were …' He trailed off, indicative of the shock at realising his godson's involvement. 'I've gone over all the information in the debrief, St John. It was the part that you didn't say that stood out to me. So, I made immediate plans to visit.'

'Didn't say?'

'Everything you did say held water. Even the mystery of your "magic carpet" to Tunis. As incredible as it was, there's nothing to dispute it.'

'So?' said Bradley, in defiance.

'So, it's just a feeling, St John, that there's something else,' responded the spymaster. 'You passed the polygraph, but even I would say, within these walls, that the lie detector used on a good man is—how would you put it?—bullshit.'

Bradley had reeled off the lines countless times in the debrief but the old man had got him—and he knew it. After all, he'd known him since he was two years old.

Bradley realised he was blinking; he felt faint and struggled to take in the emerging facts like shifting sands before him.

Maurice opened his arms. 'It may be scant consolation to you, but Hester and I thank God you're here.' His arms dropped to his sides. The atmosphere was like treacle.

Bradley's face flushed with anger. 'Thank God?' he shouted, then tried to calm himself. 'I know what

I saw, what … what I think I saw, and definitely what happened, happened. Look at me!'

Oldfield said nothing.

'Look … if they're looking for an excuse to cart me off or do away with me, this is it. It's … it's insanity, I know.' At last, the tears came. 'God knows, I know!'

Maurice stepped forward and very carefully opened his short arms to receive his godson. The young man's shoulders shuddered as he sobbed. His words were inaudible, lost within the anguished wail.

Bill, Charlie and Kal. He'd hardly known them, but they'd copped it, and that was down to him, compelled as he was to take the shot.

'The men I was with … Their deaths were on me. I decided to take that shot. One of them, the last thing he said before he died was "Timber." He gave me the range, I took the shot and he confirmed with "Timber", for fuck's sake.' For a moment, the tears merged with laughter, then he darkened again. 'That fucking cunt colonel from FT.' Guilt and anger overwhelmed him, along with the grief of losing his parents and his dead career. Rage, disappointment, embarrassment flooded him.

When the worst of his emotions were out, the weight of a granite bergen vanished from his shoulders.

'Okay, Maurice, I'm going to lie down. Pass me a cushion.' He pulled a carving knife and a WW2 service revolver from the back of his jeans and dropped them onto the sofa, widening Oldfield's eyes.

'I'll take those,' said Oldfield, picking each up between thumb and forefinger, 'and I'll get the kettle on while you make yourself comfortable.'

Upon his return, Bradley was lying on the rug, eyes closed and arms behind his head. He recounted all he'd omitted from the debriefing: the headshot; the child; the heatwave cone; vaporisation; the sandstorm; and waking momentarily in the Amazigh tent to see the child again, the explosions mirrored in their eyes.

'So, Maurice—there you have it, warts and all. You can send for the white coats now,' said Bradley, with a hint of self-pity and sarcasm.

Oldfield sat cross-legged on the sofa, holding his cup and saucer. Silence ruled for a moment before he spoke. 'St John, you know that I have beliefs. Beliefs that, to some degree, I share with millions of people. Of course, I know that you're not one of them.' He sat forwards. 'Those beliefs are based on events that can't be described as anything other than supernatural, all originating in the Middle East more than two thousand years ago. Ghosts, angels, demons, resurrections, saints and miracles … it's all there, every Sunday, including tomorrow at your namesake parish down the road.' He shuffled forwards and rose to his feet. 'But it's true. Were I even to recount witnessing such a thing today, then a straitjacket would await me.

'A medieval witness or an anonymous gardener, two thousand years ago, are deemed far more reliable. So, I would be a hypocrite if I didn't believe you. The main thing is that you know what you experienced. The events and evidence support it, but there's no point in complicating things, is there? So that part will stay between us, off the record. That's all.' He walked towards the door and opened it.

Bradley raised his head off the pillow with a twinge. 'That's all?'

'Yes, that's all, St John. Goodbye.'

'But what now? What am I going to do, Maurice?' Bradley rolled onto his chest and struggled on to all fours. 'I'm on the fucking scrap heap, Maurice!'

Oldfield released the door handle and returned to help his godson to his feet.

'That's it. There I see the man I know. The fighter…yes!' He stood back. 'It was a good move coming back here, away from Hereford. So, what are your options? To be an occasional cheap-jack assassin for your friend, Allenby, and his fascist cabal? No, not for you, I think. The Sultan of Oman? He would embrace you, but there'd be too many inconvenient questions and links to H. All those associations are over; you must cut the "22" umbilical, as if you were never there.'

Bradley looked completely distraught.

'There is a project I have in mind for you that might just be suitable. I've been looking at it for a couple of years and haven't found the time to strike the match.'

'Go on, Maurice,' Bradley urged with

understandable impatience.

'It's all been cleared at the highest level and is ready to go. It's research-based, and you'd be reporting directly to me … Interested?'

You wily old goat, thought Bradley. He laughed and nodded.

'Splendid. That's sorted, then. Jamie Wallace will get you going with all the necessary leg work. When that's done, come and see me at Century House. It'll just be us three on this, no-one else, and we'll see what you can dig up. Now for play. Your cover. Any ideas?'

Bradley shrugged in silence. The meeting had been the most emotional imaginable.

The spymaster waddled up and down. 'These are just my suggestions for you to consider: you've got a suite of A levels and you're an ex-commissioned officer, so … next stop, degree, teacher training, fun, girls, life, music.' Maurice gestured with his arms and moved his hips. 'And dancing.'

Bradley's eyes were ablaze, filling with tears of joy. He'd been in the abyss, and now he was ascending. A whole new future opened up in his mind's eye.

'You must now work on the art of living,' said Oldfield as he made his exit. 'Please give all this your active consideration.'

October 31st, 1977
Century House
SIS HQ

The full lever arch file thumped down onto the spymaster's desk.

'It's all there, sir. Double-checked and fully cross-referenced,' said Bradley. He was dressed in a skinny navy suit, a Paisley cravat and desert boots. He remained lean and fit, but he was now a healthy stone heavier. In the eighteen months since Maurice's visit to Tideswell, a new life had coalesced.

'So, BREAKSPEAR, how were the natives? What were your conclusions?'

The question took him back a little, and he laughed under his breath. 'The people were fine, the farmers accommodating. No hostility. I was nowhere near the border. But I wouldn't want to spoil a good read, sir. A deep, critical and objective report was the order, and there it is. You can flick to the executive summary if you really want to.'

The spymaster appreciated the formality from his godson; it showed his discipline. Good habits for a bright future. After all, he knew he himself wouldn't be there forever. 'While I do that'—he slid over a file of equal weight—'take a look at this. All possible cases and locations that Wallace has mined from our records. Strange events from Aberdeen to Zurich.'

Ten minutes later, Oldfield snapped the BARBELL report shut. 'Good work. No, make that excellent. It gives us more food for thought.'

'Indeed. So, what's next, sir?'

'How is the art of living going?'

'What's the expression? "All art can be refined?"' answered Bradley, beaming. He'd enrolled at Nottingham University and was one year into a theology degree. 'That's what I'm doing and I'm following your prescription, sir … to the letter.'

'Marvellous. Take that with you and continue your refinement. We'll decide on next year's project between us.'

Bradley stood up and handed Maurice another thin package. 'Happy Halloween, C. I got you this. It's to gauge the feeling on the street, the climate of opinion, seeing as though the times are a'changing. Goodbye, sir.' They shook hands, and with that, he left.

Maurice opened the package; within was an LP record, its dayglo red and yellow colours hitting him in his widened eyes.

'*Never Mind the Bollocks!?*'

Chapter 8

UT4

1100 hrs, August 8th 202?

The Hive

SIS Training Facility

Limehouse, London, E14.

Shev went again. It was four on one. She disarmed and locked the front assailant, fired two rounds on each side and to the rear, then advanced to the exit with the front assailant as cover.

On the flanks of the La Ramba cinema aisle, there were the random virtual attackers and civilians to neutralise or spare in a three-hundred-and-sixty-degree arc. She thought she'd distinguished well between them, and soon she'd find out, but she wouldn't allow speculation to distract her. The present moment demanded absolute concentration.

The instructions came through the earpiece in

Spanish, '*Go back to the mark and reload.*' She did as instructed and awaited the next engagement; the fifteenth in all. It could come from any direction, body type or weapon.

'*Salida.*' Task A was finally over; a rapid debrief would follow, covering all the attacks, weapons used, rounds spent and targets down, to be cross-checked against the footage, then it would all begin again.

This is it, she thought. Not hanging doors on a brutal building site or forcing T level carpentry into the heads of nutty kids in East London. This is living.

Every second within the Hive was accounted for. The facility was thus named not for the level of industry that thundered away behind its façade, but for its architecture, designed to train an unknown number of field agents in the hermetic quarantine of self-contained units, modelled on the inherent genius of the *appis meliffra,* the European honeybee.

The feedback was in. Shev received an aggregate score of ninety-seven percent, but she perceived that as there still being room for improvement. There was no structure or timetable to increase awareness and adaptability, but she was informed that a signals session was to follow in the afternoon. First, a shower and lunch.

The Hive's all-arms instructor, called out, 'A minute in the pod, please, 808.' His grin revealed a rack of yellow crooked teeth. His brevity was rare and a little disconcerting.

He was a man whose attributes completely belied

his external appearance: narrow shoulders, bad posture, a bricklayer's paunch, knock-knees and a bird's nest comb-over to complement a moustache rusty with nicotine. The only clue was the broken nose which pointed south-east. He was formidable in all operative areas and, despite the dud camouflage, was extraordinarily fit and agile, in both a mental and physical capacity.

As she followed him into the pod, Shev asked herself if he was about to hit her with a sickener, condemning her scores as technical faults. It wouldn't be the first time.

They sat down in unison in the transparent plastic bubble within which all two-way conversations took place. The instructor produced a clear plastic bag and emptied the contents onto the Perspex table. Out rattled an iPhone and SIM, a pocket-sized box, a blue wallet and seven button badges (spiderweb, target, bat, anarchy, smiley, pop-art-gun, and Small Faces) and pushed the pile under Shev's nose. 'Call me, Santa,' he said in his broad Welsh accent. He smiled.

She was perplexed; typically, humour wasn't his bag. Was this another test?

Time to fly the nest, 808. You've managed to grab the pebble, and now it's time to leave our little temple. There's your very own passport with Five Eyes clearance embedded. The phone is an exact replica; it has all your other stuff with our AE—added extras.' He flicked his fingers, indicating that she should inspect the goods. 'The badges are

TAVS: Total Audio-Visual Surveillance button cameras. Also used as a second layer of recognition, they will correspond in code with what your officer will be wearing, depending on the day; hence, there are seven. OK?'

'Yes. Thank you, Staff,' said Shev as she examined the passport. It looked well-thumbed and slightly distressed and had the same ID image as her Hive security pass and driver's licence.

She used the hairpin key to insert the SIM and switch the phone on. As the instructor said, everything seemed the same—the notes, the pictures, the texts, contacts and apps—as the one in her locker.

It's completely secure, with voice encryption and translation. Texts from us will delete within fifteen seconds of opening.' He tapped his temple twice, indicating memory.

The phone indicated an incoming text with the usual cat's *meow* sound as standard, which she thought strange, as they were in a basement that stretched beneath Commercial Road.

'That's the emoji code for your case officer, as well as the time, date and address. They'll give you a new SIM and fully brief you. You'll be with them until you see this emoji for exit ...' The phone *meow*ed again.

That could be a minute later, if they don't like the smell of you, or whenever. Do you understand all I've told you, 808?'

'Got it, Staff, thanks,' Shev replied as she eyed and absorbed the recognition codes on the two texts. As warned, the first disappeared, followed by the second.

'Good,' he said, and he slid over an iPad with an inventory document on the screen. 'CSD. Check, sign, date.'

She did so with her fingerprint as required.

'About the added extras!' Staff's eyes brightened, unable to hide his excitement at her deployment. 'Go to Ultra-Section, UT4, after your break. They've everything set up for you to familiarise yourself with your kit. I think you'll enjoy the new apps.'

Shev felt like it was her first day at school again, stood before a beaming Granny B with braids too tight and an oversized uniform. Since Day One, the whole thing was like a game of Jenga; as the achievement escalated, so did the risk and fear of failure. How high would she go before the pieces came crashing down and she was shown the door?

The RV location revealed in the text was a close and familiar place, too. Was this still part of the test? She knew better than to ask; such things had been knocked out of her as soon as she'd joined. Almost everything she needed to know, *they* knew she needed to know, and they'd tell her when the time was right …

Almost everything.

Off you pop, then.' The instructor leant forwards, his eyes drilling her, willing her to succeed. As she moved to leave the pod, he added with a combination of warning and command: 'Be good!'

Ultra-Section was supposed to be the real deal, the James Bond stuff that most SIS applicants had in mind before receiving a rejection email. Oddly, the fictional spy and his exploits had never floated Shev's boat.

The previous Christmas, purely out of duty, she had sat through her boyfriend Biff's complete Blu-Ray collection. Or had at least tried. Biff would recite Bond's lines off by heart for his own amusement; Shev's plan for tolerance was to prise the remote away and practise her languages with the subtitles on. She didn't even fancy any of the actors, finding them suave and cocksure turn-offs who knocked girls about and had wandering hands.

One helping of *007* a day was plenty for Shev, so if Biff was on a Bond binge, she'd go for a run up to Highgate for a lap of the Heath and be back in time for the end titles.

Robin "DJ Biffta" Clifton wasn't a vain or insecure character; that was part of the attraction. She'd never let on, but Shev would choose Biff over any macho man, Connery or the rest, any day of any week. Biff had a licence to tickle, and he was more likely to kill her with laughter.

Exiting the lift in Ultra Section, Shev found herself in a long corridor with metallic numbered doors on either side. She located the door marked UT4, swiped and entered. There were deep grey walls and a spiral staircase with LED-lit treads, which she descended into a dark open space. There were no knife throwers, exploding umbrellas or teams of nerdy technicians. The only illumination fell on a table and two chairs in the centre fifteen metres away, and she was reminded once more of the disorientation of entering a dark cinema.

In the chair facing her sat the analyst herself, ten years Shev's senior, with purple narrow-rimmed Tom Ford glasses perched on her nose. Her hair was a centre-parted bob with a corresponding streak of colour which was rendered more vivid from the light of her laptop. The white lab coat emblazoned with the Trojan heraldic crest seemed oversized and stretched to her knees, even when seated. She looked up from her screen and nodded to Shev without cracking a smile.

Shev approached. Her slight swagger was built-in, and she moved with feline-like grace. Shev found it hard to disguise the physical confidence that had been hard fought for and won on the streets of North London. But the analyst was unimpressed; her relaxed shoulders exuded a confidence all of her own.

Although physically tiny, the technician was indeed formidable, though in a completely different way. After all, that was why she was sitting there, and her hard, narrow-eyed stare made that very clear to the neophyte sat face-to-face with her first-ever Ultra Tasker.

A lifetime ago, when UT4 was just little Amira, her family had survived an apocalyptic odyssey and had arrived in the UK as refugees of war. In February '91 her father and uncles had followed the US President's advice, along with many other community leaders in Basra, and rose up against the seemingly finished regime. They thought the helicopter gunships that swooped down were those of the Coalition, and soon realised they had invited the devil.

Saddam's emissaries unleashed indiscriminate vengeance on the rebels and all that surrounded them. Those that could run did so for their lives; those that couldn't were mopped up by the Republican Guard and the psychotic thugs of the Fedayeen Saddam.

Armageddon was falling upon them, laced with black rain. They could smell the world burning. Every scorching breath was filled with tar from the smouldering oil that blew over the city to the sounds of gunfire and despairing screams.

The family piled into a van and fate allowed an escape in the dead of night, weaving through the shattered iron serpent of a vanquished army to reach liberated Kuwait. It took six months to get across Europe via Turkey and enter the UK. The indomitable will of her parents was the life raft that kept them together, along with big Cousin Nadeem, who was all of twelve years old and an orphan under their protection.

The family were disconcerted when they were told they would finally be housed on the Isle of Dogs, but soon found they had safety, shelter and nothing to fear from canines or the human equivalent. Her father, a Basran chemist, would now drive a taxi, satisfied in the knowledge that they were alive and free.

For seven years, there was normality and happiness. Amira knew no other life. Then things began to change.

There were arguments, Nadeem started drinking, and, aged nineteen, thought he should be the boss and wanted to prove it. Amira began to dread going home to the rows and the tears. It felt far safer at Langdon Park, the school where she had excelled in all subjects for two years, as Nadeem had previously. But, to her, there was never a wrong word from her big cousin. Nadeem was always kind. Then, one day, she got home, and her mum and dad were gone. Nadeem said they'd gone home to Basra. It was an emergency, and they would follow the next day.

Their bags were packed and ready. Off they went to Heathrow, and two days later they were in Baghdad. Nadeem took her to people in Fallujah that he said were family, but whom she'd never met or heard of. Overnight, things changed, and for the first time, Nadeem threatened her with what would happen if she ever mentioned her parents again. He was no longer kind to her, but life went on.

All of thirteen years of age, she preserved her memories and her mind and trained her intellect like an elite athlete does their body, but she needed to hide her capabilities, like a secret weapon, underneath a veil of subservience and stupidity. Then, another war came and never left. Carnage and terror were passed back and forth like a ball between the Americans, the Sadrists and al Qaida.

Nearly five years had passed, and it was time. It had long been made clear that, beyond her eighteenth birthday, Amira and Cousin Nadeem would be husband and wife. The time had come for *stupid* Amira to use all she'd practised and learnt in terms of science, technology and the study of people.

She located her passport and made a copy on the only day she could attend school. It was deftly replaced and locked away again, the key placed back where, of course, they thought she'd never find it. Amira obtained a phone, although at a high personal price for the suspected thief. She patched into a local network, unlocked Nadeem's computer and contacted the British Foreign Office, where contact was made with the newly formed Forced Marriage Unit.

A triangle of trust was built between a British agent behind the walls of the Green Zone, Amira and a lady in London known only as Sylvia.

Finally, her birthday came. A school day like any other Sunday, she hadn't celebrated a birthday for years. Nobody noticed Amira, even on her birthday. Alex was where he said he'd be, with four strong men. She sat between two of them in the back of the four-by-four and was covered over with a blanket before being driven towards the Green Zone. Did anybody see? Were they following?

They crawled forwards, nudging against a tide of congestion in an ocean of chaos; stopping, starting, car horns and shouts, a regular Baghdadi Sunday. Each time the jeep juddered to a stop, her fear was amplified in proportion to her sensory loss, and she pushed herself deeper down between muscled flanks on either side. Then she heard the agent's voice from the front passenger seat. It was deep, reassuring with a twang of Northern England.

'We're through now, Amira. We're in the Green Zone.'

Fifty percent of the operation was complete; the easy half. Phase Three would be getting through Immigration unchallenged, and Four wouldn't even be over when she was on the plane. Only when it left the tarmac and climbed into the Arabian sky would Amira be free. So, no celebrations; just an almost unbearable rise in tension.

An hour later, the team set off for Baghdad Airport at the time that Amira should have been heading home from school. In thirty minutes, those back at the house would realise she was late. Within an hour, she'd be missed, and by that time she'd be with her giant guardians waiting for immigration clearance.

Since dawn that day, she'd become an adult woman with her own free will but was armed only with a copy of a dual nationality passport, trying to escape a culture that could put the intervention of hostile male relatives, way above her own. There was no dramatic intervention, and the immigration clearance was given. The agent and the four giant guardians could go no further, Amira was a passenger now, and she passed through the gate and across to the aircraft.

As she snapped the seat belt closed in the window seat, she looked out onto the tarmac, expecting to see the approach of uniformed men. She was so near to the summit, where the pain was the greatest, with the prize of freedom in sight, that she felt she could almost smell it. Then came the announcements and drills, first in Arabic, then in English; the second voice she'd heard in the language following the agent for five years. She longed to listen to another; Sylvia, whose tones she'd imagined on receipt of each saviour text and wondered if she wore the 'stiletto heels that must be removed before exiting the aircraft.'

Amira felt the vibration through the floor as the engines started, and the plane taxied until it reached a string of lights stretching out like water on a cobweb. There it waited for what seemed another lifetime. Then there was the roar of the undercarriage on the concrete as they accelerated forward, and she was thrown back in her seat. Some rows behind, she heard a small child squeal in glee as if on a playground swing as the flutter of weightlessness lifted her stomach. And then the child's delight was followed by silence but for the purr of the engines.

Amira was going home.

Sylvia and two other women were waiting at Arrivals with her name printed on a sheet of A4 paper and offered her the first hug she'd received in four years. With support from networks and agencies, she healed and rebuilt. The skills and steel that had facilitated her escape allowed her to thrive. Scholarships were awarded to her, through which she ascended to first-class degrees and a Masters in Chemistry and Quantum Computing.

It had transpired that Nadeem was more than just unkind: he'd forged the required parental permissions required to take a minor out the country, made apparent by the grisly discovery soon after of the two bodies of her parents, noted by the authorities but of little concern as four fewer migrants were on the radar and a local irritant had gone back.

Only when the irritant graduated in the land of his birth from insurrection on one side to enhancing a medieval death cult with the brilliance of twenty-first century science and technology on the other, were the intelligence dots connected following the War on Terror. Nadeem's vocation had been found as Al Shabah, the Wraith of Fallujah. In time, an extra-judicial hellfire would be served from a speck in the sky, leaving little trace of the convoy in which he'd been travelling.

Though thousands of miles away and with a new life, only when informed of the drone strike did Amira feel the nightmare was truly over.

With protection and the support of the local imam, Amira was able to pay her respects to her parents. She would find solace in the arms of another family, related to that of her Foreign Office saviours, and meet her rescuing agent once again. Except this time, he was introduced to her using the codename BREAKSPEAR.

From there, Amira was given a new purpose in life, and the means to oppose men like al-Shabah.

She found her nest within the Service and the Hive had its diminutive Queen Bee.

What Shev saw in the eyes of the woman before her was absolute self-belief and the stone-cold certainty of someone who had been to Hell and back. It made her feel like a baby.

Shev sat down and placed the bag of goodies on the table, along with the phone from inside her breast pocket. 'Staff sent me here for briefing, UT4.'

The Ultra clocked the trepidation in Shev's voice and conceded a smile. She spoke quickly, surprising Shev with a strong East End accent that made Biff sound like Prince Harry.

'Okay, 808. We have four hours to get through all this and the added extras before your next RV, so let's make hay.'

UT4 illuminated the rest of the range, parts of

which were mocked-up living areas, which Shev thought reminiscent of the Jeffrey Museum where she'd taken students to on college trips. UT4 had designed everything specifically for the task, and for Shev, over the next four hours, the learning curve continued its almost vertical climb, and the Jenga tower in her mind began to sway.

Chapter 9

RV: ZIDS

1520 hrs, August 8th 202?

The Hive

SIS Training Facility

Limehouse, London, E14.

CCTV showed the coast was clear from all approaches. Shev emerged from the Hive into the arched tunnel on Ratcliffe Lane—the covert egress—adorned as usual by the dank scent of stale urine. Aerosol graffiti intermittently graced the drab Victorian brickwork, its flow covering all surfaces within a square mile like twenty-first century hieroglyphs, its message unintelligible to any soul over twenty-one and foreign to the borough, save for the sprayed red runic S and N either side of the central Venn-like overlapping letters of SOON. This was the logo that appeared on walls, windows and pavements across Europe that tinder summer, as the ominous harbinger of the Grass Riots.

Emerging from the tunnel, Shev found that the ripened steel skies had retched at last and thrown down a high-summer deluge, cleansing the stale air with a liquorice petrichor from St James' Gardens, and leaving the pavements and roads like ebonised mirrors of the corruption above. Shev passed the cover garage and walked the short distance down Commercial Road to Zids, the glass-fronted café sandwiched between a kebab shop and a newsagent.

It had long served as Stepney's haven for builders, rogues and teachers, the ranks of whom had formerly included Shev, courtesy of her position at M-City College, ten minutes down the road. This was no ordinary East End café; Suleiman and Yusuf, the Kurdish father and son owners, made sure the spoons and everything else in their establishment were far from greasy. The walls were covered in pitch pine slats, scorched and varnished, and the woodblock tables, chairs and tiled floor were spotless. Zids even offered a toilet with sandalwood handwash and a Blade hand dryer.

Daytime TV burbled from the small screen on the wall, competing with the sound of frying on the griddle. The bouffanted anchor man sounded incredulous as he reported on the phenomenal growth of the latest global sensation, the Eighth Day movement, then handed over to the weather bulletin celebrating the deluge. No one took any notice. Four tables out of the nine were occupied.

Since Shev joined the Service, her job cover was that of a construction Onsite Assessment and Training Assessor, peripatetic, hard to trace but always busy with site visits. Her rucksack contained several portfolios of fake students with fake IDs and the PPE she required for the job.

As she entered, Shev was greeted warmly by Suleiman, who remembered her regular order from the previous year to the letter.

'Bins on toast and Kit Kat, Miss?'

'Have you got crusty?' she asked.

'Karasty? Why, of course. A coffee for you?'

'Yes, please,' she said. She took a seat near the window, set her phone down and took out a portfolio from her rucksack, which she pretended to work on. Checking her watch, she found she was right on time. Yusuf, the son, placed the plate and frothy Kurdish coffee, the best in East London, down with deliberate and demonstrative care. There wasn't a peep from the phone as punters came and went, so she bagged the work and attacked the plate.

Meow! A blast of adrenaline surged through her and, with a trembling hand, she grabbed the phone in reflex. It was Biff with a nonsense joke; something about kebabs, for fuck's sake! She asked herself if she could really handle this spy-shit; after all, this was Zids on Commercial Road, not the Corniche in Beirut. Yusuf collected the empty plate, as usual enquiring after its quality, which she affirmed.

Chill, she told herself, opening the Kit Kat and dunking it in the coffee, only withdrawing on the point of disintegration. She imagined her Hive instructor saying, 'Even with dunking, 808, timing is everything.'

Meow! Shev played it cool this time, finishing the chocolate and wiping her mouth with the serviette before she checked her phone. There it was—the contact emoji:

She looked through the window onto the street— there was nothing unusual—then casually across the café to the counter. There stood a man with his back to her. He must have entered smoothly through the open door as someone left. Platinum hair touched the collar of his black lightweight knee-length coat, and he carried a large, folded umbrella. There was a white canvas man-bag over his shoulder. He, too, was greeted like a long-lost friend by the father and son, and he pulled his hand from his pocket while he spoke, revealing the thin rectangle of a smartphone. As briefed, Shev responded with the specific emoji code response. He checked his screen, then turned and faced Shev directly, his coffee in his other hand. They each eyed the other's badges: his was a target and hers a smiley.

It was the correct mutual recognition code.

The man seemed familiar. Striking and memorable, old but fit, with a lined, weathered face and clear blue eyes. He smiled broadly, sat down opposite her at the table and presented his phone screen, which showed Shev's text before it vanished. She scanned the café; the other tables were still in use.

'Don't worry,' said the man with an indicative nod. 'They're ours. Not Sully and Yusuf; just the punters. We've got the place for the next half-hour.'

He pocketed his phone.

'How's your new phone?' he asked.

Shev shrugged. 'Mine's good, but maybe yours is better.'

The man chuckled. 'I teach down the road at an ESOL school,' he said. 'Have done for yonks. It's a wonder I've never seen you in here.'

'Well … timetables, you know how it is,' Shev

answered with a touch of scepticism. 'Anyway, which one is yours? There's more language schools than chicken shops down there.'

'It was called Janley's. Exotic, eh?' He extended his hand for her to shake. She took it, and in that second, the connection was made between the photo of the cross-legged man she'd seen at their first meeting and the conditions he'd endured. The heat, the burn, the pain. She shuddered internally but showed no trace of what she'd felt. She shook firmly and released.

'I've never liked my first name,' the man said. 'In the course of our work, I'm BREAKSPEAR, or Mr B, if that suits you better.'

'Mr B will do, if you don't mind … sir?'

'Mr B it is. Although subject to change.' He sat side-on, facing the window, and crossed his legs. In a covert move, he pushed a fresh SIM along the table until it touched the tips of her fingers. She took it, mirroring his sleight of hand.

'To business. There is a small case that requires our attention. You, I and one other complete the cell. You've been selected for your suitability for this assignment. You seem to have strong intuition. Come on—let's walk down to my place. It's fifteen minutes at a steady pace.'

They set off in the direction of the City.

'As you've no doubt gathered, the learning never stops. Ever,' said Bradley, maintaining a forward gaze as he walked. 'Some of what I'm about to go over, you've no doubt already heard, but it's my take on things. If I sound like an old fart, I guess it's because I am, so I'll allow myself.'

Shev acknowledged. She was warming to her new boss; he seemed interesting, unlike those at the Hive.

'You're entitled to know some of the basics about me, and I'll share them with you as we move along—if indeed we *do* move along. I was about your age when I joined. I was in the Army first and got mangled, big time. Then I fell into this.'

Shev's grey matter started kicking in. It occurred to her that the first few pieces of a very strange jigsaw may have clicked into place. She ran over the scraps of information. The test photograph, the report requests. He was invalided out, and he's talking about intuition. Pah! Coincidence, she told herself, trying to refocus on what her new boss was saying.

'As a species, we're getting ever more technological. So, what we do in our line of work and how we do it is becoming ever more important. The Human Factor. People. Look around you. The wants, needs, secrets, desires and weaknesses. That's what we've focused on for a century. That's our area.' He glanced sideways at her. 'Do you think all the tech's made it easier for us, Shev?'

The question took her back a little. It wasn't the content; it was the fact that it was the first time he'd used her name. The first time *anybody* had used her name since she joined. Another trick?

No chance, mate. Nice try, she thought and said nothing.

Bradley looked to his left and studied her for a second.

'We're here.' They were at a building that appeared to be another East End ghost pub. Some bottle-green encaustic tiles remained out of reach, an echo of the building's past elegance. The windows were barred, and layers of bill posters for yesterday's Troxy cage fighters were plastered over every inch at ground level.

The Janley's ESOL school was above. The tatty remains of its lettering peeled away from the grime-covered windows, shamed by the neon signage of Twang Twang Chicken—London's Best right next door. Shev and Bradley were unnoticed by the usual array of youths bustling at the counter and smoking outside.

Bradley unlocked the side door and waved her in. Very elite, Shev thought as she followed him up the scabby threadbare staircase, through another code-locked door and into a musty classroom.

Bradley asked her to take a seat and continued the soft lecture on the fundamentals of espionage. 'Refining the arts of persuasion and betrayal. The exploitation of human weakness.'

Shev thought back to the training films of the Soviet double-agent Kim Philby and his smirks and blatant lies before the world's press, shown as a case study in treasonous duplicity. She'd learnt that the catastrophic betrayals of Philby and his ilk were unparalleled and had crippled Western Intelligence with paranoia for decades.

'This is what we do,' said Bradley. 'It needn't be bad or macabre … Watch, listen, learn, then we decide if time allows us to continue with the same or whether we need to act.'

Their eyes were locked for a moment, then he took a breath and braced himself, gripping the table on which he was leaning with both hands, whitening his knuckles.

Here it comes, she thought.

'In this case, time is not on our side. We—the nation—democracy and peace are under attack. We have detected a viable existential threat to all this, all that we know.'

He looked relieved, like he'd confessed to a

heinous indiscretion that had been weighing on his mind since some drunken office party.

Then, as if suddenly self-conscious of the lapse, he straightened. '808, your codename is GLIMMER. Our operation is BARBELL. Please exchange your SIM, and I will brief you fully on our mission.'

Shev listened intently and took it all in. Bradley was clear and concise, returning to the theme of exploitation in context. The term 'cover' kept reccurring like a one-word mantra. Biff would accompany her as a partner because that was who she was and part of her package; what she brought to the table. *The Shevalogue* would go live in the event of overseas deployment with funding under the cover of magazine sponsorship, and as Biff did the photography and tech, he was essential. That was all he needed to know.

As Biff was slow on his day job with his uncle, he would be ecstatic. That tight little button UT4 was part of the operation, too. At the tame end of the myriad of added extras she'd revealed were apps for airline, train and hotel loyalty reward schemes, fully loaded with points courtesy of 'the magazine', giving her instant diamond status.

She was used to pressure, stress and hard work, but this was the first time things had got weird. The weirdness was stacking up: Mr B; the test photograph; the codename GLIMMER, which was strangely familiar for no apparent reason; and now involving Biff, putting him at risk as cover. The strangest thing of all was that none of it actually creeped her out. It didn't feel wrong, and there were no alarm bells. But there was an obvious catch.

'Sounds great, but me and big Biff bowling around in his peak cap and trackies, won't we stand out a bit, especially in posh places? We're not exactly wallpaper material.'

'Exactly. You'll be the sorest pair of thumbs in plain sight … but in context. Just tastemakers from London on a jolly up, all expenses paid.'

Shev loosened her neck with a head roll, as she had a habit of doing when mulling over an idea.

Bradley continued. 'The Roma Big Issue seller who appears on the corner stands out, doesn't she … in that context. She's prejudged and rated on her appearance and her apparent situation. No one expects or suspects anything more from her. Like the dog walker, the High-Vis wearer, the Watch Tower lot.'

'Or the tattooed hipster with the waxed moustache.'

'Exactly, GLIMMER. We all see them, but we don't *see* them, only their props. How many times have you walked past this building like it didn't exist? After a while, the regular becomes invisible. As will you, and as will I.'

On such deployments, Bradley would be wallpaper; close, but at a safe distance, watching and advising. UT4 would be the same but in reach from Thunderbird 5.

Bradley's phone rang. He answered with his code-name.

UT4 explained that she had completed analysis on all the data from the deep trawl and had sent triangulation points through to him to act on the subjects.

Bradley ended with a brief, 'Roger that.'

He pulled two objects out of the man-bag beside him: an iPad and a hand-sized box wrapped in wire with two orange foam disks. He handed the box to Shev.

'What's this?' she asked.

'It's called a Walkman.'

He indicated to unwrap the wires, which were revealed to be earphones. She examined the universal symbols on the square buttons and pressed Eject. The clear plastic tray clicked open. Bradley then handed over a small plastic case; it had ballpoint writing on the note inside.

'And this is a cassette. A mixtape, to be exact. Go ahead; I need to act on something for a couple of minutes.'

Shev removed the tape, got it in the right way on the second attempt and, acting on her initiative, donned the earphones and pressed Play. The first chords of electric piano and the warm hum of Hammond organ washed over her. She read the ballpoint note: *Tin Soldier - The Small Faces.*

Bradley downloaded the message from UT4 and absorbed the content. He composed a message of his own and sent it to Shev. She opened her eyes, found the Stop button and removed the earphones.

'More on that later. Back to business.' He lifted three holograms from his phone. 'These are the subjects. I've sent you their basic info.'

Shev's phone vibrated and let out a dog bark. She grinned. Bradley pondered for a second on Shev's attribution of texts to cats and emails to dogs.

'We've got forty-eight hours clearance to operate on British soil. You've got home addresses, swipe cards and relevant ID to access their places of work.' The printer churned out three pages of A4, which Bradley collected and passed to Shev.

'First, as we did during your assessments, I need you to write a brief on what you feel from these images. Second, I need you to get eyes on in a face-to-face exchange with each of these characters and do the same.

'Two of them may be familiar to you, as they're public figures. Try to dispel anything that you think you know about them, aside from their connection to the Eighth Day thing. Have you seen anything about it?'

'Who hasn't? They were even on about it on the TV in Zids earlier.'

Bradley said nothing, but Shev could see he was impressed as she drew an image using a finger on her iPad. 'I get their pop-ups every two seconds. If it wasn't them, it was you lot,' she added with a wink, lifting the iPad to show Bradley. She'd drawn a cruciform within a circle. 'This is them, right?'

'Almost. That's a pagan sun cross symbol, beloved by neo-Nazis everywhere,' said Bradley, and he rubbed out the centre where the lines met. 'There. What does it remind you of now?'

'The crosshairs of a scope?'

'Exactly, with a space in the centre for all of us. Complete inclusivity.'

In fifteen minutes, Shev had fulfilled the first part of the task, listing her immediate impressions—which were nothing, nothing and nada—then saved and pressed Send. 'Done. Hold up. The home address for Oriel d'Orly is in Nice, France.'

'Yes, and she's there for four days from Friday in conjunction with the technology Expo, Siliconica. You can get to the London subject straight away. We'll receive your TAVS cam feed. Prime Biff, pack your bags and get booked for tomorrow night. See you here at 0730 hrs tomorrow, and we'll do Derby together. Over to Nice by midnight and back by Tuesday … maybe.'

'OK, Mr B, sir!'

Shev folded her iPad away, got up to leave and headed for the door.

'GLIMMER?' Bradley stopped her in her tracks. 'It's us lot now.' He pointed to the Walkman. 'And that's your homework.'

As it was, the French Minister for Foreign and European Digital Affairs, Ms Oriel d'Orly, who had visited Britain for the second time since June to cement a pan-European cybersecurity agreement, was utterly unfamiliar to Shev, as was *Tots TV* channel presenter Rub-a-Dub—real name James Reginald Kohler. They were just as obscure to her as Bob Distance, a builder from Derby.

Two days previously, Bob had been a chosen audience member on a weekend live broadcast of the TV programme *Question Time*. In response to the non-answer from the panel of slippery politicians, Bob had blurted out a series of numbers for no apparent reason. The presenter had thanked him and moved on, but that morning, Kohler and d'Orly had done the same in unrelated broadcasts, adding a date sandwiched between ordinary sentences before carrying on without a blink. All three wore badges denoting them as Eighth Dayers, albeit d'Orly's came in the form of a diamond-encrusted brooch.

They appeared to be disparate individuals: a plasterer, a TV presenter and a politician. The connecting factor wasn't evident, but at GCHQ, the government listening station, the board lit up.

The alert systems didn't find the outbursts nonsensical. When assembled, they made a sixteen-figure grid reference followed by a date. The reference gave the top-secret location for the servers of LINX, the London Internet Exchange, and they all marked the calendar eight days in the future, August 12th.

Chapter 10

THE MERRY DANCE

0645 hrs, October 10th, 1921

Cadogan Gardens, London, SW3.

As the dawn pushed darkness to twilight in advance of the autumn sun, a black car rounded the corner from the direction of Pavilion Road. It pulled slowly into the square of tall red-brick terraces with a fenced garden at its centre. There were six men within, including the driver.

The faces at the windows took in all they could see through the rising mist on each side. As it drew level, Spirewick lowered his head, pulling smoke from his pipe, and turned away, taking a right into Cadogan Street. He heard the vehicle crawl on and felt the stares of the passengers as they lost his silhouette. Hearing the car round the next corner, he turned on his heel and followed its route, staying out of sight of the watching men as it turned left and left again. He passed a slim man in a fedora, his head down, with a large bag walking in the other direction.

They noted each other but gave no acknowledgement or signal.

The slim man paused on the corner and lit a cigarette. From his vantage point, he saw the car pull up outside 15 Cadogan Gardens.

Spirewick waited on the other side and, knowing that a bodyguard would emerge first, his eyes everywhere, having noted a man of his size moments before. He drew back and leant on the railings of 5 Draycott Place and counted. He allowed thirty seconds and then looked again. The men were tending to the passenger as he left the vehicle; no one was covering. Amateurs, Spirewick thought to himself.

He zeroed in on the passenger as he emerged. There was the Tall Man, as described, the centre of deference. As the baggage was removed from the boot and the party headed toward the steps, Spirewick printed the form and likeness into his mind: young, handsome, of good stature, six-foot-two, two hundred pounds, dark, with a left side parting and a clipped moustache.

A merry courting couple rounded the corner, arm in arm. The revellers, looking worse for wear from a night of it, laughed and chatted. The man stopped and spun the girl, who let out a squeal and knocked his hat off, revealing a head of fox-red hair.

'FREDDY,' Spirewick hissed to himself.

He had his man, as did both Simons and Monus.

Monus—FREDDY to those monitoring his movements—knelt and picked up his flat cap, taking a good look at the Tall Man as the delegation entered the house and the door closed. The couple's happiness stopped, and, as if they were strangers, the girl suddenly turned and departed into the thinning mist without even a goodbye.

Monus stood for a moment, surveying No. 15. The window shutters opened, and the Tall Man, silhouetted by gaslight, looked out for a moment.

Spirewick's adrenaline surged. He broke a sweat, and his breathing deepened in arousal as he anticipated blood and violence. He went over C's brief in his mind, fighting his immediate instinct to approach, draw The Persuader—the razor-sharp bayonet he always kept concealed about his person—and slay the target there and then. But orders were orders; his passion for picarism would not be sated that morning. He was to shadow the Tall Man until the time came, and then this fox would be his, whenever that would be.

Spirewick pulled himself away, heading up the steps of No. 9. He had taken a room at the rear to observe the Tall Man.

On the corner, Simons, observing the couple, had anticipated the move and crossed the road to a recessed door where he was out of sight. He removed his hat and peered around the corner to see Monus heading towards Sloane Street. Simons made after him, keeping as much distance between them as was safe; the covering mist had thinned to gossamer under the freshly born rays of morning. Keeping sight of The Fox was a constant gamble against exposure as he headed at pace down the length of Sloane Street towards Hyde Park.

Simons kept his gaze to the left of the shoulder so as not to alert the target's sixth sense, whilst also being in a position to take cover against any backward glance from the target if required. Monus made no attempt to look back, crossing Knightsbridge and entering the park. Simons swallowed the risk of allowing his quarry more distance, then crossed the road and followed. Seeing Monus had turned left and was skirting the river, Simons chose to hang back until he reached Carriage Drive and continued. On he went through the arch under Serpentine Bridge.

Hidden high in the sweet chestnut and oaks, the song thrushes greeted the new day. The breeze whispered through the reed beds without troubling the trace of errant mist clinging to the riverbank and hazing the morning light. It was pushed by a sudden gust off the river, stripping the first browning leaves from the trees to flutter to the ground and lodging the mild pepper of autumn's nascent decay in the pursuer's nostrils.

Simons noticed that, as the man passed ahead, the weeping willows and the procession of reedmace seemed to sway, almost in salute, and an array of peacock and cinnabar butterflies, flashing amber and crimson, rose as ripples in his wake.

Rounding the next corner, Simons stopped in his tracks and pulled back. Monus was stationary, looking to his left. With his back against the bridge, Simons scanned the route they'd taken for pursuers. Finding none, he turned again, edging forwards, his heart pounding, until he could see Monus, still as transfixed as he had been a moment before.

Monus then walked forwards, putting himself partially out of Simons' sight to survey that which had waylaid and fascinated him. A lifetime of five minutes later, he was off again at a stride.

Simons gave him the extra distance in the open area before setting off once more, allowing himself a glance to his left at where Monus had stopped. He saw a conical bronze statue entwined with small winged beings and topped by a boy, his horn glinting in the rising sun. As Monus made a beeline for Lancaster Gate, Simons quickened his pace as the risk of losing his man in the surrounding streets and buildings increased with each stride. He was nowhere near within touching distance of the target, but he was as close as he had been since the chase had begun forty minutes before, and now the destination became clear: Paddington Station.

At last, cover wasn't a problem for the slim, hatted man; the soldier-like rows of cream studded iron pillars that stretched up to the gallery roof provided all that was needed. Simons spotted Monus, stationary once again, on Platform Four. Simons saw another person joining him, and, from a distance, he could make out the same flame-red hair beneath her bonnet; it was the girl from Cadogan Gardens. They said nothing but stood stock-still, square to one another, as if communicating without words.

A porter passed by Simons' shoulder.

'Excuse me, sir? The next train on that platform—where's it heading?' Simons asked.

'That's the 07:30 Great Western to Bristol, sir,' replied the porter, pointing up to the large station clock. 'You'd better hurry; it leaves in five minutes.'

Simons walked briskly to the ticket office, keeping the couple in his peripheral vision as he made the purchase. He could see their backs as they acted like lovers once more, but he was beginning to lose them in the bursts of steam from the funnel as the train stoked up.

When he caught sight again, they were halfway down the platform. As the next blast of vapour cleared, they had vanished, and the porter was closing the doors. Simons dashed aboard as the whistle blew and flags waved, and he slammed the carriage door shut behind him as the train pulled away.

Simons lugged his large carry bag onto the rack above and took the seat nearest the window. He kept the fedora on his lap, a useful prop to cover his face and feign sleep to avoid conversation with the four other occupants, who were all male and of advanced years. The target and his companion were perhaps four coaches ahead.

The tactic with the hat worked well on the early train. At each stop, Simons removed a vanity mirror from his breast pocket and held it out the window to view any exit from the carriages ahead. On the first two occasions, politeness didn't necessitate a query, though Simons noticed his fellow travellers exchanging curious glances. On the third stop, at Chippenham, one of the gentlemen piped up, 'So, what on earth are you up to, old man?'

Simons ignored the inquiry until the train had built up enough speed to deny a late exit, then replaced the mirror and closed the window. He had planned his cover for all eventualities, or so he thought. He considered pulling Browning and C's favourite Bronx American out for airing but settled on Oxford English for his reply.

He mopped his brow for diversion, then conspiratorially said, 'I'm looking after the … interests of my client.'

The passenger's eyebrows rose, so he added an exaggerated wink, eliciting boorish laughter from those present.

'Indiscretions?' said the conversationist, with rising pitch.

Simons touched his nose and addressed them all. 'Let us say guilty until proven, my dear sirs. Guilty until proven.'

Satisfied with his response, the gentlemen let the young man be; he was no doubt working, after all, possibly for a man of considerable wealth and taste.

As the locomotive pulled into Bristol Station, Simons readied himself to advance as soon as possible to a vantage point, rather than waiting to tail the target. In one movement, he raised his hat to his travel companions and was out the door, his bag in hand. He made his way through the crowds in front of him at speed, passing through the gate and leaving the station to observe the exit from the corner. Five minutes passed before the couple emerged from amongst the throng and headed towards town.

The handsome spy bagged his coat, replaced the fedora with a brown flat cap and gave chase. The couple spoke to no one as they made their way along Temple Gate to Victoria Street, where they crossed the bridge, continued to St Augustine's Parade and finally reached the harbourside.

Crowds were manageable, but risk of exposure on the quay was now at its highest. Simons pulled back to wait on the corner, lit a cigarette and checked behind him, but when he looked again, they were gone.

At the jetty, there was a row of docked steamers along the quay, made up of large ocean-going vessels and shorter-range freighters. Within the forest of masts, the billowing funnels indicated imminent departure. The quayside was a melee of activity as the dockers rattled along gangplanks loading and unloading vessels by hand-to-hand or from hoists connected to towering black cranes.

'Damn it!' Simons growled under his breath, as despair passed over him. A mid-sized steam freighter was pulling out from the quay when a movement flashed by him; it was some distance past before Simons could make out a man running at full bore along the dock. The man leapt over the edge, clearing the range across the water, down to the freighter's deck and rolled across its beam before rising to pirouette as if to an amassed audience. The man replaced his cap and, with hands on hips, turned to look back at the quay. Simons thought he saw a glimpse of gold in the broad grin as he waved goodbye with his cap in the direction of the wharf.

Crushed with failure, Simons averted his eyes, remembering the Chief's implicit warning. The steamer pulled into the centre of the canal and sounded its horn as it headed out towards the Avon, its gate to the open sea. Simons suddenly felt the strain of the last seven hours that adrenaline had kept at bay, and sweat poured from his skin and stung like vinegar as it ran into his eyes. A weight equal to his seemed to grow on his shoulders, followed by guilt swelling like an acidic tide in the pit of his stomach. His hands began to shake.

'You OK there, sir?' a teenage boy called up from a facing deck.

Simons pointed to the shrinking shape of the freighter and its grey and white plume.

'W … where's that t … tramp heading?' he stammered, then doubled over with his hands on his knees, the sweat from his brow spiralling down to dash the cobblestones like ordnance from a Zeppelin.

'That one? Straight to Tivoli docks, Queenstown, I'd say.'

Further along, a gangplank dropped with a crack as loud as a shell burst. Simons had clung to the edges of sanity for those desperate moments as the feelings flooded back, but the impact threw him straight back to hell; back to Black Tom. He recalled plunging into the ice-cold water of the Hudson, its infinite blackness drawing him down, while above its shimmering surface, the world was engulfed in flames.

His form curled into a ball, but his arms strained to pull his knees ever tighter beneath his chin as he rocked back and forth on his haunches. The sickening sound of a grown man's weeping filled his ears, until he slowly realised it was his own. The barbed whip of guilt stood back from beating its victim to allow shame to take over, egged on by terror.

Through his fingers, Simons could see the legs of the quayside dockers now gathered around. A nervy man was nothing new, but no one came forward to offer comfort to the stranger, and they soon filtered away, shaking their heads. He clamped his eyes shut again and sank deeper still.

Then there was a touch. He felt its warmth on his arms, then his hands were gently taken. He felt like he was rising out of the abyss of pain; out of the black ice and fire. He felt fingers running through his thick black hair, stroking him, and he realised that he was no longer drowning. The sickening sound that was coming from his mouth eased to silence.

'Shhh now, eh.'

The voice was comforting, like the warmest blanket. The soft hands took hold of his face, and he opened his eyes. Windows to the soul of the deepest and brightest green met his; they were set wide apart within a pale, heart-shaped face framed by red/gold locks.

The rescue was complete; he was enveloped in bliss, and at the back of his mind, C's warning echoed to silence …

Chapter 11

TEN MOONS

The sounds of the surf and calling gulls filled his ears, and the cold tide chilled his ankles. His lungs full of salt air, he held a smaller hand that gripped his fingers tightly. The hand belonged to Garrett, who giggled and jumped as the froth of the tide surrounded them. The laughter, further along, came from his mother, Roisin, who was holding his brother's other hand.

The tide receded down the smooth shore of Dalky's Whiterock Beach. There was a large hand on his shoulder, pulling him close to a warm body. Looking down into his eyes was a face like his, only fuller and topped with greying hair; it was his father, Abel. The sun emerged from a small vale of cloud, bathing the family in the glow of high summer, and the chorus of joy continued as Abel lifted little Garrett onto his shoulders and led his clan towards the shore.

There was the shock of cold water up his back, to which he turned, and the spray struck him in the face, momentarily blinding him. He heard the high giggle of a girl, and as his eyes cleared, he saw the tousles of red and gold touching the water as she cupped her hands to douse him again.

Simons awoke with a start.

He was on his feet but staggering, and the ground beneath suddenly moved and sent him crashing to his left. Rubbing his eyes, Simons regained his footing, only to stumble again in the other direction, like a pugilist on the threshold of defeat.

He caught the combined scents of salt air, coal, and oil, then heard the thresh of the paddles to the rear, all informing his senses that he was indeed at sea.

As he scrambled to his knees a third time, there was laughter behind him. He spun to confront his tormentor and staggered once but managed to remain upright. It was the girl from the Bristol harbourside, the girl in his dream, full-grown.

'Where am I?' shouted Simons, his fists raised as if he were facing an invisible enemy.

The girl smiled and regarded him with curiosity and some amusement. Her voice absent of mockery, she said gently, 'Well … you're here, with me.'

The voice that pulled him from the fire on the Bristol quayside melted his heart. He gritted his teeth and strained to focus. Dropping his guard almost entirely, he looked through the square windows on either side to see giant plumes of the Celtic Sea, shifting in constant movement below a leaden horizon.

'Please … where is here?' he pleaded.

The girl gestured for him to sit down. Simons,

with few other options, obliged. The young woman reached for his hand, and he pulled his own away in reflex. 'We're crossing to Queenstown as you wanted,' she assured him, 'just as you told me.'

'As I told you?' snapped Simons, his mind racing. Slowly circumstances came back to him; the turn at the water's edge after he lost Freddy; the girl comforting him; being lost in the green vales of her eyes—then nothing.

Christ. The mission. The mission!

'Yes, you told me everything,' the girl continued. Without intending to, she'd now filled him with dread; only her beauty and aura held him back from the cliff edge of despair. He began concocting his cover to trick his way out, a fail-safe combination of lies and truth.

'Everything?' he repeated.

'Yes,' she affirmed. 'You were hurt in the other war. You're a Dublin man—a doctor—and you wanted to cross to Queenstown to help them that needs it in this one.'

My God, he thought. That was the one he'd just cooked up! 'My bag?' he asked, his eyes desperate.

She pointed across the cabin. 'Just there.'

He grabbed it and checked its contents, keeping one eye always on the girl. His clothes and books had not been removed, and his medical instruments were all intact. The false bottom containing his papers, lock picks, cash and revolver was undisturbed.

The shifting peaks of the sea grew in height and depth, challenging his footing once again as the steamer plunged. Simons figured they were at the centre of the crossing. Still transfixed by the girl's beauty and manner, he went into character.

'I'm so … I'm so sorry … about …'

'You did take a turn. Jabbering like a goose, you was,' she said with a chuckle. Simons touched his belly. 'You ate like a horse, then slept through the night like a baby. So kind of the captain to feed us. Shame you couldn't heal yourself, eh, Doctor?'

'How did you get us on board?'

'Well now, I heal, too, you see. I asked them nicely, they let us on, and that's that. My brother took off and left me, the wrong 'un that he is.'

Of course, thought Simons, remembering Freddy vaulting onto the steamer.

'Your brother?' he said, feigning ignorance.

'Less said, eh?' She pointed to the bow. 'Look—not long now.'

The land of Roche Point and Fennel's Bay sloped on either side of the channel, like an embrace drawing them past Spike Island and up the River Lee into Queenstown and a berth at Tivoli docks.

'So, how do you feel now, Doctor …?'

'My name is Finn,' Simons answered, holding out his hand, which she took with a gentle shake. He was compelled to revert to honesty. 'It's so strange, but I dare say I've never felt better!'

They emerged from the cabin and weren't noticed or challenged by the deckhands; it seemed almost as if they didn't exist. The girl led, and they ascended onto the dockside. She nodded a way forwards, and they walked together until they reached the top road, saying little. Despite his companion's claim of his gluttony during the crossing, Simons felt he was flagging and needed sustenance, but the girl seemed indefatigable and carried him along in her presence. They reached a wooded path with tall cedars thick on either side, rich in scent and full of bird song.

'This is beautiful,' said Simons as they walked.

'Indeed, it is,' said the girl in immediate response. 'As are you.'

Simons burst out laughing, doubling over. 'Well, I … Well, I …' He was lost for words.

The girl maintained her quizzical smile. She took a deep breath and gestured at the woodland. 'Yes, I can see a difference,' she said, as if answering an unasked question.

'A difference?' quizzed Simons, close to regaining composure.

''Tween you and these. Do you have a favourite?'

'They're just trees, dear. Very nice and all, but...'

She set off again, and he followed, like a moth to flame, in silence until they reached the road.

She gestured back with her thumb. 'They calls that Lovers' Walk, you know.'

'Well, that's very apt, regarding you and the trees,' said Simons.

His wit was lost on his companion, but she sang a lilting melody as if in answer to a question he hadn't voiced: '*In the willow, you look for me. In the willow, you'll find me.*'

It was now late afternoon. As they walked, side by side, hunger, thirst and fatigue were beginning to get the better of him, despite his fascination with the girl. His body exhausted its scant reserves of fat, his cheeks felt hollowed further, and his empty belly moaned in protest up to his dry tongue and lips. He'd set off in pursuit of Freddy the previous dawn with no mind of his destination. The following day had been the most eventful for many a year. He had endured a hellish crisis at the Bristol harbourside and been redeemed at the hands of the young woman.

The girl halted at St Patrick's Bridge and turned to see Simons twelve paces behind. His head was bowed as he hauled his bag, the picture of exhaustion. 'I'm going this way,' she said, then pointed in the opposite direction. 'The town's that way. Good luck with your healing, Doctor Finn.' She proceeded across the bridge.

'Please. Wait!' Simons called in pursuit, adrenaline granting him energy once more. 'Please?'

She stopped and turned with raised eyebrows, nourishing him again with her broad smile.

'You didn't tell me your name,' he added as he staggered toward her.

She spent a moment considering, then responded flatly, 'Myra.' She turned to leave once more.

'Dear Myra.' The infatuated Simons couldn't disguise his plea. 'Could I see you again, please?'

Once more, she stopped but this time she didn't turn entirely. The pause seemed like minutes before she spoke again. For Simons, any moment in her presence was to be bathed in, and, despite his need for sustenance, he had bizarrely never felt quite this way before. Still side-on, she said, 'On the full moon, *Cuan Dor*. The tall willow, I'll be there.' before shaking her head and giving another gentle laugh. She sang the song as she had in Lovers' Walk, this time with more intent to her erstwhile companion, and added a verse before continuing on her way: '*Ten moons, I'll promise ye. Ten moons, I'll give ye.*'

'Full m– Myra, wait!' called Simons, but she would wait no more. She was soon over the bridge and gone.

He set off for the town, his mind whirling as he focused on being back in the land of his birth and concocting the layers of cover he would employ to bed in for the duration of the BARBELL mission. He established accommodation at the Mutton Lane Inn. Speaking in his mother's tongue, he began to carefully relate his story in confidence to those he knew would disseminate it. He was ready for the local inquisitors and all that they would throw at the fictitious doctor, and he adjusted his tone and body language to that of a pacifist who posed no threat.

He was the Dark Invader now.

Simons' reality was his alone. He was no doctor; just the son of one with three out of the eight years required to qualify as a medical student before the war.

Were it not for that conflict, he would now have been in his final months of study. He had forged papers as cover and references that would patch through from the Royal College of Surgeons to the Admiralty, which would corroborate everything in his legend. His encyclopaedic mind absorbed the basic knowledge of physiology to get by, but that was all. So, the story was that he hoped to resume his studies at the university.

A spy in his element—and following much-needed sustenance and having secured a room in which to reside—he focused on his mission. Locking the door, he removed the false bottom of his case, checked his map of the country, cleaned his revolver and stashed it and the rest of the kit where no one would find it. He then headed around the corner to the Post Office on Plunkett Street and requested a phone call. He called the agreed number, letting it ring twice before hanging up, then he dialled again, and it rang ten times as agreed before it was answered by a female. '112 Harley Street.'

'Hello. May I speak to Cathal, please?'

'One moment.'

A minute of silence passed. Simons scanned the office, almost certain there was someone out of sight with a phone to their ear and a sharpened pencil in hand.

'This is Cathal.' C's voice gave immediate relief.

'Cathal, this is Heath, Stanley Heath.' Silence. 'The accommodation you advised is fine, as is the weather. Mutton Lane is perfectly central in Queenstown, and I'll inquire about my studies at the university tomorrow.'

There was a pause as Simons imagined the broad smile of his master above the lantern jaw. The long sentence allowed C to discern Simons' tone beneath the strong Dublin accent on the other end of the line. He heard C draw a breath.

'Good … good, I thought you'd like it.'

'Freddy and I got parted in the rush, but I met a girl claiming to be his sister on the Bristol quayside. I'm to have tea with her down in Glandore.'

C got the hint; he would have received Spirewick's report confirming that the target had arrived in the company of a girl who had later departed.

'Glandore? Well, I'll pass this on to your brother, and I'll cable any news if there's a change in his condition. Goodbye, my boy. God bless you.'

'God bless you, Cathal.'

The line clicked dead. Simons gave the telegraph address of the Mutton Lane Inn to the Post Office staff to convey any messages for the attention of Dr Stanley Heath.

Simons' felt self-satisfied with his innovation on the hoof; indicating to C that the line was insecure, by changing SHEATH to Stanley Heath, his well-used and given legend. C had immediately called the Admiralty to inform them of the recognised change to Simons' cover.

Simons went back to his room, washed and slept, his dreams full of the encounters of Myra at the harbourside, the crossing, Lovers' Walk and the bridge. When he awoke, he checked his watch and found it was 20:37. After passing through the boisterous bar to get some air, he surveyed a waxing, gibbous moon, close to completion, set in the dark velvet clouds overhead.

The following night, the bar was half-full when Simons came down and took a drink. The debate between those for and against the Treaty settled and flared like the coal fire. Head down, he shrugged and stayed impartial. When pushed, he said he'd carried stretchers and dug out bullets in the French Republic for four years, but at heart he was a man of peace.

Word spread fast, and, the following night, the inn was visited by IRA rebels who insisted that the new guest Stanley have a drink with them, swiftly followed by another and then another. His cover story held water, but he was dragged outside and beaten regardless, and his room and bag were ransacked. The men found none of his kit and only basic funds, from which they took a 'donation'.

Rifling through his pockets, they produced a white feather, which only intensified the attack. Before the final punch reduced Simons to slumber, he told them through split lips that should it come to war, if they could find no other vet or butcher to deal with bullet wounds and amputations, they knew where to find him. The innkeeper's wife kindly patched him up. He had her sympathy as well as, he suspected, her heart, as her husband, was a much older man.

All that had unfolded had played out like a script from Simons' own pen. As the university had accepted his references and fees, his waking hours would be spent either in the library or attending lectures, and when darkness fell, his composure would dissolve as he stared at the golden disk in the night sky, transfixed like a lunatic.

In six days, he estimated it would be time, the moon would be full and then he would travel to find *Cuan Dor,* the Harbour of the Oak Trees, and search for a beautiful girl waiting under a tall willow.

The personal and professional had intertwined, and there was nothing the spy do about it.

Saturday brought the full moon. C had furnished him with funds for all reasonable eventualities via a healthy Munster and Leinster bank book. Simons would withdraw all he required from the Bank at South Mall.

He considered the options to get himself to Glandore. A bicycle would raise no eyebrows, but the distance would be a considerable strain: three hours each way. Any financial arrangement at all would involve risk and pique the curiosity of those who had interrogated him. He decided to 'confide' in the innkeeper's wife that he needed a vehicle for a day to go upcountry to visit his mother in Dublin. He would be attending his first local mass the next morning, and he would await the inquiry that would surely come from the curious and those pitying the bruised but handsome young man.

As he left the church, a local garage owner, approached and sounded him out with the usual questions. He had invested in a new vehicle and needed the business, so he asked for a substantial deposit, to which Simons agreed.

He collected the shiny black Model T Ford, all of three months old, and set off at 2 pm in the direction of Dublin. He was tailed, of course and, as 'luck' would have it, he broke down at Glyntown, with the car shuddering and lurching along for half a mile. The tail passed him by, then appeared up the road as Simons, exasperated, inspected the engine and tried in vain to restart her with the handle.

Their patience clearly exhausted after thirty minutes, his observer drove past him back towards Queenstown. When the coast was clear, Simons restarted the car and drove at a steady pace. Keeping a wide berth on the outskirts of the city, he crossed the river at Leemount Bridge and raced south against the dying light towards Glandore.

His map and compass took Simons down through Crossbarry, along the Bannon river. On either side were the green patchwork fields of Clonakilty and Owenahincha, where he caught sight of, and the salt air from the grey ocean again.

On the straight, with his destination in sight, his mind was free to reflect on the *années folles*, those crazy years in Paris after the war; the gilded cage C's telegram had rescued him from.

In a post-war Paris that crawled with international adversaries, the spy vs. spy game continued, minus its previous deadly intent, as the Great Nations tried to define themselves in the name of peace. As a "Passport Control Officer" at the British Embassy, Simons accessed International High Society via The Frolics, the new establishment at 30 Rue de Gramont on the corner of the grand Boulevard des Italiens. The establishment became the centre of Simons' universe, as the gambling and reading rooms of *Le Cercle Hippique* and *Sportif* were soon to be found under the same roof. His reports on England's adversaries and the climate of opinion were sent to directly to C as required.

With the arrival of summer, the doors to The Frolics were closed until the autumn, so Simons dressed down and crossed the river to soak up the other side of life, blending in amongst the poets, writers and artists of the Left Bank. He befriended a man who's work he'd been gifted by a discarded lover a lifetime ago. They were both Belvedere old boys though Joyce was ten years his senior. The author drew succour from his pal "Heath's" unveiled tone, reflections on their old city and its characters. Simons soaked up his take on how things were and the hopes and fears of the new world, all adding colour and flavour to his climate reports for C.

When night fell, he ventured further out to the *bal de barrière*, seedier hangouts frequented by low-lifes and bohemians. He often recognised upper-class Parisians from the finer haunts, including "diplomatic personnel of significant interest", who, like him, were looking for amusement amongst the pleasures of the poor and the downtrodden.

When the first leaves of autumn fell, Simons returned once again to the gleam and embraces of The Frolics and its flapper girls. They were exquisite fluff, especially Phaleana, fun and entertainment in female form, with her bobbed hair, pearls, silver cigarette holder and dress with ease of access. There was no shortage of laughter to vent the anxieties of his operational wartime activities.

He laughed off the recalled gaiety of Paris as he sped down the road, either side of patchworks of green fields. But thoughts of others loved and lost rose for a moment, revolving like a spectral carousel: Aveline, Oona, Lotti, and Edie. The wonderous Edie. They were beauties, one and all, but none was as strange or as captivating as his journey's objective, Myra, all red hair and rags.

Above the rattle of the engine, Simons could discern the sound of church bells carried on the wind. He rounded the corner to see a white spired miniature cathedral, slowed as he approached and pulled alongside. The clanging peels of the bells filled his ears, but his sight was drawn to his left.

A field rose to a hillock that formed a close horizon, on the top of which stood two figures, both still and staring at him intently. There was an older woman of striking beauty, evident even at that distance, dressed in field green garments that seemed to grow from the hill. Long red hair flowed down below her waist and tussled in the breeze, and in her right hand, she held a branch-like staff. By her side was a stick-thin boy in ragged clothing; late teens, deathly pale, with the same hue of hair. His arms hung by his sides as he glared.

The hairs on the back of Simons' neck stood on end. Disconcerted, he looked to his right to see if someone had emerged from the church and was the object of their attention, but there was no one. His view snapped back to the hillock. The onlookers had gone.

Simons shook his head to clear it, crunched the car back into a higher gear and accelerated down the track towards Glandore. The bay was to his left, and as he sped along the road ahead of him, he could see the horseshoe-shaped harbour, with its moored boats and the stone pier protruding out into the bay. He spotted the spire of another church, set into a rising verdant slope that graduated to a wooded hill. Its bells were also peeling out as the day began to die.

He had reached The Harbour of Oaks.

Simons drew to a stop in front of the pier and checked his watch. It was 17:20. The detour to shake his pursuers had cost him valuable time; he estimated he had an hour left of daylight. He pulled the car in and walked out to the pier to survey the area, doubting the likely success of his search. Looking for a willow in an oak stack, he thought to himself.

The car had gained some admirers when he went back and took out his gas lamp. When asked, he gave the bizarre reply that he was a tree doctor looking for a tall willow, which provoked hilarity among the growing crowd in awe of the young man with the latest in modern machinery. They pointed to different parts of the surrounding hills and began to argue among themselves as to where the tallest willow could be found.

Simons rechecked his watch: 17:38. This was attention he did not need. He headed off in the direction of the church on the wooded hill, accompanied for part of the way by the small crowd, but the assistance soon melted away but for one old man.

'Young fella,' he called out to the stranger ahead of him.

Simons stopped and turned, annoyed by the delay as the light died by the second, and caught the caller's eye.

'I think I knows what you've seen,' said the old man in a grave tone, 'and what it is that you seek.'

Simons said nothing but raised his lantern to discern the man better. The flickering flame showed the lines of concern etched into the old man's face. He could now see his shaking hands were grasping a rosary that glinted in the lantern's light.

'Take yourself and your fancy machine away right now, before it's too late,' the old man warned, 'and don't look back. There's a cost for messing with the glimmer folk … A *terrible* cost.'

Simons stepped towards him. 'The *glimmer* folk?'

'Get you gone, boy. That's all I need to tell you. That's all you need to know.'

Simons nodded his thanks, and the man departed, shaking his head and mumbling to himself.

Dusk had set in as Simons reached and passed the now silent church. He ventured inside the woodland, where what remained of the day was banished by the layers of endless branches. He felt no insecurity as he went deeper and higher, from tree to tree, further up the hill.

Within an hour, he'd reached the top and looked out across the bay to the sea beyond. The massive tawny moon hung in the heavens, a perfect circle that bathed Glandore and reflected a golden track that shimmered on the surface of the waves, out to the horizon. Its beauty rendered him breathless, and Simons leant on an oak, its bark pressing into his back through his cold, sweat-soaked shirt. He tried to rationalise the scene he beheld and the improbability of his journey's objective.

The dusk chorus of feathered evening song gave way to an owl's hoot and the creatures of the night, with which he felt at one. Time meant nothing now, so he sat for an hour before nodding off into a dreamless sleep. The screaming jeebies that had woken him every night following *Black Tom* had not returned since the crossing, and he pined for the source of his redemption: Myra.

Sometime later, he woke gently and rose. He could see some dancing light—fire, perhaps?—on the downlands over to the east. Estimating the distance to be around three or four miles, he descended the hill and considered whether to make his approach by car or on foot.

Back down in the harbour, all was silent. He detoured to the end of the pier to get a better look at the position of the fire, but he'd lost the advantage of height. Feeling defeated and foolish in such an abstract endeavour, he turned his back to the village and sat on the horseshoe wall, staring at the moon and out to sea. If this could be bottled, he thought. His bruised body reminded him of every blow of the rebel scourging two nights previous, and his head felt heavy again.

'In the willow, you'll look for me. In the willow, you'll find me.'

His eyes snapped open, and he spun around to find Myra standing before him. Her beauty was amplified by the moonlight that pulsed and flowed through the flaming gold hair and the reflection of the shattered moon that danced on the water in her verdant irises. The lantern's flame burnt a luminescent green as she drew closer, and Simons was able to see that the gown she wore was similar to that worn by the apparition on the hill.

'Myra!' Simons was filled with joy and relief. He stepped forward to embrace her, but she raised her hand, then took his.

They sat together, not saying a word, alternating their glances between each other, the bay and the moon that had brought them together. Whenever he tried to question her about the woman and the boy on the hill or the glimmer folk the old man had mentioned, his breath left him and he couldn't get the words out. Myra would just smile gently or beam, disintegrating his senses.

The moon moved across the sky and began to dip as dawn crept up from the hills above the village. At last, she spoke. 'I must go now, Doctor Finn, and so must you. Come on.' They walked to the end of the pier, where she released his hand.

'Myra …' He managed to speak her name, and she saw the yearning and the question within his eyes.

'Little by little, Doctor Finn, this was our first. I promised ten, remember?' she said, then sang the song again as she walked away and headed up the lane into the dawn. '*Ten moons, I promised you. Ten moons, I'll give you.*'

Simons stood stock-still, replaying the night's events until the approach of the early fishermen snapped him out of it. He made for the Model T, cranked her to life and set off up the hill on the drive back to Queenstown.

As he approached the small cathedral before the

bend, his hairs stood on end, and he looked to his right. He expected to find the woman and boy staring silently back at him, but there was nothing but brightening sky. He didn't notice the old man with the rosary peering through the hallowed tall doors of the cathedral to his left as he drove past, closing them as he crossed himself.

Over the next eight months, undeterred even by the outbreak of civil war in midsummer, Simons made the same journey, dictated by celestial movement, and each time the intimacy grew.

With the tenth moon due, Simons set off again via his usual circuitous detours.

When Myra appeared, he presented her with a piece of paper. 'What's that?' she asked.

'Look at it.'

She did as he said. 'What does it say?'

You bloody fool, thought Simons to himself. As if a creature like this would require the written word. 'It's an address; a place we can go, no matter what. Whatever should befall us—' He looked up. '—as this is the tenth moon.' His eyes filled with tears. He gently took the paper from her hand and pushed it inside the breast of her tunic. They walked arm-in-arm through the woods, and Simons finally asked the question: 'Myra, what of your family?'

She laughed. 'That's why I meet you here like this.'

'Your brother?' pressed Simons. She laughed again with no answer. He persisted. 'Mother?

Father?'

'Mother? As I say, that's why I meet you here. As for my Father? Fathers pay the cost.'

The cost. The last part intrigued him, but at the top of the wooded hill, bathed in the light of their tenth moon, she took hold of him, and their feelings were given full vent beyond worldly expression, above and beyond the carnal ecstatic to a plane beyond spiritual.

Simons lay in slumber on his side of a bed of wild moss. He felt Myra's kiss, on his eyes. She dressed and padded away down the hill.

The Dextroamphetamine he'd swallowed as he'd parked the car hours before had done its job, keeping him on the edge of consciousness. Leaving the lantern, he followed silently at a distance, through the harbour and then up the lanes, across the fields towards the small cathedral, then across the hillock where he'd seen the apparition on the night of the first moon and the area where he'd approximated the dancing fire had been.

After experiencing sensual joy beyond imagination, Simons now grappled with terror as he crawled on all fours to the brow of the hillock and peered over. In the distance, he could see Myra walking towards a circle of standing stones, and, as he watched, she went left to a matted thicket and disappeared within.

He stood, ran down the hill and peered inside. Beyond the branches and the undergrowth of the thicket, he could see green fire, light and movement.

Simons pushed apart the branches and foliage and made his way silently through to the clearing.

There he saw it in all its magnificence, set between three standing stones: a tall, shimmering willow, its branches swaying and twisted like the limbs of a Hindu deity assailed by a gale-force wind, on a night where there was none. Simons could hear strange music, indefinable from horns, strings or drums, which came from no clear direction.

The bass vibration tickled his stomach and sank through to his bones. Around the swaying tree danced Myra, Monus, and the boy. Between them, green pillars of flame sprung from the ground, took on human form and joined the dance before spiralling back into earth, only to reappear in another area. But where was the woman?

The spy strained his neck and peered further through the veil of boughs and foliage. His eyes met others in a direct gaze as a figure emerged from behind the tree; its intensity pole-axed him onto his back. He scrambled back away from the perimeter, tearing cloth and flesh against resistant branches and thorns, expecting the figure to alert the others and force an immediate pursuit. Neither happened.

Simons glanced back to the edge of the thicket and could see that a fourth figure had joined the dance with a celebratory vigour.

It was the woman from the hillock.

Sat at his desk back in London, C's eyes burned with excitement, and his heart raced as he digested the content of the latest cable from Simons:

Cathal have the source. The glimmer tree. Send apostles with coal and candles. SHEATH

He placed the telegram inside the open book at a page headed *Faeries*, then snapped it shut and slammed his fist like a hammer on the words of the frayed and tattered cover of *Daemonologie* by King James VI.

At last, he met the gaze of the handsome uniformed young man in the portrait.

'Now, my son. At last … it is time.'

Chapter 12

THE NAKED I

1830 hrs, August 7th 202?

London, W1.

On leaving Bradley, Shev headed straight to the DLR. Once on board she texted Biff with a list to pack for a fully funded holiday and said she'd explain later. She was now en route to make contact with the first subject, Mr James Reginald Kohler, aka Rub-a-Dub.

The file said that Kohler lived in a mansion block off Wigmore Street. She got there for 19:30 and saw him approach from the other direction and enter the building. Walking around the corner, she opened a pouch containing a nest of lanyards with various ID tags that granted inspection authority. She'd already decided on the Anti-Social Behaviour Officer one back at Bradley's yard. It was much more bankable than the others for domestic entry. Not even the feral mums on the estate ignored ASB officers, as court appearances, injunctions and, ultimately, evictions could follow. He'd be curious about a complaint if he'd been naughty, or he'd be glad to put the boot in if his neighbours had been at it.

Shev dropped the lanyard over her head, pulled her clear lens glasses on, tied her hair back and went for it. She pressed the intercom once, waited five seconds with no response, then pressed for a second time and sustained the buzzing.

'Yes?' said a guarded voice.

'Mr Kohler? I'm Emma-Jane Briggs from Westminster ASB.' Her ID blocked the intercom's camera view for a couple of seconds. 'I need to talk to you about a complaint that's been made relating to your property. It's just procedure; shouldn't take long.'

The door buzzed and Shev entered. The interior lighting flickered and pulsed as if an electrical storm was overhead. Fixed to the lift with masking tape was a notice printed on A4 paper— "APOLOGIES. OUT OF ORDER"— to which someone had scribbled underneath 'Fuck your service charge,' beside the obligatory sketch of male genitalia. The vinyl stairs stank of plastic and disinfectant, and the failing lighting became blackouts as she ascended, leaving her in total darkness for seconds at a time. With a shaking hand, she drew her phone and used its torchlight application, the web-like halo enabling her to reach the third floor. She entered a well-lit communal hallway blessed with a pedestal table on which sat a basil and mandarin diffuser and ornamental lilies.

She located Kohler's flat. As soon as she reached for the bell the door clicked open. 'Come in, shoes off,' a muffled voice shouted from inside.

Damn. She'd hoped to collar him on the doorstep.

She pushed the door open to find a dim hallway. There were two closed doors on either side, and one at the end of the hall which was ajar. A fillet of light bled through the gap on a ream of incense smoke. Adrenaline gave Shev the sensation of looking down the wrong end of a telescope. Her mouth was dry, and she swallowed as she advanced, her senses heightened to the max.

'In here,' shouted Kohler. His voice was deep, yet subtly effeminate with a north-western twang. Shev recognised the tone as the one she'd heard on *Tots TV* saying an inane catch phrase.

Shev pushed the door open and caught a glimpse of herself in a large floor-to-ceiling mirror. The place was sparsely decorated but illuminated by a myriad of candles. To her right, silhouetted in front of a large, muted TV showing *Tom and Jerry* cartoons Rub-a-Dub sat in the lotus position, dressed in pyjamas. She walked alongside and saw a man-child face, pudgy and round with flushed cheeks. The blond curly wig from his TV appearances was absent, revealing a bald head with a star-shaped tattoo adorning the crown. His eyes remained closed.

'Mr Kohler?'

'Yes,' lisped Kohler exaggeratedly, as if is dealing with someone with low understanding.

Shev stepped past and squatted down at a safe distance between him and the TV. 'There have been some complaints, and we need to get your side of things,' she said, pulling a clipboard from her rucksack.

'Hmm. It's not him across the hallway, is it?' Kohler enquired, without moving. 'He has the most insane parties, and I know he's really pissed off with me.'

'And why would that be?' asked Shev, taken aback.

'He keeps inviting me, and I won't go.' His eyes snapped open, glassy and doll-like. An unnerving broad grin broke across his face, and Shev drew back. 'Just yesterday, he said he was throwing the ultimate party. Dancing, drink, drugs and lashings of sex. I said, "Really, how many are coming?" He replied, "Oh, it'll just be the two of us." Kohler let out a guttural laugh. 'Only a jest. Oh, really, I can't resist that one.' He sighed. 'Really, I can't.' Then dialled himself down to a chuckle.

Shev was entirely disconcerted and couldn't reconcile what she saw and heard in front of her with the benign and dungareed Rub-a-Dub on *Tots TV*.

Kohler composed himself but retained the

unsettling grin. 'But seriously, there's no trouble here anymore. We've all crossed over as far as I know.'

'"Crossed over?"'

'*The Eighth Day*, of course,' was Kohler's stark reply.

'Er … there must be some mistake then.' Shev pulled some documents from her backpack. 'If there is any more trouble, Mr Kohler, log it here and send it to the address at the top. OK?'

Kohler took the document and threw it over his shoulder, where it fluttered to the floor. His eyes narrowed, and the smile was gone. 'Do you think there's been a mistake, Miss … Briggs?' The tone was suspicious and accusatory.

Shev's mind raced. She looked into his eyes and saw a level of depravity the likes of which would make Caligula puke. 'Maybe it was an old case that wasn't closed properly,' she said. 'So sorry to bother you, Mr Kohler.' She stood up and stepped back.

Kohler's eyes widened, and his grin returned. 'Over the threshold, the *naked i*, all is all right.'

'Naked eye?' Shev's voice rose in pitch in enquiry.

He pointed to his chest. 'That's *I*, not eye. Naked, stripped back.' He tapped his nose. 'True, pure.' Then, like a Gregorian sermon, he sang, 'The Naked I … Isla, oh, Isla.'

'Isla? Well, er, thanks for your help, Mr Kohler. I'll see myself out.'

'Miss Briggs,' called Kohler as Shev reached the door. She turned back to see him straining as if to hear or to find his words; he stared in her direction, unblinking, as tears welled in the widening glassy orbs. '*Night … night … twinkle.*'

On her return to the Cally flats that night, the revelation of the sponsored *Shevalogue* went gone down very well. Biff had it down as a wind-up until he saw the confirmation emails. They were flying business class and staying at the Hotel Negresco in Nice, opposite the beach. He was ecstatic and started singing '*Ruby, Ruby, Ruby, Ruby,*' signalling his intention of an Indian take-away to celebrate.

Over the meal, Shev found herself chuckling in a combination of terror and hilarity as she ran over the Rub-a-dub/Kohler experience in her mind.

'What is it, babe?' asked Biff with a mouthful.

'Nothing. Just something I saw at work today.'

'Like what?'

'It's nothing; it's just tickling me, that's all.'

'C'mon, babe, you's lockin' me out. I want in.'

Shev dead-armed him.

'Ow!'

'Nope. It's girl stuff, I ain't, and that's that. Anyway, you'd better be ready for tomorrow night, no messin'. I'm out of town all day.'

'It's hired, you're driving,' said Bradley. 'I'll take care of the music.'

The keys were already sailing in her direction, and she felt like she'd necked a neat cocktail of fear, dread and excitement as they chinked into her palm. There were no butterflies in her stomach, just a swarm of enraged African bees. Don't look down, Shev told herself. If she did, she'd surely fall. This single thought swamped her, as the Jenga tower in her mind grew higher and higher, piece by piece.

She'd passed the Hive's evasive driving course, no problem, but hadn't owned a car or driven regularly since passing her test at seventeen. Facts laid bare. If she couldn't drive her boss up to Derby on the M1, handbrake turns were completely useless. She belted up, adjusted the mirrors and her driving position, then punched the address into the sat-nav and they were on their way.

The musical education continued throughout the drive, punctuated by cultural commentary from Bradley. They'd got through *Kind of Blue, Birth of the Cool, A Love Supreme* and were midway through *Catch a Fire*. Bradley hadn't mentioned the previous night's mission once. An icebreaker was required.

'Do you always hire cars, Mr B?' asked Shev, pulling the question out of the air.

'Well, buying them's the best way of burning money, isn't it? Unless you want to open a restaurant.' Bradley glanced across at her. 'Now I'm domiciled abroad, I don't need to bother. I've a little runabout over there.'

'Over there?'

'Jamaica. The North shore.'

Shev was impressed; it explained Bradley's baked-in tan. She ran through the mental images that could depict his lifestyle. Guns and ganja or white sand and rum? 'This was well-timed, then,' she added, referring to the Wailers' warmth and rhythm lilting through the dashboard speakers.

'Commercial Road keeps my feet on the ground when I come back to work, which is rare and hopefully, quite soon, never,' said Bradley. 'I'm a widower.'

'I'm sorry, sir,' Shev replied, cringing internally, lost somewhere between good manners and over-familiarity.

'No kids. It never happened for us. Just a smattering of nieces and nephews.' He tapped the dash. 'I immerse myself in this lot now. If things work out, you could visit some time … if we survive.'

There was nothing creepy in his suggestion, and she figured it was just kind lip service. Me and Granny B rocking up in Kingston, Shev thought. Sod Adam Clayton, this bloke was right up her strasse.

The sat-nav indicated that they'd reached their destination. The car coasted alongside a blue painted hoarding with 'considerate construction' notices. Behind the hoarding were three tower blocks that stretched into the sky amongst a nest of cranes positioned like giant sentry guns. Shev sought out a parking spot and pulled in.

'What's it going to be today, then?' asked Bradley, regarding Shev's cover.

'Health and Safety Exec, what else?' Shev smiled.

'I'll inform UT4 now, and she'll smooth over your credentials.'

Shev got out, took her rucksack from the boot, donned her ID and personal protection equipment and walked over to the site entrance. She was now in her element, secure in the knowledge that the HSE had immediate access to all areas on construction sites, striking fear into site managers everywhere due to the potential for instant shutdown, if anything untoward were to be found.

There was a fifteen-minute wait at Security as the site management had a meltdown at the impromptu HSE visit before Shev was granted access and inducted. She examined the progress charts and drawings in the site office to establish the whereabouts on the site of her target, the second subject, the plasterer Bob Distance.

Shev held no fond nostalgia for the harsh new-build environment as she made her way via the cordoned-off green route up to the plasterers' work area. She asked about her target's whereabouts, and two men gave directions with a snigger. 'He's in plot two, luv, but he charges for autographs and extras.' Shev noted the reference to Distance's *Question Time* appearance.

As she approached, Shev could smell the unholy mingling of fresh and stale sweat from hard labour, and the emissions from an unhealthy diet. The unit had a bare concrete floor and grey plasterboard walls and ceiling. In addition to the smells emitted by the workmen, the air smelt dank and moist from the shuttered concrete that wrapped the building.

Bob Distance was standing with his back to her on a low scaffold, working furiously with his trowel, spreading deep terracotta plaster onto the ceiling above his head. She studied him for a few minutes as he worked the area.

'HSE,' Shev said, by means of introduction. 'How's it going, Bob?'

Distance didn't miss a beat. 'Okay, luv. I'm all right.' To Shev's surprise, there was no attitude or aggression behind his words.

'Are you blue-carded and NVQ'd, mate?' This was usually a sore point that triggered a rant among construction workers, especially when quizzed by a woman.

'Aye, luv, I am. It was a grand well spent.' The response was almost automatic as he splashed water on the plaster and worked it to a finish.

'You obviously love your work, Bob.'

Distance stopped at last and dropped the trowel and hawk with a clatter onto the scaffold boards. His arms hung by his sides as if he'd suddenly received some shocking news. His shaven head slowly turned until Shev saw his profile; his eyes were closed and sweat dripped like a slow tap from his chin. When he opened them, he revealed the same glassy, dilated orbs as Kohler. 'No, luv, but now I can live with hating it.' His blissed-out grin hardened to a scowl.

Distance leapt off the scaffold and landed with a thump in front of her. Shev stumbled backwards, then regained her footing. The plasterer straightened up and remained motionless. She was terrified but focused. If he came at her, it would be groin, then throat with all she'd got. There was a clear link with Kohler, but he'd shown no physical hostility compared with Distance's movements. She decided to gamble.

'The … the naked I?' she stammered.

Distance grabbed the Velcro on the front of his high-visibility vest and tore it open. He revealed the broken cross logo of *The Eighth Day* tattooed across his chest and the words *Night Night Twinkle* around his flabby navel. The plasterer broke into a decayed grin and said, 'Isla … and I've gone one better than the tee-shirt!'

Shev fastened her seat belt and started the car. 'Did you get all that, Mr B?'

'Every second,' said Bradley, tapping his phone screen. 'UT4 will be doing a deep analysis on the footage.'

Shev reset the sat-nav and pulled away.

'What did you think, or should I say feel so far?' Bradley asked.

'Last night, Kohler seemed potty … and proper sordid. You name it, he's into it. Totally off-road.'

'Way down the rabbit hole, eh?'

'Down the rabbit hole? He is the rabbit hole.' She shuddered. 'As for Bob Distance, a bit of hedonism at weekends, full throttle for forty-eight hours, all straight for Monday, that kind of thing. Nothing too dodgy. That's what I felt, but I could be wrong. But now you're asking, they both scared the shit out of me.'

'Me, too, for what it's worth and I even wasn't there,' Bradley added with sincerity.

'They're both blissed-out on the *Eighth Day, naked-I* thing, and they both mentioned Isla, whoever she is. Neither of them was discreet about the subject at all, sir. It was almost as if they were expecting me. And their eyes …'

'Go on,' urged Bradley.

'Yeah, they were glassy, like a kid's dolly. You know the ones where you pick it up and they click open? Like that.'

Bang! There was an impact on the front of the car. Shev checked the mirror and screeched to an emergency stop. She was out of the vehicle in an instant and saw a shopping trolley on its side on the grass verge. There were no groceries but the paraphernalia of a street person lay sprawled along the road; blankets, duvets and a filthy quilt. She spotted a figure in a stained sheepskin coat on the verge, struggling to rise.

'My God!' Shev shouted to Bradley. 'I've hit a bag lady!' She ran towards her at full sprint and reached to lift her arms.

'GLIMMER, no!' Bradley yelled, waving his arms and running towards them. 'Get back! Get away!' He pulled Shev clear as the old lady reached for her hands, leaving her to paw at thin air. As Bradley dragged Shev back towards the car the victim straightened, unaided, and the two BARBELL operatives could see she was smiling; the picture of serenity considering the near miss.

The duo watched in horror as the bag lady's eyelids slowly rose.

Shev hunched at the wheel in silence as they sped down the motorway, with just darkness, orange strip lights and the white lines ahead.

'What'll it be, then? Replay or new stuff?' Bradley was referring to the music, his area of responsibility.

'Oh … I'll go for new. Just like everything else, why change the flavour?' said Shev with a hint of annoyance and sarcasm.

'*Revolver*. This one's by George. You need to remember, as I'll be testing you.' Taxman counted in, the staccato beat began, and they began to nod their heads in unison.

'Mr B?'

'Yes, GLIMMER?'

'How did you know?'

'About Nan back there? Where do I begin?'

'At the beginning, I suppose. What was it?'

Bradley took some time to consider his words, allowing McCartney to complete his raga guitar solo. 'When I started with BARBELL, way before you were born, it was a kind of inheritance project. The task was to research an origin story, and it carried on from there. Over the years, I've seen many things that were beyond rational explanation. Right now, I don't know what it was back there, but what I *do* know is that … when the sky goes black, rain is very likely. You can smell it on the wind before it falls. And judging from all I've seen over the years, with the last twenty-four hours thrown in, you—or should I say, *we*—were about to get wet. Very wet, indeed.'

2300 hrs August 8th 202?

Hotel Negresco

Nice

France

Biff was on a three-stage circuit. He bounced, rolled and wallowed on the king-size bed like a giant grey porpoise. Next, he bowled into the bathroom and marvelled at the jacuzzi before proceeding to head out onto the balcony, where he sat at the table for a moment and gazed up and down the promenade at the traffic and palm trees below. Once satisfied, he returned to the bed.

All his Christmases and birthdays had come at once. He'd been meek and mild at the airport, sticking close to Shev through Security; but in the VIP lounge he got merry on bottled lager, followed by the flight champagne on the plane which had ended up in a bollocking from Shev. Now, at half-past-midnight, he was burning off the last of his nervous energy and sugar rush from the hotel's complimentary Belgian truffles.

Shev was exhausted. She laid on the bed in the white towelling dressing gown, her ribs aching from Biff's comedy performance. Everything was plush and shiny; it felt, smelt and tasted expensive. A text came in from Bradley, requesting an RV time in the upstairs restaurant before Biff rose in the morning.

When Biff hit the balcony again, she texted *0700* hrs as her 'boyf' wasn't an early riser. She got up and checked the bathroom; the expensive bubbles were high and fine. She slipped out of the dressing gown, lowered herself into the bath and called out to Biff, 'Robin, jacuzzi time. Come and get it!'

The alarm buzzed on silent at 0645 hrs as planned, and Biff remained rooted in the land of nod. Shev freshened up, pulled on her navy Adidas tracksuit and taekwondo trainers and made her way up to the restaurant on the next floor. She spotted Bradley in the corner, sipping coffee and reading *Le Monde* as the uniformed staff buzzed around the central buffet.

Shev made her way over to Bradley and sat down opposite him.

'Morning, Mr B. Did you have a good night?' she chirped.

Bradley looked up, fixed her with his gaze for a moment and then returned to his paper.

'Mr B?' There was no response as he took another sip of his coffee. Shev resisted the temptation to take the cup from his grasp and demand attention, followed by another impulse to grab the paper and screw it up. She stood up, sliding the chair back as she did so, and waited for a response.

Nothing.

Enraged, she stormed out of the restaurant and ran back up to the room. What the fuck is this? she kept asking herself. Biff hadn't even changed position. Shev carefully lay back down beside him on the bed, seething, and looked straight ahead at the widescreen TV. She studied the room, thinking it was nice while it lasted. The answer hit her like a punch in the eye. Her jacket was flung over the dresser chair. 'The badge cam. Fuck!'

She rolled off the bed and rifled through the case. 'Thursday, Thursday, Thursday. There, *Batman=pop-art-gun!'* She sped out the door and ran back up the stairs, as fast as she could go, clearing three treads at a time and pinning on the badge cam as she went, and tore into the restaurant. Bradley was gone.

Her heart sank, and she cursed through gritted teeth, imagining a shower of giant Jenga blocks raining down on her head and clattering on the floor. She turned to leave and found Bradley stood before her, this time offering a broad, gentle smile. He indicated the way back to the table with an open palm and requested more coffee.

Shev's eyes said it all.

'We've lost eight minutes, GLIMMER,' said Bradley, 'but you've learned something, eh?'

She nodded and the old spy continued. 'This is the kind of environment to learn such things. I wouldn't bet on it happening again, though. This is why we have procedures. Both our lives could depend on them.'

The coffee arrived and Bradley began his briefing. 'To business. The next subject's residence is three kilometres away, and the Siliconica Tech Expo is the same distance west, forming a triangle with this hotel. There's a scooter and helmets outside for you and your partner. UT4 will message its whereabouts and be your comms director. I'll be watching your feed. If you need me, call. If not, I'll see you here at the same time tomorrow.'

'Haven't you forgotten something, sir?' asked Shev, looking at the floor. 'I can't give Biff a backie while I case out d'Orly, can I? He'll love the Expo, and we can do a feature, but …'

'Of course,' said Bradley, and he drummed the table with his fingers, appearing to be giving it a degree of serious thought. He already had a plan, but as usual, he'd put the ball in Shev's court.

'I know,' sparked Shev. 'The spa. I'll book the spa for him in morning, while I'm out doing the interview. Massage, steam, sauna—it looked great in the brochure. He'll love it. What do you think?'

Bradley opened his mouth to answer, when—

'Who's this?' A groggy Biff stood before them, rubbing his eyes and thumbing in Bradley's direction. Shev said nothing and felt like she'd suddenly shrunk an inch.

'Who is this, babe?' Biff repeated with more agitation, then asked Bradley directly, 'Who are you, mate?'

Bradley rose and extended his hand. 'You must be Boff. My name's Brad. I'm from the magazine.'

'It's Biff. What magazine?' He addressed Shev again. 'Who the fuck is he, babe?'

'The magazine,' Bradley continued, withdrawing his hand. 'You know, your sponsors for all this, for your *Shevalogue*? Great work, by the way.'

Biff was unconvinced, and Shev recognised all the signs of his stress. His eyes had narrowed and darted from side to side, his shoulders rolled, and his left knee began an involuntary tremor.

'What's it called, then? The magazine. What's it called?'

Shev shrank another inch. 'It's called *Modger*,' said Bradley. 'It's for modernists, hipsters young and old. Food, travel, fashion, music—the finer things in life. Shev wasn't allowed to tell even you until you got here.'

Shev broke out in a shit-eating grin and nodded furiously. Biff took out his phone and searched: 'Mod … ger, mod … ger. *Modger*. It's here!' he blurted.

'Can you see the link to the *Shevalogue*? Pride of place on our home page,' said Bradley.

'Hang on … yes. Yes, it looks great, babe!' Biff was elated and the stress signs dissolved to be replaced by the wiggle, a familiar body language telegraph to Shev that signalled all was well. Shev gave Bradley a look beyond words as her pained grin remained fixed. His eyes told her, Trust me; you've had forty-eight hours in this game. I've had forty years.

'Shev, do you want to tell Boff …'

'It's Biff,' Shev interjected.

'Sorry, do you want to tell Biff about the other

crucial clause in the contract?'

Shev took a deep breath and collected herself. 'Well, I think I'll let you explain … *Brad.'*

'Oh, OK. This is absolutely crucial if we're to continue sponsoring all this.' He waved his hand, indicating the opulent surroundings. 'Biff, as you're the tech man, we need to keep Shev anonymous. No images, video or audio. Just a silhouette at best.'

Biff stroked his chin, and his brow crumpled in thought as he nodded his agreement. 'Like that other blog,' Bradley continued, '*Secret Moona.* We need to keep the mystique. What do you think? Of course, we can pull the sponsorship if you'd rather…'

'No, Brad, we're down with that,' Biff jumped in. 'Totally down with that, aren't we, babe?' He looked to Shev for approval and got a thumbs up. 'Abso-bloody-lutely!'

Bradley checked his watch. 'This calls for a celebration. Sod the fact it's ten to seven in the morning! Mademoiselle, champagne, *trois verres, s'il vous plait!*'

Chapter 13

DARK RESURRECTION

0730 hrs, August 9th, 202?

Nice, France.

Bradley asked Biff to do the honours and open the champagne, which was to be another first for him. Shev recognised Bradley's tactic of inclusion, keeping Biff at the centre of things while he was present.

There was no consideration that in the hands of a French Polisher from N1, the magnum of Dom Ruinart 2007 had the potential to impair someone's vision permanently. Off it went with a pop, the cork ricocheting off the ceiling and, surprisingly, leaving everyone's eyesight unharmed.

'No spraying, Biff; you're not Lewis Hamilton,' laughed Shev as he filled her glass.

'To the *Shevalogue*,' toasted Bradley, and he and Biff drained their glasses. Shev passed hers back to Biff, who added, '*Modger and* the *Shevalogue,*' before knocking it straight back.

Here we go, thought Shev. 'That'll be my last,' she said with mild sarcasm. 'I've got work to do.'

'Where we goin', babe?'

'Not we; I. I've got an interview lined up. You're booked in at the spa, if you can walk straight when you've finished in here. Then, when I get back, we're off to the Expo.'

Biff gave Shev a quizzical look.

'Really, Biff? Don't fancy a massage, nice smelly stuff and all that? You'll be fine, and it'll sort your back out. My turn tomorrow. Pace yourselves and see you later.' She grabbed a croissant and was out the door before Biff could protest.

'Another? Shame to waste it,' said Bradley, lifting the bottle.

'Okey-dokey, Brad. Then I'm gonna get stuck into that buffet.'

'That'll soak it up, eh?' said Bradley with a wink, which he got in return.

Back in the room, Shev checked the contents of her Samsonite rucksack, which consisted of a *Time Out* guide, a map of Nice and the essential tech kit needed for the operation.

She assembled disparate kelp components taken from her make up bag, resulting in a palm sized insect with small propellers at each end-the locust drone, then placed it her jacket pocket. She fixed a tiny communications bud in her left ear, paired it via

Bluetooth with her phone and grabbed the complimentary water bottle off the dresser.

Meow! UT4's text landed. According to the message, the scooter was around the corner on Rue de Rivoli. The message also gave the location for her next stop; Chemin du Mascon, St Antoine, the residence of the French Minister for Foreign and European Digital Affairs, Ms Oriel d'Orly, who, unbeknown to Shev, was awaiting an exceptional guest.

Leaving the hotel foyer, Shev stood on the step for a moment and took in the warm salt air. She squinted, dazzled by the French Riviera's greatest attraction, its blinding crystal light. The brightest azure sky she'd ever experienced reflected in the shimmering sea, which, according to *Time Out,* had delighted Matisse and impressionists a hundred years before. On went her new *Jackie Ohh* sunglasses, part of her duty-free essentials, and she turned left on the corner into the shaded street where the scooter awaited.

The keys were under the rear mudguard, and she freed one of the helmets, which was colour coordinated with the mauve and cream Vespa. As she secured the chin strap, she considered how vital taste and style seemed to her new boss.

Shev mounted the machine and clipped her phone onto the handlebars, removed and switched on the locust drone. The gadget picked up the phone's signal, whirred to life and left her palm quickly climbing above her out of sight, where it would remain with her below in its gaze. The sat-nav gave a fifteen-minute journey time, enough to consider her strategy on arrival. At the push of a button, the Vespa purred to life. Shev revved up, swung a U-turn, then turned right onto the Promenade des Anglais, passing the hotel and marvelling at the classic structure crowned with a terracotta dome that would be her home for the next few days.

She wonder what state Biff was in now. How many moves ahead had Mr B planned? Did he have the champagne waiting on ice from the off? She stopped the supposition, realising one answered question would lead to two more in a swirl of terminal paranoia. In truth, she'd received a masterclass in planning and manipulation. She still felt no guilt at hoodwinking Biff; he was having the time of his life and wasn't in any danger … yet.

Shev maintained a steady speed, heading south down the Promenade des Anglais. The beach was to her left, the palm trees towering overhead like elongated pineapples on the opposite side. The road was quiet, with only a smattering of joggers up and down a route punctuated by international flag poles and beach huts.

She couldn't help but smile as she passed the Union Jack dancing in the warm breeze. From the Cally to the Hive to this *and* she was getting paid. But she was under no illusion about her role as a field operative; she wasn't even a tiny cog in the wheel, maybe just a ball bearing or a squirt of oil, but she intended to prove her worth on this mission if it was the last thing ...

The sat-nav indicated a right turn. She weaved up a narrow road on a gradual climb, blocks of purpose-built flats giving way to thick vegetation and purple-flowered hedgerows of Campanula. Finally, she arrived at several large, gated, stand-alone houses, indicating that she was close to the target. She pulled over, rocked the Vespa back onto its stand and dismounted, leaving the engine running.

She took off her rucksack, checking both ways, and fished something from the side pocket. A tractor approached from the opposite direction; instinct told her to keep her head down and rummage in the bag until it had ambled past. On the all-clear, she walked over to the verge and fixed a button-sized object to the tree bark, where it became all but invisible; the first miniature observation cam was in place. She resumed her journey, and thirty seconds later, the sat-nav's voice came through her earpiece, '*Vous avez atteint votre destination.*' She slowed and carried on.

To her right, in her peripheral vision, she saw a driveway sat back from the road, guarded by two uniformed men. She maintained her speed until they were out of view of her wing mirror, then she turned, pulled in and repeated the process with the second camera. Her orders were to establish direct contact with the subject, d'Orly, just as she'd achieved with Kohler and Distance, but politely asking the security if she could see the minister for five minutes wouldn't wash. Bradley was relying on her initiative.

'GLIMMER—UT4. Are you receiving? Over.'

The voice gave her a start; she hadn't heard UT4's East London tones since leaving the Hive three days before, Shev blocked the view of the button badge-cam twice with her open palm to signal, *Affirmative.*

'GLIMMER—UT4. The cams are up. I have one-hundred-and-eighty-degree coverage. Over.'

Again, Shev acknowledged receiving the transmission. As Amira had explained in their training session, the Ultra would now become another pair of eyes; she also had the overhead locust drone's view to cover movement to and from the target house.

Shev eased forwards on the scooter to the point closest to the gate, then pulled in once more, staying out of sight. In her mirror, she saw a vehicle approach from behind, then slow until it was parallel with her before it stopped and ticked over.

It was a black Suzuki jeep; the driver, who was alone, studied Shev intently from behind black aviator shades. Her mouth dry as ash, she broke into a sweat, her heart hammering against her chest as she looked straight ahead. She asked herself if evasive riding was next on the menu, but if it came down to her scooter versus the Jeep on the country lanes of the Côte d'Azur, she didn't fancy her chances. She reverted to her training and decided to position herself solidly in the centre of the road when she pulled away, like a ringmaster raising a chair before a tiger, bullying a greater force with presence and confidence.

The nearside window descended and the driver removed his shades and smiled, drawing Shev to meet his gaze with her own. He was dark and handsome, with shoulder-length greying hair. Despite his looks, Shev sensed a wave of hostility seeping from him, forming invisible tentacles that stretched through the open window with evil intent. 'Are you OK?' he asked in English.

He's taken a wild guess, she thought. She nodded.

The driver squinted his eyes. 'Sure?'

He wanted to hear her. The tentacle's invisible suckers latched around her shoulders, chilling her to the bone. The temperature dropped, and an inexplicable cold shade killed the crystal sunlight. Shev nodded once more, cool, calm and clear, then revved up the scooter and took off, free of the chilling shade and the grasp of the invisible squid. She shuddered in instant recall as she passed the gates of d'Orly's residence and purred back down the sloping lane towards the coast.

Checking her wing mirrors, she was relieved by the absence of the jeep. She took further comfort from the voice in her ear: '*GLIMMER—UT4. Thirty metres ahead, take the next left and wait. Over.*'

Back at the Hive, deep below the streets of Limehouse, Amira sat before the six screens in a state of near shock.

She took control of the locust drone and saw the jeep set off, then stop at d'Orly's gates, to be waved through to the building. She wound back Shev's button cam feed fifteen seconds, zoomed in and ran the footage on a loop before pulling down footage from the second bud-cam. He was naturally older, greyer, and had no beard, but surely it couldn't be, could it? The March 2016 drone strike had been inconclusive regarding the identification of remains, although the ensuing silence had indicated success. But the glacier rising from the bottom of her heart told her she was not mistaken.

Amira had indeed just got an eyeful of her supposedly deceased cousin, Nadeem.

'Are you getting all this, sir?' UT4 asked Bradley from the corner she occupied on his Surface screen.

Bradley sat on the balcony of his room, overlooking the crescent coastline. For the first time since working with her, he sensed a slight panic in UT4's voice as he viewed the real-time footage from Shev's button-cam, showing she was stationary as instructed by the Ultra. 'Indeed I am, UT4,' he replied with emphasised calm.

'It's a red development, an X1. I've done facial recognition on the driver. We have confirmed with ninety-eight percent certainty the ID of NaS: Nadeem Al Shabah …' Amira fought to retain objectivity, and, despite the personal gravitas of the revelation, it was a fight she was winning. She'd given Bradley direct, unemotional facts that negated ridiculous questions like, 'Are you sure?'

'What about vehicle?' asked Bradley.

'Rented to one Mr Maximus Lane. Owner via various proxies and shell companies of a substantial real estate portfolio in the Docklands. The need for cable and server space has placed the UK tech industry at his beck and call. Most notably the LINX, the London Internet Exchange,' Amira confirmed.

'Interesting. Can you confirm a visual on Lane's current location?' Bradley requested, putting the evidence together and eliminating the vague possibility of ID fraud.

'Lane's personal Gulfstream 650 flew from London International to Nice three days ago but his yacht the *Astrid* is currently berthed in Nice harbour,' said Amira. 'CCTV and financial records and SIGINT confirm Lane is residing in the penthouse suite of the Negresco, E445. He is your neighbour, sir.'

'Isn't that convenient?' A little too convenient. He was in their lap. Or they were in his. Bradley focused on the livestream from Shev's badge-cam, which was undulating due to her steady breathing. He settled on a plan of action and related it in detail to the Ultra.

'GLIMMER-. Return to base and standby for a P11. Details will follow.'

Shev acknowledged and pulled away. During the fifteen-minute journey, she tried to process the intervention of the mysterious driver and mentally prepare herself for her first Protocol 11; the three-step drill to undertake the unlawful entry of a property.

The procedure consisted of compromising the security of a target's dwelling in order to enter, to obtain any incriminating evidence and, finally, to leave undetected. It was basically a non-destructive breaking and entering in a luxury hotel overseas. What a wet dream this would be for that king dealer, the little-big-man-would-be Mafiosi from the Cally estate.

Shev left the Vespa where she'd found it, retrieved the locust drone and went to meet Biff, who was sizzling on a sunbed by the Negreso's roof-top pool. He looked unconscious beneath his blue Beats earphones and sunglasses. Shev pulled the umbrella over to give him some shade, but her hospitality went unappreciated as Biff let out a low grunting snore. She kicked his ankle, and he spluttered awake.

'Now then, Rock Lobster.'

'Hello, babe. I must have nodded off.'

'You'll nod off to sickbay if you're not careful, Biff. You're always forgettin' your whiteness. Sorry, bright redness.' She pulled up a sunbed. 'So, how was the spa, mate?'

'I'm a new man, babe. Especially now I've had chance to chill in the sun. I bet we'll match completely by the time we go back.'

'Mad dogs and Englishmen, Biff. Any sign of the old boy?'

'Nah. He had a bite at breakfast and pissed off. You've played a blinder with this though, babe, I gotta hand it to you.' They bumped and slid hands.

'So, what shall we do for the rest of today? Chill or head to the Expo?' asked Shev.

Biff thought for a moment. 'Let's chill for a bit, eh? No rushing round; it's too hot. We can get some footage of all this if we want and play it by ear.'

'Fair enough.' Shev bent down and gave him a peck on the cheek, getting a greasy nose for her trouble. 'I'll go and get changed. Back in a minute.'

She arrived back in the white complimentary dressing gown, which she peeled off to reveal a bikinied heptathlete's body, all six pack and curves. She buttered up with sunscreen with the help of Biff and settled down with the Walkman.

As Bradley had predicted, all eyes were on them, all envy from the female guests and furtive lust from behind the shades of the males, one of whom she identified from the file received from UT4 as Max Lane, a rotund, tan-tastic individual with a blond mid-eighties mullet.

While she was soaking up the sun, Shev received UT4's message ordering the Protocol 11 to be enacted on Suite E445 immediately.

'Biff, I'm nipping back up to room,' she said as she pulled the gown back on. Biff pulled a face and wafted his nose as she headed indoors.

Once inside, she donned her trackies and refitted

the earpiece, to be greeted by Amira's dulcet tones once again. *'GLIMMER-. CCTV on the apartment is clear, and I have eyes on Lane. Go ahead. Over.'*

Amira put the plan she'd briefed Shev with into effect, requesting a magnum of Pol Roger Brut vintage 2009 to be left in Suite E445 on ice, as Lane's profile indicated he would not refuse entertainment. Shev hung back out of sight until the maid arrived to deliver, then shadowed her with expert timing and distance as she approached with the trolley and entered E445. She placed a chip in the swipe gap before the door clicked shut and was back out of sight when the maid emerged.

The first phase had been practised countless times in training at the Hive. Now she'd succeeded for the first time in the field without issue, but this was only the beginning.

'GLIMMER—UT4. You are now clear to enter. Go.'

Shev sprinted back up the stairs and to the door. This was it; her first run in the field with UT4's added-extra phone apps. She selected the key app, held the phone to the lock, swiped top to bottom and the door clicked green. She pushed the door open, selected the scan and extended the phone across the threshold. A ring pulse displayed on the screen, then presented clear. Shev entered with caution, keeping her arm extended until she'd entered the open-plan lounge and got a second confirmation of a low probability of erroneous digital signals that might indicate internal bugs and surveillance. She remembered what UT4 had told her at the Hive AE briefing: 'If they're using Stone Age analogue shit, we're fucked; the apps won't cut it. So be quiet, quick and keep your head down.'

As she pulled on the essential latex protective gloves and light rimmed full-face surgical mask, Shev noted that the decadence within—all black marble, gold, chrome and glass—was on a different scale to the room she and Biff were staying in. She hit the drawers first. Nothing. The clothes were on hangers; with care, she checked the pockets: all clear.

The cases were directly below. Genuine Louis Vuitton. Very nice, locked with twin four-ring combinations. Her thoughts delved back to the training session with Staff at the Hive when he'd emphasised most people go one digit either way of their numerical passcode.

She hoped that Max Lane belonged to the category of most people. Using her phone, she took pictures of the first case's current settings and got to work. This was pressure, and a bead of sweat dropped from her forehead onto the mask below, which soon began to fog. It took twenty-five permutations, but eventually the first case popped open.

She opted to search and photograph one case at a time before moving on and found nothing untoward in the first two. The third case contained a wash bag with something out of the ordinary: five small cellophane packets containing fine pink powder.

Via the CCTV hack, Amira observed Lane being

woken from his slumber by his Vertu phone. He struggled forwards on his sun lounger due to his opulent gut, then sat bolt upright. The caller had clearly piqued his interest. He stood up, pulled on his dressing gown and hurried indoors, out of camera view.

'GLIMMER—UT4. *Red alert: he's coming back. Estimated sixty seconds until entry. Withdraw. Over.*'

Shev acknowledged, checked her watch and moved the two other cases back to their position in the wardrobe. She took a table knife from the dresser.

'GLIMMER—UT4. *Forty seconds until entry. Withdraw. Over.*'

She stretched the index finger of the left latex glove and cut it free, took one of the packets of pink powder, shook it and then opened the top. Using the end of the knife, she scooped a small mound onto its tip, then, with exquisite care, transferred the sample into the latex and replaced the packet with its companions.

'GLIMMER—UT4. *Fifteen seconds until entry. I have a visual at the end of the hall. Withdraw. Over.*'

Shev tied off the latex finger and pocketed it. She returned the packet to the case compartment, zipped and closed the case, and checked her phone to ensure she reset the previous combinations as she'd found them.

'*Ten seconds until entry.*'

Shev slid the case in the wardrobe and closed the door.

'Five seconds.'

Shev placed the knife back on the dresser in its exact position. She looked at the champagne bucket, then the balcony glass door left ajar and the breeze billowing the curtains.

As she heard the door click open, she remembered the games she'd played as a little girl, when she'd squeezed her eyes shut and imagined herself to be invisible. Granny B had always said it worked because she'd wished so hard.

As she lay flat and closed her eyes, Shev imagined the floor growing reed grass up around her arms, legs and head, knee-high so that she was unseen by the approaching predator. One of the old tunes on Bradley's mixtape came back to her, and she focused on its lilt and mystical rhythm to block the fear from her mind, the deep voice singing something about '*the end, beautiful friend*.'

Lane stared at the champagne bucket for a moment and went straight to the bathroom, sharply pulling back the shower curtain. He then wobbled out onto the balcony, looking down over the edge to those far below. Unable to find a cat-like intruder, he returned inside. His gammony features were streaked with sweat as he dashed to the wardrobe and withdrew the third case. He clicked the combination, opened it and scrambled his way to find his prized packets as they should be, with no discernible difference. Lane sighed with relief, wiping the sweat from his face with his towelling sleeve, and replaced all as it was.

The champagne magnum, speckled with condensation in the ice bucket, beckoned him over, and he succumbed and snatched it free. A smile spread across his face as he pressed the cold glass to his shiny pink cheek. The door buzzed. 'Company!' he said, rubbing his hands, as he went to receive the visitor with the magnum under his arm.

'We are so sorry, Mr Lane; there has been a mistake.' The Room Service girl's eyes were full of apology, verging on tears, as she stood before him. He was expecting to welcome a prostitute of the highest order, courtesy of his benefactor, hence his presence in the hotel as opposed to his yacht. Lane really couldn't afford another divorce along with his crippling gambling debts and expensive bad habits.

'The champagne is for another guest, Mr Lane. We took the wrong room number. We are so, so sorry.'

'What? Er, OK,' bumbled Lane. 'It's fine. I'll hang on to it, just bill the room.' His tone was weighted with disappointment.

'Please accept it with our compliments, Mr Lane.'

Lane gave a lame sympathetic smile, and the door clicked shut.

Shev had used the AE to record and stream the audio directly to UT4 from her hiding place beyond the field of Lane's perception. Lane muttered a racist curse under his breath, popped the cork, poured and sank two glasses in succession and then flopped down on the bed. His Vertu phone rang with a choral burst of *Hallelujah*.

'Yeah, N. Not bad, mate,' chuckled Lane when he answered. 'I've just been given a £200 bottle of shampoo on the house due to some fuck-up, hah. I thought it was you spoiling me with another luscious takeout.'

Streaming directly to UT4, Shev adjusted the app to enhance and pick up the accented voice at the other end of the conversation.

'Needs are needs,' the voice said. 'd'Orly was very appreciative indeed; putty in our hands. After the Expo tomorrow, your jet must be ready for my next destination: a three-hour flight, due north. Make it so.' Silence.

Shev heard Lane mocking the caller's accent to himself as he rolled from the bed to his feet and refilled his glass. 'Make it so, make it so … oh, yes, yes, *very, very good* … you ounce cunt.' He went out onto the balcony, taking the champagne bucket with him.

'GLIMMER—UT4. Stand by to exit.'

Shev considered the unparalleled level of trust she had placed in her distant colleague, much more than she could ever have imagined when she'd first faced her hard eyes two days ago.

'GLIMMER—UT4. Go!'

As Shev rose from the floor, she could make out the silhouette of Lane through the floating drapes, and he appeared to be slumped at the table. She was up and out.

Shev tore down the stairs, feeling weightless

from the endorphin boost of terror, imminent capture and escape. She called Bradley. 'Mr B, I have something.' She refrained from the urge to tell him she needed to see him right away but was relieved when that was what he requested.

In his room, Bradley examined the tied-off latex teat within the quarantine bag, along with her gloves and mask. Shev recounted the actions and events in a thirty-second debrief, not all of which was clear from the badge-cam feed. The old spy seemed impressed with her initiative but added a note of caution.

'A close call, GLIMMER. Think about "what if" and "then what"; that way, you'll ride the flux when it all goes wrong, because it sure as hell will, one beautiful day … as I'm sure UT4 will explain.'

His last words were ominous; Shev was in the Ultra's bad books. Satisfied she'd taken the feedback on board, he beamed. 'But very well done. I'll see you in the morning ... if not before.'

Back by the pool, Shev threw her gown back onto the sun lounger.

'Some dump that was, babe,' commented Biff the sun-potato as Shev plunged into the cool blue water.

She revelled for a few seconds in the pure, cold silence of immersion, then she kicked and stroked four times and went over an image she'd registered as she'd dived: a man caught in profile across the pool, who seemed strangely familiar.

She surfaced and wiped her eyes, but he was

gone; she turned to catch a millisecond of him from the rear as he entered the hotel. She banked the image in the back of her mind for future reference, flipped, dived and kicked back down to touch the bottom of the pool, kicked again and zoned out for a moment of peace and calm as she'd done in the imaginary Kenyan savannah in Lane's room, to that old song, so limitless and free.

'UT4, go onto H channel, please,' said Bradley as he stood back from his Surface on the dresser. A face-to-face was essential, in the circumstances. He needed to read her expressions due to the personal element of the revelation.

'Thank you,' said Bradley, as the Ultra's head and shoulders were projected out before him. 'The vocal on the caller?'

'It's a positive match against what we have for NaS, sir.'

'You've seen we've recovered a material sample from the P11,' said Bradley. 'Analysis and identification are an immediate priority, and there's also the time factor.' He held up the sealed bag. It was time to broach the personal element. 'I'm trying to imagine how you must feel, UT4 …'

'I'll be on the next available flight, sir,' UT4 interjected. 'I have no reservations.'

'What about the kit needed?'

'I have the basics. Some specific hardware components will need to be sourced and obtained in situ. We have a vessel moored at Marseille with an onboard lab; I can direct it to the harbour there.'

'Go ahead, UT4. Thank you. Oh, I'll also need triangulation of the movements of Lane, the *Astrid* and his private jet over the last three years and possible destinations that are a three-hour flight time north of here. Check all flight plans and manifests.'

'Yes, sir,' answered Amira. 'Will that be all, sir?'

He thought he caught her smile as he answered but was unable to detect its nature as her image flickered and vanished.

Dewhurst observed the exchange between the two from behind her desk at Vauxhall Cross.

'Day 6, BREAKSPEAR.' She spoke the two syllables of his code-name like a boxer administering a jab, finding range before landing a decisive blow. She steered clear of his former military rank. If it was intended to rattle him, it had no effect. The Regiment had been three years of his life, decades before, and it had ended in tears. He wasn't a TA reject or flak-jacketed loser logging into forums, unable to let go of something they never really had. He'd moved on, a long time ago.

In the Chief's office, Bradley's hologram shimmered as he turned to face her.

Bradley imagined lining up charger to charger, lance to lance across a medieval tournament field as he always did when engaging this particular C.

'We're still in Day 5, actually, ma'am. GLIMMER's surveillance of d'Orly gleaned an unanticipated return.' Bradley proceeded to tell Dewhurst what she already knew, in his own words, as was her wont. 'And, following analysis of the footage, we have a confirmed ID of X1 terrorist Nadeem al Shabah, previously presumed dead.'

The Chief drew back. 'A dark resurrection indeed,' she said, clasping her hands together and resting her chin on the mid-finger knuckles in a moment's contemplation. 'Any theories as to his status in all this yet?'

Dewhurst was following her mantra, adopted from Ariel Sharon of always escalate. It had never failed her and usually resulted in the other side blinking first. Usually.

'There's a triangulation between Al Shabah, d'Orly and the LINX vice-chairman, Maximus Lane.' Bradley employed the politician's trick of avoiding the main question and giving an answer that suited his own purpose. 'I won't bore you with conjecture, ma'am. The common link is the *Eighth Day* cult. UT4 is in-bound to analyse the material sample obtained by GLIMMER.' Bradley involuntarily swelled, revealing a hint of pride in the new operative, then quickly normalised, knowing his every nuance would be under Dewhurst's microscope. 'We are moving apace, ma'am.'

'I stand corrected, BREAKSPEAR, but we're now only four days away from *what, when, how*?' scolded Dewhurst. Her hologram flickered and was gone. She'd lowered her lance; there would be no charge or single combat today.

Bradley opened the live feed of the *Shevalogue*; it was coming from the pool upstairs. Biff was waxing lyrical on the virtues of the view, hotel and pool with Shev doing filming duties, silent and invisible behind the camera.

The old spy appreciated the momentary distraction from the gravitas of the situation by the joy of youth. He'd neglected to mention to Dewhurst that the London Internet Exchange had last convened eighty days ago, and the *Eighth Day* movement had manifested twenty-four hours later. Or that the next LINX meeting was to be chaired by Max Lane in three days, twenty-four hours after the Pan Europe Digital agreement was due to be signed off by d' Orly, tying in with the deadline involving the mysterious Isla.

This was all hidden under the convenient umbrella of conjecture, acing the next escalation from the Chief along with his suspicions that between Dewhurst, UT4 and Nadeem al Shabah, the SIS was possibly at the point of the longest sleeper sting in history.

He could discount nothing but felt he was approaching the summit of the threat's true nature. He'd identified three sides of the pyramid that contained the Invisible Storm, but it was the content of the fourth that filled him with the most diabolical dread.

Chapter 14

BEAL NA MBLATH

August 19th, 1921.

1, Melbury Road, London, W1.

It was C's force of habit, on the eve of operations, to pore over his plans in forensic detail, the components of which sat neatly arranged on the green leather of his desk. Central was the black letter, as forewarned by Lloyd-George and Churchill, which had arrived a fortnight before. C's hands shook as he removed it once again from the envelope and read the name, as he had done countless times since its arrival, in the vain hope that the type would revert to John Smith, a nobody. He fed the letter back into the envelope and pushed it back into position.

To its left sat a green folder labelled DIRK. He removed its contents and leafed through the notes of Spirewick's reports and telegrams. The assassin had followed his orders impeccably and had maintained his discipline as his large, deadly shadow had moved between Cadogan Gardens and Liverpool, where he had seen his subject off and had greeted him unawares on his return to continue the Treaty negotiations.

In the dusk of the last December, the Tall Man had been unaware of the motorcyclist already ensconced on the boat as he'd returned to Dublin with the signed Treaty. The shadow had stayed close, invisible, for the next eight months, which was some feat for a man of his size and aura.

C turned his attention to the SHEATH file on the right and fanned out the series of Simons' telegrams, culminating ten days previous with the location of the source, which was most timely following the arrival of the black letter.

He found use for the final message as a bookmark within an ancient tome, sitting above the black letter. C's face had reddened with embarrassment the first time he'd leafed through the arcane relic. He chuckled with disgust at its malign diagrams and horrible absurdities, asking himself if the Scottish Monarch had ever, in truth, had any supernatural encounters beyond his rabid superstition and grotesque imaginings. He had considered there was something of value under a passage which had alluded to the thin time, dawn or dusk, when, according to King James VI, elemental beings are at their weakest.

C aligned this information with excerpts from other works from the illustrious bookshelf behind his desk, this time from the East: Sun Tzu's *The Art of War* and Musashi's *Book of Five Rings*. Each volume was concerned with military strategy and the key aspects required for victory: weather conditions, time and place of battle and the assessment of one's forces and those of the enemy.

C's plan was complete. He composed and sent the following telegrams to Queenstown and Dublin:

DIRK- supper on 22nd Aug. FREDDY will carve 19:45. Your brother lights candles a 19:45 + 30. You pour wine thereafter and say grace. Call. CATHAL.

SHEATH-cousins arrive QT 06:30, 22nd Aug. with coal and candles for supper. you light the candles at 19:45 +30. Call. CATHAL.

The first call came and was connected via Ann. 'CATHAL speaking,' said C in a measured tone.

'CATHAL. This is DIRK,' said the high, lisping voice of Jonah Spirewick. 'The invitation is accepted. I look forward to supper, and I have fine fare for the evening.'

'Excellent, DIRK. In three days, we'll dine together. Your brother will light the candle first. No matter what you see, you must not pour the wine until FREDDY has carved. No matter *what* you see. Do you understand? You must let Freddy carve at 19:45. When he does so, you can pour the wine, but not until.'

'I fully understand, CATHAL. My guest will be at the table.'

'Remember, DIRK, Lady Liberty awaits …' said C, and the line clicked dead.

Simons' call followed. C noted a slight tremble in his voice and how tired he sounded, the strain of such an unusual mission clearly taking its toll, even on one as experienced as he. Simons made clear his understanding that he would meet a steamer at Queenstown with twelve men equipped with munitions for the task.

C emphasised the timing of detonation was everything, and it had to be thirty seconds beyond 19:45. He assured Simons that the men would follow his commands and directions without question. He was then to return with them on the crossing from Queenstown back to Bristol.

Since the night of the tenth moon, Simons' perception of colour and taste had dulled, his senses blunted like an overused razor. He felt strangely weaker by day, as if his strength was somehow linked to the waning moon. From Myra, he received all that was promised in her song and much more beyond imagining. His professionalism remained in spite of his malady, and through his patience, the completion of the mission seemed close to hand.

Following Sunday's Mass, he made an arrangement with the garage owner for the hire of the car once more, all covered with an eye-watering enhanced payment and an agreed bonus upon the return of the vehicle. The businessman was more than happy to oblige with a fee strong enough to seal his lips.

From London, C had confirmed arrangements with the man who controlled Queenstown Harbour, Vice Admiral Charles Coke, for the safe passage and docking before dawn of the Q ship, the *Gold Star*. Twelve men would disembark with their kit, dressed in Free State army uniforms, while hidden on the Q ship were twelve blue tunics of the Royal Marines Artillery. They would rendezvous with and be under the command of an old dinner guest of his, the Captain of the *Sayonara* who, under C's command, would require a tender to be left fuelled and ready for the transport of the Gold Star's party.

At the dockside, Simons sat safe and dry in the cab of the Model T as rain swept in from the River Lea. It was the blackest hour before sunrise, the moments when hope can be lost and exchanged for depthless despair. He heard three funnel horns, the agreed signal that the apostles had crossed and would disembark with their candles and coal. He wandered down with his lantern to the foot of the gangplank and exchanged the agreed clearance lines with the man who stood awaiting his arrival.

Upon first sight, Simons felt assured that the men C had sent could deal with any opposition, Free State or Irregular, should it cross their path. They were mostly silent, questioning nothing. Their leader, Jones, only emphasised to him that the steamer would remain berthed until 2100 hrs, when it would return to Liverpool with the thirteen of them on board. There was no doubt in Jones' demeanour that the mission would be an unqualified success.

As Simons had planned to stay behind to be with Myra, he'd prepared a bogus coded cable, which, of course, Jones couldn't decipher, saying that he'd received revised orders that he was to remain in Queenstown following the operation to observe. He then gave his orders. 'Tell the men to load the tender, Jones. I'll lead the way to the target. We need to cross the countryside and be in position as early as possible.'

He also warned of roadblocks and agitation between opposed armed parties but Jones was fully aware of the dying embers of the civil war. Soon, the two vehicles were heading south through the breaking dawn, and the lone driver in front felt weaker and heavier than ever.

By 8 am, the car led the tender off the road to the small white cathedral. The deluge of rain died down to slight drizzle and sunlight broke through the clouds, granting a rainbow over the bay of Glandore down below them. As the men disembarked, Simons looked to the mound over the way. The woman with the branch staff stood there, as she had on his first visit, months previous, and she was staring directly at him with the same intent as when she'd discovered him spying in the thicket. His skin prickled as before. She was alone this time but still seemed rooted and grown from the crest of the hillock like a verdant totem crowned with flame.

He thought he could discern a smile as she turned her body, then finally her copper mane descended the other side, out of sight.

'Sir? Sir?' Jones' voice snapped him out of his trance.

'Yes? Er, yes … it's over there.' Simons pointed to the hillock. 'Ten minutes on foot. We'll shuttle the gear over the hill, then set up.'

The thirteen men worked as a group, struggling, slipping and skidding in the rain-softened mud and grass but managing to get the crates over by the stone circle in a couple of hours.

They saw no one and Simons led them into the thicket and through the undergrowth, in fear of what he would see and find. But there was not a soul in the clearing on the other side; just the three standing stones with the tall, still willow at their centre.

No shimmering, strange music or dancing flames; just the wilds of nature. In another hour, the ordnance was through, and the men, torn, scratched and bloodied by the undergrowth, set about strapping the explosives to the tree and filling its hollow boughs with dynamite.

'When this goes, sir, it will really go,' said Jones. 'So, we'll take the wires and detonator through to the perimeter next to the stone circle.'

'Yes, splendid,' affirmed Simons, his gaze constantly drawn to the surrounding undergrowth for any flicker of golden-red hair or watchful green eyes as the men worked.

'We'll keep four men on the detonator out there,'

Jones said. 'Four on the wire in the undergrowth and the rest in here until it's five minutes before the time.'

The wait in position was the longest twelve hours of Simons' life. He became familiar with the three standing stones and their inscriptions, every branch, leaf and twine of the thicket and even the minutiae of insects and small creatures that inhabited it.

The recitals of the thrush, wren and blackbirds suggested a sweet lament, and as he sat against a standing stone, he experienced *ciúnas gan uaigneas*—quietness without loneliness. In reminiscence, he compared the fauna there amid the willow and verdant thicket with the gaudy debauchery that had surrounded him at the central tables of The Follies a lifetime ago, but his mind returned continually to Myra, the tenth moon and her beautiful song.

Since C's final order three days earlier, Spirewick, as the Tall Man's shadow, had been dragged across the country from Dublin down to Queenstown. He moved swift and low in the saddle of a khaki Ace Four motorcycle. His frame dwarfed it, but its four cylinders still afforded him agility and speed. The Ace's length could also accommodate the fine fare he'd mentioned to C: his battlefield favourite, a Browning M1918 rifle, wrapped in hessian and strapped to the flank, masked as fishing apparatus.

In Queenstown, Spirewick took shelter in a safe house in sight of the Tall Man's HQ, the Imperial

Hotel. Under each arm beneath his greatcoat were twin shoulder holsters adorned with Mauser C96 pistols lifted as trophies from the hands of the Tall Man's hit squad.

He would leave nothing to chance in completing his mission by eliminating FREDDY and anyone else standing between him and a new life with Lady Liberty across the Atlantic. He found himself sleeping rough in fields through the sweltering nights as the Tall Man weaved across the countryside on a strange tour, but then came the day.
Spirewick woke at dawn and cleaned the weapons with a particular purpose, his stone heart filled with excitement and yearning for the hours to pass until 19:45, when the longest thirty seconds of his life would follow, after which he would carry out his purpose of living.

The late summer evening was drawing in, the dawn showers now a distant memory. The day's sky was closing in powder blue, flocked with amber clouds, the emissaries of autumn.

The assassin had ridden to and fro through the lanes some way back from the rear of the Tall Man's small armed convoy. He noted the familiar scenery as they'd headed back the way they'd came, across Alhalarick Bridge. The convoy slowed to a halt. Spirewick took the opportunity to check his wrist and pocket watch for the fiftieth time that day. It was 19:29. Fifteen minutes to go. Fifteen minutes before it all happened, but with no sign of what was to unfold.

The vehicles ahead revved hard, the bestial roar of the engines echoing down the lane as the convoy surged forwards with acceleration. Then came the crack of single shots, joined by a burst of automatic gunfire; a concerto of battle had struck up. It was happening …

At his desk, C withdrew the candle from the drawer, followed by a small stoppered bottle containing a slither of paper, and rested both on top of the black letter. The clock's chains released and chimed 19:30, driving his hands and eyes to his pocket watch. Satisfied, he sat back and loaded his pipe, then struck a match, studying the phosphorus as it flared and then settled. He transferred the flame to the candle's wick, as he had on three other occasions, then to the stuffed bowl of his pipe, which crackled with his sharp draws of air.

Standing stiffly with the aid of his stick, he moved free of the grey fug over to the large Georgian window. With the stem of the pipe, he pushed back the net curtain and surveyed the sunset above Earls Court, an imperial scarlet mottled with a tide of yellow. In the windowpane, he caught its glint off his monocle, braid and buttons. 'Shepherds delight,' he muttered to himself.

BARBELL had occupied every moment of his mind since its other working parts, Spirewick and Simons, had slipped away from the office ten months previous. The operation was like a favoured child, adored before its siblings. The hundred or so other Secret Intelligence Service operations across the globe couldn't find such a place in his heart. As the constant witness pendulum clacked back and forth, the old man's adrenaline amplified with each pass. C, along with his colleagues over the water, SHEATH and DIRK, readied himself, second by eternal second, as the moment drew near.

*

Spirewick gave chase around the bend and, catching sight of the rear vehicle, braked hard into a horizontal skid.

He recognised the familiar crackle of a Vickers machine gun, punctuated by what he thought was rifle fire, but he could see nothing. He couldn't expose himself by advancing up beyond the rear vehicles. Two hills rose on either side of the narrow, snaking road. He needed higher ground.

He turned the bike and set off back around the track, looking for a route up the hill to his left. *There!* Again, the rear wheel swung out at a right angle to the road, leaving a haze and stench of burnt rubber in its wake as he took off up the trail rising up the hill. He was now on the highest ground with only the mottled twilight sky above him. From this vantage point on the crest of the hill, he could now look down on the winding valley, and he could see the two groups exchanging fire further up the track. Confused by the early opening, he remembered C's specific order: 'No matter what you see, you must not pour until FREDDY has carved. No matter what you see. You must let FREDDY carve at

19:45.'

Spirewick dismounted and checked his watch; it was 19:41. He pulled out his field glasses and unsheathed the Browning from its hessian coat, resting it against his shoulder as he ran forwards, then plunged down to his knees and sank into the sodden turf to prepare the weapon, all the time keeping one eye on the battle unfolding in the valley below.

The heckling of the Vickers suddenly ceased. Spirewick lay on his chest, and through the field glasses, he could see the party ahead of the convoy retreating around a bend towards rising land. On the road below, an officer ran to the rear of the armoured car, took cover and continued firing at the party in their new position above him.

Spirewick focused the glasses and could clearly see the battling officer's face. Spirewick the shadow had now found his sun. A man of action. It was him.

It was the Tall Man.

*

Simons surveyed the tree wrapped in a girdle of ordinance.

'It's almost time, sir,' said Jones, presenting his watch to Simons. 'We need to make for the detonator,' It was there to the second—19:42

While Simons checked the synchronisation with his own watch, Jones ordered his men to withdraw from the clearing and watched them filter out through the thicket.

'Yes, Jones—go to the firing position with your

men.' Simons looked up at the dusk sky and sang an ancient rhyme to himself, '*I see the new moon and the moon sees me. God bless the moon and God bless me.*' He called out to Jones as the man entered the thicket, and pointed to the sky. 'Look, it's cradling the old one in its arms. It's a portent.'

Jones misheard and shouted a warning in exasperation, 'Make sure it is a moment, sir, or you'll get a much better look at the new moon.' With that, he crashed off through the undergrowth to join his apostles.

The irony of Jones' comment wasn't lost on Simons. He was alone before the strapped-up great willow—or was he? He saw a flicker, then flame approaching like a tiger through the foliage.

'Myra!'

*

C removed the glass stopper and emptied the slither of paper onto the desk. He lifted it with his paperknife, accompanied only by the rhythm of the clock.

Tock-clack, tick-clack, tock-clack.

'Almost eight years, Ally,' he said gently as tears welled in his eyes. 'Just a few seconds more, my son.'

He lifted the slither towards the candle as the clock's chains released with a metallic rasp, and the bells struck on the quarter-hour. A tear rolled from his cut-water chin and hit the green leather of the desk like a transparent bomblet.

In less than a second, he would ignite the remnant. His voice would break with the pain of what was in store for a great and noble man, a former enemy whose fate was now entwined with his vengeance. The kind of man who his son was denied a life to become.

He spoke his name and the paper burnt to ash.

*

Below him, Spirewick could see the skirmishing parties moving down the road, drawing parallel to his position on the hill. He extended the forelegs of the Browning and took a prone firing position in the mud and grass. *Watch check: 1944 hrs.*

In amongst the exchange and all around, he searched in vain for FREDDY with his field glasses. The Tall Man was now standing bold as brass and straight as an arrow in the middle of the road, engaging with a sidearm. 'The damn fool …'

The Tall Man seemed to take an age to fall. The grace remained, just as in every movement Spirewick had witnessed over the preceding months. He was going down as if cushioned by a caring wind, almost floating, still gently, forwards, facedown, then motionless, at peace in the epicentre of chaos, as if in a deep sleep.

*

Myra stood on the other side of the clearing, still partially hidden by the undergrowth. She was not alone; at her shoulder, like a second torch, was The Woman.

Simons sprinted forwards as far as the last standing stone, screaming and waving as he went. 'Go! Back, go back!'

Myra did not move, her eyes questioning, uncomprehending. He stopped; the distance was too great. With a pleading scream, he yelled, 'Myra! Please, go! Go to the place I told you! The place on the paper.' He struck his chest with his right hand, then flapped in her direction, as if beating down a raging fire. 'Go! Now, go!'

In the face of his panic, The Woman, gazing over Myra's shoulder, wore the fixed, knowing smile he'd glimpsed when he'd been discovered spying in the thicket on the night of the tenth moon; the same smile he'd also seen as she stood on the hillock that very morning. She wrapped her free arm around Myra's waist and led her away. There was no resistance, and Myra didn't look back.

Simons watched as the two copper manes melted into the darkness of the thicket. He turned and ran back the way he came, checking his watch before slowing to a walk. Finally, in surrender, he slid down the last standing stone and watched the second hand's movement with tear-filled eyes—19:45. *28. 29. 30.*

'The bloody fool,' uttered Jones on the other side of the thicket. He raised his eyes from his watch, met those of his lead dynamiter with a nod.

Down went the plunger.

*

The body on the road was completely motionless.

Through his field glasses Spirewick spotted two men descending the opposite hill toward the road, one a stick-thin younger version of the other with the same flaming red lid. They were celebratory and jubilant. 'There you are, FREDDY boy,' whispered the assassin, as he set him in his crosshairs, before losing him to the bushes on the hedgerow. Spirewick clicked the Browning onto automatic, readied for their reappearance.

There was a *thump* like a thunderclap in the distance. Its report echoed and drew near. The pair emerged onto the road and stood still, blank, pale and stunned as if they'd heard terrible news, the worst imaginable. Spirewick squeezed the trigger and emptied the magazine. The rounds raked a diagonal line through Monus, hip-to-shoulder, flipping him, arms flailing, around and back like a rag doll. The burst echoed across the valley and blended with dwindling cracks of small arms fire down the lane as Monus and his companion hit the ground.

Spirewick rose with a slip on the sodden turf, ran back to the Ace, holstered the Browning, kick-started the machine and tore down the hill track to his stricken victim. He was grinning ear to ear with pleasure and arousal that only cold-blooded murder could ever illicit for him. When he reached his target, the guns had gone silent, replaced by the wails of men further down the way.

The assassin rocked the bike back onto its stand and patiently surveyed his quarry at the side of the road, Monus' legs were sticking out of the undergrowth, the younger man whimpering as he cradled him. Spirewick approached with a slow swagger and pulled out each of the Mausers from his shoulder holsters. FREDDY had carved; now, he would finish the pour. Spirewick considered C's orders had been followed, but his bloodlust had drowned out a crucial element of their detail.

There they were before him, at his feet. He aimed the first Mauser at Monus. 'FREDDY, this is Peter.' He chuckled, then levelled the second. 'And for you, boy, this is Paul.'

Monus opened his eyes and stared deep into those of his assailant.

At that moment, Spirewick heard, in unison, the screams of every soul he'd dispatched since the age of eight. They shrieked through his head, threshing his brain like wheat sheaves. All were heard; from his incestuous father/grandfather, to the butchered Elephant Girls and all those in between from the back streets of London, to the innocents of Sinai and Palestine, along with those across the Green Isle. The yells and squeals that once gave him sexual pleasure now converged to destroy him as he knelt, helpless, his own cries of agony drowned out by theirs, his massive hands clamped over his ears.

'Come on now, Declan—home,' wheezed Monus, on his back. 'Home for us. Help me now.'

The younger man did as he was asked and helped his wounded brother to his feet and leant him against a tree. They paid no regard to the huge man writhing incapacitated before them, drawing breath only to wail again. Declan ran around the corner and returned a moment later on a motorcycle showing signs of crash damage. With tender care, he helped

Monus onto the rear, and wrapping his arms around him, he set off down the lane.

As the distance between himself and Monus grew, Spirewick's senses returned. The screams of his victims, though dulled, remained in his ears. He wiped away the third set of tears he'd ever cried and studied the pool of blood in the bushes and its trail over the white petals of hawthorn, picked up and holstered the Mausers and mounted the Ace. 'I'll chase you to hell, Freddy boy,' he growled and screeched off in pursuit. A scattering of gold and brown leaves circled in his wake.

Spirewick's superior machine caught the Triumph with its wounded passenger in no time, but the closer he got, the louder the infernal screams in his ears became. On every straight, he drew and fired, but each round missed its mark. He rounded the corner with the small white cathedral. The road down to Glandore was clear. Turning back, he saw a line of tracks carved into the grass up and over the green hillock, where the darkening sky glowed from a fire beneath a column of smoke.

The scent of burning wood filled his nose as he drove the Ace up and over the hill. As he sped on, he saw the Triumph abandoned on its side, the wounded man leaning on the younger as they disappeared into the thicket by the stone circle. He gave a burst of acceleration and skidded off the machine, sending it into its inferior cousin and himself tumbling through the mud.

Sudden relief. The screaming vanished from his

ears, and only the crackle of the fire beyond could be heard. He drew one of the Mausers and entered the thicket as the twilight edged its way to darkness.

He emerged into the clearing to see a split bough, crowned with emerald fire, embers settling through the air to die and the remnants of charred and burning leaves and branches scattered on the ground.

Squatting on his haunches against the facing stone was Monus, wounded, trembling, his head in his hands. Spirewick caught his eye again and flinched for a moment, expecting a renewed torment of screeches of the damned, but felt nothing, only his own contempt and joy at imminent slaughter.

He took aim and paced steadily toward his target, drawing the second gun for cover. He couldn't see the stick-thin boy, but he was no threat. His mocking grin was fixed, and his breathing was deep in arousal for the second time, as it always was when blood was about to be spilt. He slowed, step by step, savouring the moment, close to climax. Point-blank now. His target shook his head as he wept.

'America, FREDDY … Here's to America,' Spirewick hissed, pulling the trigger and creating a third eye for his victim.

The head dropped, as did the arms. Spirewick's hateful boot met the shoulder, sending the body over onto its side. But its blank eyes, punctuated by a bullet hole, were now brown, not green, and the tear-strewn face was now fine-featured with high hollow cheekbones and a joyous, peaceful smile. The shock of hair above the bullet hole was lamp black, not red.

He was standing above the body of his brother, SHEATH—Lt. Finn Mallow Simons.

*

From within the undergrowth, Monus hugged his brother as he supported him. They sniggered as Spirewick dropped the guns, head on chest, transfixed by the sight of his fallen comrade.

'Now, Declan, that's the way to do it, eh?' said Monus, tapping his forehead. He stood independently, and Declan took a step forwards. His eyes narrowed and fixed on Spirewick, but Monus took his arm. 'No, no, brother. It's the badger in his hole, that's for you. I'll finish this; off you go. Right now. Go!' Silently, as ever, the boy departed through the dark thicket into the growing night.

Monus emerged into the clearing and approached Spirewick, wearing his maniacal grin. Spirewick turned, startled, and, seeing him, went to pick up the gun.

'No, you don't,' said Monus, his words freezing the behemoth. 'You've put enough holes in me today.' He drew near, beheld the terror in the lashless eyes and reached up with his talon-like hand. He did what no other had done and gripped the broad, ox-like throat, his long nails digging into the flesh. Spirewick whimpered, unable to move. 'Now I'll put some in you.'

Then Monus' eyes opened wide, and he released his grip and jumped back. 'No!' he shouted, turning side-on, then he took a step. 'No! No, Ma! Please, not again!' He took three more wooden strides, then stopped.

Spirewick, finding he was released, looked down again at the gun, then remembered The Persuader, his only constant companion in life. He reached into his greatcoat, unsheathed the bayonet, raised it high and unleashed a slash with all his strength to Monus' back.

At the moment of contact, Monus stepped forward, the blade cut air, and its wielder tumbled and rolled several times involuntarily with his momentum. All the while, Monus' protestations continued. Spirewick rose to his feet, red with rage, drew close and struck again with the same result, his greatcoat fanning as he span like a dervish into the ground.

Monus set off, walking towards the thicket and through it, cut and torn by branches to the other side. Spirewick was in his wake, slashing and stabbing, but always short.

On and on they went, through the night, into the rain and mist, across the fields and over hill after hill, mile after mile.

The footing became softer as they entered the bog land's embrace. It drew them down, covering their knees, then their waists. Still Monus protested. Still, Spirewick attacked with tiny prods, hardly able to lift the now leaden Persuader. He missed again until there was silence ahead and the pleas ceased. Spirewick sank deeper and deeper with the vain struggles of a fly in a web, up to his neck, then above his nose, the blinking lashless eyes full of horror, until the mists and clouds cleared to reveal the lone bayonet glinting in the light of the new moon.

*

The hearth was full of emerald flame, in a parlour adorned with the spoils of the owner's prosperous occupation. The fire illuminated the red Afghan rug and the flock-covered walls, upon which hung framed paintings between gaslights which flickered in verdant unison.

'She was beautiful, Ma. So sad, it is,' said Myra, regarding the central photograph of a family, the mother and baby seated and the proud father stood behind them, his hand resting on the woman's shoulder.

'It is that, and the child as well, him being a physician and all.' Myra's smile melted and gave way to pain once again. 'We found this place, Ma, but it's not for us; we can't stay here. You've seen what they done; you always said the tree was all. We saw it, the bang. Terrible what they done. Killed the glimmer and us with it.'

The Woman turned side-on. 'Not so! You saved us. All is well now.'

Myra shook her head. 'We're as done as these.'

'Did you not hear me, child? It's you that's saved us, but you're right about one thing: we can't stay here.'

Myra was lost, her eyes asking the question that her mouth could not.

The Woman drew her closer. 'We find ourselves here, but the slumber time is upon us, child. What your brothers did in this world of men, well … And what Monus stole from me has not been returned, so he'll enjoy the bog, and the bog'll enjoy him.' The last words brought the trace of a smile.

'But the glimmer?' exclaimed Myra.

The Woman pulled her closer still and spoke in a whisper, knowing the chamber maid's uncomprehending ear was fixed to the door. 'The glimmer wasn't lost with the tree, not one branch or twig. You were right; you and I can't stay, but it's made for the pair of you.' She placed her palm on Myra's belly. 'The glimmer is here.'

There were no words now, but more tears, this time of joy, as Myra placed both hands on top of Ma's and sent warmth to the spark which grew within.

It may have been moments or hours later when Myra asked, 'But how can I—we—live in their world of men alone, Ma?'

'The cost has been paid. It's the blood that will protect. But this night, I, too, will be gone to sleep,' said The Woman. 'This will be the first and last time you hear this, so listen carefully. Right now, a charming man approaches a kind man, the master of this house.' She tapped the photograph on the mantlepiece with her staff. 'This man.'

Myra studied the photograph more intently.

'He has been visited by tragedy … not of our making, I might add. Sickness came upon the girl and the babe, that even he, as a healer, couldn't defeat. His heart is broken. Shattered.' She grasped Myra's shoulder. 'But this night, he will return here, see you and be mended. He will love you and believe whatever you tell him, as will all his kin. You will take his name, and he will take the child as his.

'You will pass our song on to the girls—that's bloody important, only the girls—and they, in turn, will pass them on, until the slumber time is over. The cost is paid, and the blood will protect … That's all.'

The Woman broke free and pulled open the door, startling the eavesdropper. She was along the hall and out through the street door, slamming it shut, cutting off Myra's pursuit. The door seemed stuck fast, but finally, it freed, and Myra ran out the pavement of St Stephen's Green and found it deserted. The only movement was from a bundle of swirling willow leaves, early for autumn. They glinted in the emerald lamp light and dispersed in the August wind.

*

C sat in great anticipation of the visit. The mission appeared accomplished, but at great cost. Admiral Coke had recorded that thirteen men, including a man of Spirewick's description, rather than Simons', had boarded the *Golden Star* at Queenstown, but the ship had been found adrift in rushes near the mouth of the River Avon, bereft of its crew.

The saddest thing of all was that it appeared that Simons, his own man, had bought it, though C lived in the hope that Ann the secretary would announce his arrival out of the blue and he would appear at the office door, as had happened following previous successful missions in New York and Mexico. In his heart, though, C felt this wouldn't transpire and he'd drafted a letter of condolence to Simons' next of kin, listed as Dr Garret Simons of Dalkey, Ireland.

Sometimes hope is all, he mused to himself. But within the details wired to him by Simons throughout the mission, there had been a glaring omission. It was clear to C that Simons had indeed been compromised by the Sister on the first day of the operation, but for him, there was no turning back. As far as Lloyd George's black letter was concerned, BARBELL's mission was accomplished, and the events at Beal na mBlath had got as far as the newsstands of London and New York.

Despite C's personal loss and the end of the waking nightmare he'd endured with Monus, he could still feel sorrow that his masters had reasoned it necessary to deprive a people of such a magnificent leader as the Tall Man, whose crime of victory against the Crown could not be forgiven. Still, his was not to reason why, only to serve the King and his Empire.

The BARBELL log's final entries were complete, and it was laid to rest by its author in its secret place beneath the hearth in front of the fire. Its very creation presented a great personal risk to its writer. Political manoeuvring and jousting with MI5 were one thing; dealing with foreign enemies was quite another.

The contents of the log, if discovered, could see him ridiculed at best and confined to an asylum at worst. It was all in there—from the night in Meaux, the fevered dreams, the phantasmal assassinations, BARBELL, Simons' reports and the final reckoning, with as much detail as he could muster.

Although he had lost something truly priceless, his son's gaze from the portrait could be enjoyed at last to join his memory in the silence that greets and closes each day. But what about the part that he could afford?

Physically, his leg, taken as a trophy. Psychologically, rationalising the interaction and existence of the fantastical without entering Bedlam while maintaining the Service. He paused and asked himself a question that filled him with dread and for which a definite answer could not be found in this world: what was the spiritual cost? What the hell were these people—these things—really?

Ann's signature knock rapped at the door. 'It's Lt. Spirewick for you, sir.'

'Send him in,' called C as he filled his pipe. Closure, at last.

The door opened and Spirewick's form, still and foreboding, stood in the light of the hallway, reminiscent of their first meeting. He stood regarding the old man for what must have been three seconds, then stepped across the threshold and towards the desk. C drew a match from its box.

'Damn good job, Lt. Spirewick. That creature dispatched and the whole business put paid to. I knew you were the man. There's a fellow named Nathan Hart who will see to your needs in Liverpool. Your pardon, ticket, passport and funds are in the envelope.' He pushed the package across the desk. 'Take them and be off with you. Good luck!' said C, pipe in mouth.

'Yes, sir,' lisped Spirewick.

C detected a slight echo to the voice, which he subconsciously tried to rationalise as he struck the match. The phosphorus sparked and livened to a flame. *Green!*

Spirewick drew his swordstick and, in one movement, struck both the matches from C's hands and the pipe from his mouth, the tip glancing the bridge of his nose in its arc. The old man was sent to the left with the force of the blow. As C's monocle flew from his eye, the attacker's right sword arm simultaneously drew back, cocked to deliver the killing blow.

But where C had been, his assailant now saw The Woman sat behind the desk. How beautiful she was, in her dress of glistering green and willow, her eyes pools of turquoise and teal but rimmed with emerald flames of anger. Above and to the left, a pipe, matches and monocle were suspended in flight. She rose to her feet. 'You have been such a bad boy, Declan,' she scolded. 'You listened to your brother, broke your Ma's heart, hurt the glimmer and now … Now you'll pay, boy. You'll pay and sleep …'

C instinctively raised his hands to his face in fear

and defence as the pipe, matches and monocle clattered to the floor. He anticipated the skewering strike that would end his life there and then, but he felt nothing. The attacker stood poised but frozen, transfixed, breathing quickly through gritted teeth. Now C could see the green of the eyes in place of the dead cobalt of those belonging to Spirewick. At once, he reached for his own swordstick and pushed to his feet. He unsheathed the blade and, with all his might, launched himself across the desk, plunging the steel deep through his assailant's chest, running him through, right to the hilt.

No sound came from Spirewick's mouth, but tears streaked from the jade eyes as they turned a dead brown from iris to the whites. He fell to the right like a felled oak as terror and shock overwhelmed the old man. He sank back into his chair and then flopped forwards. He was out.

He lifted his head to see a woman of mature years but astounding beauty standing before him. Long wild hair of flame and white hung to her waist, and she wore a shimmering dress of emerald that matched the colour of her eyes. She leant on a willow staff and spoke in a gentle Irish brogue. 'What has befallen us should not have come to pass … but it's over now. The cruelty of your kind and mine shames all, but it's over and done with now.' She moved forwards. 'Over!' She raised and slammed the base of her staff on the floor. 'DONE!'

C woke with a start and sat up, his sticky brow

detaching with a dull pop from the green leather of the desk. Besieged by cold sweat, he focused as best he could and found he was alone, the office empty. He saw the debris of the engagement: the cane scabbard, the scattered matches, his pipe and monocle on the floor. C knelt and retrieved the last, fitting it snuggly into place. Struggling to his feet, aided by the desk, he limped around to its front. There he regarded his swordstick, laid on the floor amongst a pile of dried, dead willow leaves that appeared to be roughly arranged in the shape of a man. He looked to the hearth.

The BARBELL file would receive one final entry and encryption, after all, and thence be closed, concealed and forgotten by its only living witness. Until somehow fate would demand its discovery more than fifty years later, when its revelations would reach another singular man who would also sign off with the simple green ink inscription of "C".

Chapter 15

SILICONICA

0700 hrs, August 10th, 202?

Nice, France.

Bradley looked up at his companion. 'Beach and Expo today, I presume?'

Shev nodded, but her expression was grave. A great night had followed yesterday's chill out at the pool. She and Biff had showered, then took in the Promenade des Anglais on foot, freewheeling and filming more footage before gorging on posh pizza at *Edusa.* Back at the Negresco's bar, Biff had ordered a vodka martini, shaken, not stirred, as a final pleasure to top off this day of firsts. All this blotted out Shev's absence during the morning and ensured he was snoring in oblivion by midnight, when Bradley had decided it was time to disclose mission-critical information regarding her colleague UT4, who would be arriving from London at 0930 hrs the following day.

Shev now had the charge-sheet of the handsome stranger in the black jeep's activities, and she'd seen the footage of the atrocities in Syria and Iraq interspersed with the badge cam footage of her encounter. There was no dramatic music or captions to inspire or corrupt like the radicalisation videos she'd viewed in training at the Hive, just plain facts; everything from the murders of UT4's parents up to the drone strike that had supposedly extinguished his flame. After the maddest of days, even the late message and its lurid content hadn't prevented her from a deep sleep and lucid dreams.

Midnight, in the midst of a savannah. A warm breeze waved the tall gold blades of grassland where she lay, carrying the purr of nocturnal insects. Constellations spattered across a sky of stirred purple. A super-moon bedded on smoky clouds bathed Mount Kenya and the surrounding plains and flat topped acasias in refracted silver. A black dot crossed the moon's cratered face and sent forth a streaking arrow to the ground. *'Direct hit,'* crackled the commentary, then she saw grainy footage showing a black plume in the crosshairs of the Reaper drone, containing the vaporised elements of what was once Nadeem al Shabah.

The dreams continued until she rose like clockwork at 0645 for the RV.

'So, which first? Business or pleasure?' Bradley persisted, teasing the froth of his latte with a spoon.

'I checked the programme. D'Orly will speak at 11.00 hrs, followed by a Q&A, so we'll start at the Expo.'

Meow! Shev checked her phone and opened a selfie of UT4, barely recognisable from their encounter in the Hive, with cap and wraparounds. The message was immediately followed by a second.

'That's the address and the pinpoint for the brush pass,' said Bradley. 'Be at the Dive Shop for 10:00. Where's the sample?'

'Don't worry,' said Shev. 'It's secure.'

There was a touch of defiance. She decided not to voice her thoughts on this occasion, and she didn't need to; it was in her eyes, the understanding that her boss had weighed the elements of risk between the pair of them. Everyone is expendable, but some are more expendable than others. That was why she'd secreted the sample bag in the lining of the passenger helmet and, of course, he knew that. Total surveillance, wasn't that what they said back at the Hive? Leave nothing to chance.

Yes, Bradley saw it in her green almond eyes; the first flash of discontent and attitude. In truth, he liked it, but he only responded with cold blue indifference in his.

Shev's fifteen-minute ride to the RV with UT4 was a

scenic pleasure. She was guided by the sat-nav into the city along Rue de la Buffa, across the pedestrianised slab of Place de Messina past the Towers of Meditation and the verdant garden stretch of Promenade du Pallion. She threw a right at the Museum of Modern Art, cut across Place de Garibaldi and cut round to the rear of the harbour until she approached a glade of singing white masts of Port Lympia's Marina.

She made a pass along the length of the quay and saw the small, capped figure emerge from a white taxi at the designated spot by the Dive Shop. In her wing mirror, she saw the driver remove a case from the boot, receive his payment and leave. Shev U-turned at the end of the quay and pulled over. UT4 was staring straight ahead at the harbour thirty metres away. It was adrenaline time again. All that was required was to pull in and complete the brush pass. She elected to ride closer, as the walk with the second helmet would seem to take forever. She purred to a stop and dismounted the Vespa. Her colleague showed no recognition. The same inverted telescope vision, courtesy of the adrenaline, made her seem much further away. Shev unclipped the passenger helmet, loosened the tape and carried it under her arm as she took the ten paces in UT4's direction that would put her elbow-to-shoulder.

UT4's rucksack hung by a single strap over her right side and, in a move crossing the back of UT4, Shev made the transfer into the open side pocket.

'On a P11, when I say pull out, you fucking pull

out,' hissed the voice in which she'd placed absolute trust. Shev smirked internally, as if on the receiving end of an irate school teacher's rant, then stood and watched the reflection in the plate glass window of the small, determined figure strutting away across the road in the direction of the marina. Bradley had hinted at UT4's displeasure at the P11 debrief but had now got the message, loud and clear. She was just thankful that UT4 hadn't insisted on knowing why she hadn't followed her direction.

A police vehicle rounded the corner, cutting off her view of UT4, raising her stress level again for a moment before it picked up speed, passed by and continued on its route. Shev felt greatly relieved to be free of the sample, and she set off back the way she'd come, considerably lighter and thankful of the preview of the area before the ride out to the Expo.

Biff's rock lobster look was toning down to, in his own words, 'a nice Cuban mahogany,' and he was the healthiest she'd seen him, despite his indulgences. The comedic value of Biff riding pillion on the back of the Vespa wasn't lost on either of them; he was winded when Shev thrust the spare helmet into his chest, and the Vespa groaned as his weight dipped the rear suspension. After several attempts, Shev managed to pull away, en route to the Plaza where the joys of the Siliconica Expo awaited them.

As they crossed the threshold, the couple pulled closer together, short of holding hands, as

Siliconica's sensory onslaught hit them in unison. The Expo was making good on its promise to reveal 123 innovative new technological breakthroughs via interaction, demonstration and presentation, the crackle and gleam of tomorrow splinted with silicon and ultra-def screens. Pixilated wonders refined the failings of organic matter as the latest in AI interaction was embedded throughout with human and holographic presenters balanced evenly at a ratio of 1:1.

The base algorithm driving the presentations was way ahead of the human speed of thought as it scanned, decided and delivered a fitting pitch to each heartbeat and digital profile within a metre of a projector, reconfiguring the holographic presenter on the nano-second decision of the customer's visual preference data.

Within an hour, they had ample footage of the Expo and its wares. It was Shev's intention to busy Biff later with condensing and editing the content before posting. He was happy to do some livestreaming of the event as it trended in real-time all over the world.

The audio countdown to the main presentation began over the speaker system, corresponding to archived NASA numbers on the screens beside the stage. The Shevaloguers were in their front row seats when it reached '5' and the lights went down. When she emerged to a standing ovation Shev was impressed by Oriel d'Orly's appearance in the flesh. She was a former model who Biff cruelly likened to the Clare Blunderwood drag act, due to her angular blonde hair, stilettos and clinging skirt. With feline grace, she received a kiss on each cheek from the host, glided over to the chair, crossed her legs, lifted the microphone to her glistening lips and uttered an intentionally seductive, '*Bonjour, Siliconica.*'

The crowd were ecstatic on hearing the minimal, husky tones. As the digital Q&A began, there was no doubting her charisma and intelligence. Oversized Run-DMC style executive glasses obscured her eyes, even in close-ups provided by the massive screens. The sparkly *Eighth Day* brooch was there for all to see, and talk of collaboration and a new digital dawn for Europe went down well. When pressed by the enamoured hipster host for more detail as to when the big announcement would be made, she playfully chided, 'Now, now, Tangui, you must be patient.' She then addressed the audience directly. 'And all of you, too. In only a few days, it will all be worth the wait.'

There was a trickle of crimson from her tiny nose and she smudged it away with the back of her forefinger, but the flow increased. Tangui passed tissues and called for assistance, and d'Orly was ushered off-stage the way she came, with no mention of the mysterious Isla. The lights dimmed again as a string arrangement of *Are Friends Electric* came over the tannoy, reinforcing d'Orly's teased promise. The show was over, and the audience shuffled, conflicted between excitement and concern for the style icon turned politician. Shev discreetly scanned the crowd when they rose to leave; Lane and al Shabah were nowhere to be seen among the throng and displays of a better tomorrow, so Biff soon found himself clinging on for dear life once again as Shev rode the Vespa back to the beach.

'You'll be two of the sorest thumbs hiding in plain sight,' had been Bradley's words, what seemed like a lifetime ago. So, Shev saw to it, armed with an inflatable unicorn for Biff and a Godzilla for her, as they took two recliners on the Negresco's private beach. In turn, they took cooling forays into the surf and recorded more stills and vids for the *Shevalogue*, along with a few personals for themselves.

It was when Shev was twenty metres out from the beach that she looked back to the shore and saw the man, conspicuous in his stillness, as he stood and stared. She struck into a forward crawl as fast as she could, but when she was ten metres from the shore, the man suddenly turned and headed away, lost amongst the oversized umbrellas that stretched back to the promenade.

But she'd caught his profile, just as she had as she'd dived into the pool the day before, and she was sure now. The man she had seen was Mr Snow.

Bradley had also witnessed d'Orly's meltdown at *Siliconica* before slipping away under his Panama hat and venturing on foot to find the green flag vessel at the marina where UT4 was waiting below the deck. The lab was compact but impressive, and UT4 seemed happy, almost animated in comparison to the hologram he'd seen the previous day as she came to terms with the revelation of Nadeem al Shabah. She drew up a screen to present her findings.

'The sample meets the compound profile for the illegal street drug "pink", a synthetic cocaine derivative,' explained UT4, bringing forth a range of supportive images of captured hauls, individuals in the act of consumption and a geographical map of the UK. 'As you can see from the footage, "pink" is taken intranasally, the dopamine blockers absorbing into the blood stream through the nasal passage and delivering the hit. But there's something else. When I increased magnification, I got this.'

The image looked like a metallic equivalent of the coronavirus: spherical roundels bristling with silver protein spikes. The Ultra waited for Bradley's question because, as far she was concerned, she would be the first person in any intelligence service to answer it, and she was savouring the moment.

Finally, he cracked, 'So UT4, what is it?'

'This is a scanning probe microscope, sir, enabling the heterogenic identification of materials at an atomic level, and I believe this'—she jabbed her finger at a projected spiky sphere, now the size of a football—'is non-organic, an alloy-antenna. It's twice the size of an average virus, one micron in diameter. There are at least a thousand in this sample alone, forming a network and responsive to a larger signal,' said UT4 with a grin. Bradley looked puzzled. 'I'll be explicit. I think it's nanotechnology, sir. *Narcotic* nanotechnology. NNT. *Night Night Twinkle.*'

Bradley had agreed with Dewhurst that UT4 would immediately send the sample to the UK via the Diplomatic Bag, then on her arrival collect and take it by chopper to Porton Down for further analysis with all the technology available.

The old spy sat at the beach bar and studied the on-screen data UT4 had sent on the movements of Maximus Lane. As suspected, the data dictated a pattern that linked him to other existing evidence: unaccounted-for killings, thefts and signal disruptions. He received another message and checked his watch before opening it, figuring UT4 was in the Departure Lounge ahead of her flight to the UK. He then glanced at the clustered block of umbrellas stretching down to the water's edge, somewhere under which his young charges were having the time of their lives.

The message read: *'Lane's jet confirmed landed at Reykjavik thirty minutes ago, refuelled and hopped across the island to the Skagafjörður airstrip, which serves the bay and village on the north side of the island. Maximus Lane is aboard the Astrid, which has left French waters and is according, to SIGINT, en route for the UK.*

Regarding the syntho-narcotic, "pink", the first agency identification was almost three months ago: London, UK, June 23rd.'

Bradley shuffled on the stool and rubbed his chin as he digested UT4's intel-bomb. June 23rd. Three days after the last LINX meeting and synching with the emergence of *Eighth Day*. His intelligence matrix had taken on the form of a pyramid. Another message appeared from UT4: a grainy photo lifted from cheap CCTV.

'FRS gives 98% match of the passenger on Lane's jet. I can also confirm the aircraft flew twelve times between London and Reykjavik within the last three months.'

Bradley received and downloaded a clear second image of an all-too-familiar face.

The face of Nadeem al Shabar.

'Yes, sir, what is it?' Shev laid back on the lounger as she saw Biff stumble down the cobbles into the surf with his inflatable unicorn for company.

'GLIMMER, are you free to speak?'

'Yes, Biff's having a last splash around. He insists that I watch our gear, even though this is the hotel's private beach. Go on.'

'I'll get to the point. We're leaving, going north, far north, to Iceland. NaS landed there less than an hour ago by Learjet, and we're in pursuit. Sort your flights out ASAP. I've reserved you a room at the *Odensvig*.'

Shev sat up, her iPad already open. 'I'm looking now. There's no direct flight to Reykjavik; it has to be via either London, Budapest or New York, an eight-hour journey. Can I ask a question?'

'Of course.'

'You said NaS has a Learjet. If we're travelling domestic, couldn't he be back here by the time we're half-way?'

'Good point, GLIMMER.'

'But not if we keep him there.'

'Go on.'

'My old boss used to go on about a boxing fight that was cancelled due to an ash cloud.'

'That's right; the volcanic ash cloud back in 2010 grounded a lot of flights,' affirmed Bradley. 'Major disruption.'

'Well, when we were behind on the job, he say we needed an ash cloud to keep the clients off our backs.'

'That's all well and good, GLIMMER, but we can't conjure the weather.'

'No, but if I may, sir, we might have someone who actually can … in a virtual sense.'

'Very good,' laughed Bradley. 'Deep fake a hyper-object such as an ash cloud, localised in some way, enough to keep him there and let us in. It would be one hell of a hack, but you're absolutely right; if it is within the realms of possibility, we may have someone who can look at that, but carry on with the booking as advised.'

Shev spotted Biff stumbling back down the cobbles with his purple and silver companion as he tried to exit a wave crash.

'There's one more thing, GLIMMER.'

'I think I know …'

'As you've seen, a route via London is on the menu. So, with Biff or not with Biff, that is the question. It's yours to answer, so do so with haste. I'll see you there.'

Chapter 16

DAY ZERO

August, 12th 202?

Reykjavik, Iceland.

She'd gone from the smog of Britain's capital to the crystal light of the Cote d'Azur and now stepped out into air to match, fresher air than she could ever imagine back home. 9.00 am in Iceland, cool and cloudless, the fetid hairdryer of parched London now felt as distant and as alien as Mars. By 1700 hrs the previous afternoon, they'd disembarked from the flight from Nice for a stay over in Budapest, zombie Biff was pushed onto the plane at dawn, and here they were. With Biff, it was.

BREAKSPEAR had advised if you create the legend, own it. Biff had swallowed it all, and it hardly touched the sides: Business Class travel, lounge access, the lot. This time, Shev suggested a day's chillout time at the *Odensvig* to edit and explore while she nipped off and did "her bit" and was met with no resistance. They'd meet later in the centre of Reykjavik and revel in *Menningarnótt*, Culture Night, Iceland's biggest night of the year and one tailormade to crown the *Shevalogue* adventure. She'd created Biff's itinerary, beginning with another spa session, followed by all the go-to bars and the sickest mixological dens, which would keep him occupied until she returned. Biff was impressed with Hotel Odensvig, which once again they shared, two floors apart, with Mr B. Shev suspected that despite the wad of *krona* he had secreted about his person, and with Room Service at his disposal, Biff wouldn't go far. The late Icelandic summer was kind, and the weather app Shev consulted showed a potential eighteen degrees and solid blue sky overhead.

At 1000 hrs, Shev emerged from the hotel. Bradley waved to her from a hired Range Rover. She opened the back door to see all surfaces of the interior had been covered in plastic film, threw her rucksack in and joined Bradley in the front.

'That's ominous,' said Shev, thumbing over her shoulder.

Bradley ignored the comment. 'It's a three-hour-plus drive overland to *Skagafjörður*, hence the airstrip at that end. Our man's still there; miraculously, the volcano flared up again. All flights grounded,' he added, with a wink.

'What happens when we get there?'

'We've got time to think about that. Enjoy the

scenery. This whole country is an area of outstanding beauty. You're on the decks today. When we're close, I'll brief you fully.'

Thirty minutes out, on either side of the road flowed an undulating scrub of green below grey outcrops and glimpses of the sea to the left. To the right sat the valley, the skirt of the mountain and its waterfall.

'I've been here before, you know, for work,' Bradley said.

'Your … er … research project?'

'That's right. Hot off the back of the Cod War, believe it or not.'

'What's that? It sounds like a mass pillow fight with fish instead of cushions.'

Bradley chuckled. 'It was a bit more serious than that; a conflict over resources, as most wars are. This time, it was fishing quotas, but there was a specific kind of interference that required us—BARBELL— to investigate. That's what led me here in 1978. How many years before you were born?'

'Only twenty. So, what was it?'

'It's a story better told before a roaring fire on a cold winter's night, as with all BARBELL stuff, but seeing as you've asked me … There's something known around these parts as a *draugar*. Such things have different names in other cultures,'

'A drugger? There's plenty of them where I'm from.'

Bradley went on, undeterred. 'There were reports of a specific attack where ships were boarded, which lead to physical engagements. It was the one time where actual firepower was used against the natives, but there were no injuries or fatalities.'

'Why was that?'

'Because there was an arguable case that they were never really alive. Draugar are known as zombies or the undead in our parts. In the debrief the stories of all the marines involved concurred. Rounds spent, targets down, then no bodies. Marines fighting undead zombies is laughable, isn't it?'

'A nice ghost story.'

'Story?' Bradley looked out across the landscape. 'You know about superfoods?'

Shev thought for a moment, jarred by the change of subject. 'Sure, wheatgrass and all that. From shops in Crouch End that smell like rabbit hutches.'

'That's right. Food, models, dare I say it, sex—they're all part of the melee. Once, on the 263 bus to Highbury Barn, I earwigged a recollection of the post-office engagement in the battle of Waterloo by an old man sitting behind me.'

'He must have been very old, bearing in mind the battle of Waterloo was in 1815,' said Shev with more than hint of scepticism.

'That's just it. When I rose to leave, there behind me was a spotty eighteen-year-old. Speaking in tongues, I believe is the expression. No spinning heads or family insults; just the two of us. I got off, so it ends. Just a very strange five-minute London experience on public transport, a place where we can even fall in love, several times a day, every day.

Exclusive to you, undiscussed before now. So-called *supernature.*'

'You're saying supernature is just nature, like food and the rest, part of the mel–'

'Part of the melee, that's right. Normality is the filter required to see clearly and retain your sanity, because in the course of your profession, you'll be watching, listening and seeing everything in ultra HD, and without the filter, you'll see Pan and then there's no way back. Add *Arthur Machen* to your homework list, by the way.'

Shev shivered. 'Arth …? Well, you did make it back, so what did you find?'

'That knowledge and interference come at a cost, as with all our investigations. The report got squirrelled away in Registry, deep inside the wedding cake with all the rest.'

Shev was on a roll now—they'd known each other all of a week and she'd served with him at the sharp end a handful of times—so she continued. 'You said "our." So, it wasn't just you?'

'BARBELL is unique in the sense that there's always only three of us. This is, ironically, only the third line-up in a century. When I came in, it was the Chief, me and my colleague/field officer, Jamie Wallace, but we were more like partners really. He was an FO pen-pusher who got caught up in my story. He paid the price on our final operation; lost the filter and saw Pan, just as I just mentioned.'

What the hell, thought Shev. Go for broke. 'And you?'

'I paid it years ago; that's how I got into this. There's never a day when I've not asked myself why the world spun on one action, as it does for all of us really, but this was so, so … singular. The answer has always eluded me. Maybe it's up ahead, eh?'

They now had a visual on the harbour. Bradley put the hazards on and pulled in. 'Now, you know what you know, and that NaS is ahead, so talk. Tell me the story so far.'

'OK,' said Shev. 'He's a bad *hombre*, a murderer, child abductor, terrorist, tech-wizard, dead but now … somehow alive.' She paused, recalling Bradley's ghostly story vignette about the *draugar* legend and the BARBELL operation. She shrugged off the chill and went on. 'He's connected with the London Internet Exchange via Maximus Lane. I saw him RV with the French Tech Minister, Oriel D'Orly, in Nice. D'Orly's part of the threat, wrapped up in this *Eighth Day* shit along with those other two plums and we're here to …'

'You're nearly there,' interjected Bradley, as if pushing her towards the answer like a coach on the sidelines.

'Whatever NaS is up to, it's now-ish, and today is the eighth day,' said Shev in response. 'The *Menningarnótt* festival can't be a coincidence; it's cover. It's the ideal distraction, especially here at the other end of the island, right on a deep-water bay.'

'There's more,' Bradley cut in. 'Analysis has confirmed the sample you lifted is the designer drug "pink," a brand-new synth-narcotic. It's laced with nanotechnology, which we can afford to assume is to communicate with and influence the user. UT4 is continuing work on it as we speak.'

'So that binds it all together.'

'How and what?'

'Pink, *Eighth Day*, NaS, d'Orly, Rub-a-Dub, that plasterer and the threat.'

'That's all in the box, but we need something else to bind them.'

'Of course. Isla. The mention of Isla by Rub-a-dub and the plasterer'

'That's right; the identity of the mysterious Isla. Our main suspects are d'Orly and NaS himself. Do you remember the walk from Zids last week? What we discussed?'

'The fundamentals of espionage. We're here to get the intelligence for others to choose whether to act or not … and it's down to me, I guess?'

'To confront NaS and identify Isla, *who, what, where, how*. We've a Duke-class frigate close by in international waters off Greenland with SBS on board for the heavy lift. When we give the signal, they'll be within a thirty-minute range by chopper. You're going in unarmed, save for your AE. Look, listen, secure evidence and get out. UT4 is our eye in the sky and our ear on the wire. I hope it's going to be that simple, but we both know it won't be.'

Shev nodded her approval. This was it; the sharpest end so far.

'A lot can happen in thirty minutes.' Her voice betrayed her unease and self-doubt.

'You're highly trained and have proved your capability. All things in relativity, you are now an experienced field operative. Your skills and your heightened intuition are why I specifically requested you for BARBELL. We're waiting on an exact location from UT4, and from there it's route one. I'll be close. In the meantime, let's check and set our tech, then get into the village and look round. It's time we ate something.'

*

Mid-afternoon, Biff finally opened the hotel room's window.

The morning had gone well. He'd caught up on his beauty sleep, had Room Service breakfast and a touch more kip. The texts had gone back and forth with Shev; the usual emojis, hearts, balloons, dumb GIFs and kisses. Then it was down to business; a couple of hours of editing and rewards basis visits to his vintage porn favourite, Mary Millington, as he did whenever Shev wasn't around, which was becoming more and more often. A *Shevalogue* post, a joyous shower of likes—then came the siren call, from the seductive trio against whom resistance was impossible: Heineken, Pringles and Toblerone beckoning from the mini-bar. Would it be rude not to answer? Abso-bloody-lutely.

*

'This place looks good; it's up the road in Hofsos. According to *translate,* it does a mean fish and chips,' said Shev after consulting her phone.

'That'll do, then,' Bradley agreed.

They completed a reccy around the outskirts of town and up and along the central street, Hólavegur, and found it unremarkable in its normality. Low-build houses with red and green roofs set in a cradle of craggy mountain tops, the green-grey sea of the bay and an infinite sky.

'It … They seem so ordinary,' said Shev.

'It is, and they are. The Icelanders are wonderful people with an amazing history, culture and environment. They've no idea of what's in their midst today.'

They enjoyed the finest cuts of lightly battered *Skagafjörður* cod with sides of chips and veg and pancakes for afters then the message from UT4 came through.

'HMS Somerset is confirmed offshore. Heavy Lift is on standby for your signal. I have the location—grid refs and GPS pin to follow.'

The location was an industrial area back down the coast between the Tannery and Black Beach.

'This is it,' said Bradley, rising from his seat and leaving several Krona notes on the table.

They drove towards the target in silence. Upon arrival, Bradley pulled up fifty metres from the hanger-like warehouse, one of several which made up an industrial estate that was interchangeable with any other the world over. He used bounce-back to get confirmation of the correct building.

'You're straight with it all? Every minute, tap your badge-cam. If you fail to do so, I'll send the signal for Heavy Lift. Stick this on the door, sleight-of-hand, before you go in.' He passed a palm-sized triangular reflective patch. 'It's an LTM, laser target marker.'

'Charming,' exclaimed Shev. 'I'm not gonna be wearing a drone strike, am I?'

'Drone strikes are anti-material. How could we explain that away? This isn't Raqqa. The whole point is pure HUMINT, human intelligence. There'll be a precision Electro Magnetic Pulse via your locust drone to kill bystanders' devices and any CCTV coverage, but it shouldn't trouble our tech. We don't want any mistakes when Heavy Lift comes in. Believe me, we are not above farce, and we're not cleaning chandeliers, Rodney.' Shev smiled at the reference to *Only Fools and Horses*. 'I'll be less than a click away, OK?'

Shev nodded, unclipped her seat belt and left the vehicle. She approached the warehouse door and heard the Range Rover pull away. She remembered the teachings, but not which sensei had said it: 'Be there a fifty percent chance of success, think of nothing, brace yourself and proceed.'

The Asian Cockney voice in her ear was as coarse yet comforting as ever. '*GLIMMER—UT4. I have you on visual, and all your feeds are live and clear.*'

Shev fixed on the distant door at the end of the long telescope in front of her. With a deep breath, she gripped the steel slider, placed the sticky LTM and pulled. The door was unlocked and slid back with ease.

Shev pushed the internal steel door inwards and

entered.

*

The cascade of hits and likes on the *Shevalogue*'s latest post continued.

'Mission Accomplished!' Biff shouted to himself with his arms raised, Banzai style. More rewards were in order, and he was feeling lonely. He checked his phone; it was half-past-four. 'Where the bleedin' 'ell is she?' he muttered, then he checked the itinerary on his phone. 'Hmm … first stop kicks-off at 6pm. A warm up's in order.'

On went his cap, his gold chain and his Burberry scent, and he checked his wad of krona before toddling off down to the bar.

*

The hanger's interior was lit by strip lighting, and there was a sweet, roasted scent in the air, like the hot-nut trays that come out at Christmas around the West End. There were glass partitions on either side, but there was no sound or sign of life. This only heightened her senses further, which were so charged to the max that a dropped pin would sound like a thunderclap.

In spite of the badge-cam, she took several stills and checked her phone for surveillance signals. It confirmed ten signal feeds, and she understood that someone else apart from Bradley and UT4, whether close by or on the other side of the world, was watching with intent.

As she moved forwards, she could see that behind the partitions to her right was a large amount of laboratory equipment; elongated bottles, tubes, measuring instruments, and scopes. Centrally, there was a spine of monitors that topped the desk-bench with high chairs along its length. There were looped attachments fitted into the table at each station that appeared to be securing devices for whichever poor souls would have been working there. Behind the left partition were also banks of tables with IT terminals. It had the appearance of a disused call centre spliced with a college laboratory. She proceeded to the end and turned the corner, tapping her signal on the minute as agreed.

A burst of volume hit with a clang that compressed her eardrums and gave her such a start that she felt nauseous at the thump in her chest. She drew breath and the clatter continued; it was music, jangling guitars, then that voice. Of all the voices, in all the places, at this moment, it was that voice. Her old boss's idol, Elvis, was in the building. She pulled her nerves back from the sensory assault and kept going forwards past the corner of the lab.

The eye contact was immediate, as was the chill and serpentine sensation around her neck and shoulders she recalled from d'Orly's chateau. Nodding in time and lip-syncing to the King, as alluring, dark and sinister as memory served, there, at the end, was Nadeem al Shabah. He was sat at a transparent acrylic desk housing two computer monitors. Above were two massive screens which broadcast Shev's head and shoulders from two vantage points. She was her own audience.

Al Shabah killed the music, leaving a few seconds of foggy white noise to ring in Shev's ears.

'*Góðan daginn*,' he sneered in the vernacular dialect, his tone laced equally with sarcasm and condescension. 'That was a long scooter ride, eh, Miss?' He averted his gaze back to the monitor and tapped the keyboard.

Shev said nothing.

'Ah, Miss Siobhan …' he continued, smug in the correct pronunciation of her name. 'Well, I never, and the plates and the paper trail had me convinced the scooter was hired by someone else. A friend of yours? She bears a stunning resemblance.'

He was trowelling the sarcasm on inches deep.

'An occasional borrow doesn't hurt.'

'I play for keeps!' Al Shabah spat the words, jumping with intention. He settled back down. 'Facial Recognition software. Total surveillance—where will it end, eh?' Into the mix went mock concern amid a liberal sprinkling of camp.

Shev did not respond to his statement.

Al Shabah rose, standing feet apart with hands together, as if he were about to plead. 'What happened to the mystery of life, eh?'

'Where's Isla?' snapped Shev. The question was direct and weaponised, straight from her diaphragm like a *Kiai*.

It had the desired effect, shunting his composure off balance. Shev took three steps forward and anchored each word with stated gravitas. 'Where. Is. Isla?'

Al Shabah looked at the floor. 'Isla …' He snapped his eyes back up to Shev. 'I'll tell you mine if you tell me yours.' He nodded over Shev's shoulder. 'Who is that?'

She was wise to the distraction tactic, so she dropped down low and looked back. There was a man, tight on the corner of the lab, with a Tavor submachine gun trained on al Shabah.

'Mr Snow!' said Shev in disbelief. She rose again, side-on, so she could alternate her vantage point between the two men.

The gunman said nothing but kept his sights

trained intently on al Shabah, who parroted, 'Mr Snow,' in a mocking tone as he leant down to his keyboard. The interloper's features replaced Shev's on the massive dual screens. 'Well, well, well … Eli Snomis. Israeli national, Sayeret Matkal, then Mossad. They held a funeral for you in 2003. How very interesting, Lazarus Man.'

Al Shabah addressed Shev but kept his eyes fixed on the monitor on the desk. 'From your reaction, Miss Uhuru-Behan, you are as surprised as I am.' He looked up at the gunman. 'You should leave, Mr Snomis … Now.' He came back to Shev. 'But I did say I'd tell you mine, so I'll start first. Isla is long gone, I'm afraid, but what a mind she had! All this architecture'—he tapped the top of the monitor—'the finer details, it was all her, way beyond my capabilities … But once it was done, she had to go, as I'm sure you understand. I'm not the sentimental type, although … family has deep meaning for the likes of us, does it not?'

Shev was completely confused and felt those tentacles from the day in Nice tighten once more around her neck and arms.

Shouting 'What the fuck are you doing here?' at Snow wouldn't suffice, but Mossad? Missing, presumed dead, in 2003? It made no sense. Mr Snow had moved in when the Olympics were on back in 2012. 'An inherited tenancy,' he'd said. There had been no reason to question it.

Al Shabah showed no fear at the weapon being trained on him and gestured to the interloper to approach. Snow moved forward, maintaining his bead but not his resistance, like a noble carp fighting against the line, reeled in with sinister ease by the beckoning rod of al Shabah's finger until he was within arm's reach.

'Shev, I think you should leave now.' Snow forced the words out through gritted teeth, and she drew comfort from hearing his accented tones once again. 'Go back, Shev, the way you came. Right now.'

She stood motionless, rooted to the spot out of both fear and loyalty. Al Shabah snatched the weapon and lifted its sight to his eye. Snow's hands remained in position as if he were a second-rate mime artist. There was a burst of automatic fire. The velocity lifted Snow off his feet, and he flopped down hard on the concrete. A crimson pool spread from beneath him.

Shev's hands covered her mouth in reflex, stifling a yelp. Wet heat tricked down her inner thigh, and her eyes welled. The stench that combined a butcher's shop and firework sparklers filled her nostrils. Al Shabah, grinning, transferred his aim to her. She forced her hands back down to her sides and did as she'd been trained. She thought of nothing. Not dying. Not running. Not Granny B. Not Sensei. Not Bradley. Not UT4. Nothing.

Al Shabah cackled, clicked the safety on and threw the weapon to the ground with a clatter. 'I thought I'd mellowed with age, but it appears not. Now, where were we?'

Shev's eyes darted back and forth between Snow's body and his slayer. She cleared her throat and got it together, imagining every teacher she'd ever had barking at her to do so, and the gnashing spittle flying off the instructor's yellow crooked rack back at the Hive.

'As the man said, I'm leaving now. That's it.' Shev turned to make her way.

'Of course, but not yet, Miss Uhuru-Behan,' urged al Shabah. She paused and turned back.

'Although I see you are a carpenter and a teacher.' He gestured towards his monitors, which seemed like they might reveal the key to her very soul. 'It's quite obvious what your current vocation is. You're a spy, sent by your service and whichever nation state they serve. So let's not go there as time is of the essence.' He took a vial and a straw from his inner pocket, sprinkled the pink powder on his desk and fashioned it with a razor blade as he spoke. 'And I've got to fly, too. What I'm about to say is the basic overview; an executive summary for your superiors.' With his free hand, he gave an exaggerated, sarcastic wave intended for the button-cam. 'Simple and quick. In common perhaps with your profession, by whatever gateway, all followers of the cult and enjoyers of this stuff, volunteered!

'All I offer with the *Eighth Day* is a peaceful world; an end to war. Who needs it when you control an outcome, pebble, pond and ripple? Be it a tick in a Hartlepool ballot box, a stabbing in East London, a Commons vote, a little "grass riot", a cough here, a sneeze there; all pebbles and ripples.' He picked up his mobile. 'No more questions of fake or real. Just actions, on request. Just like ordering a cab.' He slapped the phone back down. 'Utopia. That's what I wanted to name it, but Isla deemed it far too elitist. Too many syllables, can you believe?'

I can, thought Shev. Unfortunately, I can.

'That's why we settled on "pink." Oh, Isla and I did quarrel over that one.' He let out a long sigh. 'That's the size of it; the whole shooting match in a nutshell. It's a big, big night tonight and I don't want you to miss it, but there is something you need to do before you go. it won't take a moment.' He continued to fashion the powder as if he were unsatisfied with the shape of the line.

Shev moved closer to get better footage on her button-cam. Al Shabah went silent, lost in his work, then muttered, 'What of me? Al-Shabah? *Al-Jamie?* Did the ghost become the collector or the collector become the ghost?' Done with the momentary reflection, his black eyes flicked back up to Shev's, and the intensity of his stare caused her an undefinable pain. He shifted back to control and aggression and jabbed a vicious finger. 'I need you to come over here and hoover this up, right now! Then you can go, safe and sound. A little bump, I think they call it.'

'Nah. It looks a bit moreish, and I'm bad enough with Digestives.'

Her response stunned him; he was clearly unprepared for Cally wit and hands-on-hips sarcasm in the face of cold-blooded murder.

'You really are fucking mad, aren't you? It's not happening, and I'm off. Fuck ya.' She turned on her heel and headed off, carried by terror and the stark reality of imminent death; she'd never walked so fast whilst feeling so slow in her life.

She was almost at the corner of the labs when al Shabah called after her, 'Perhaps I can persuade you. Look.'

Shev glanced over her shoulder and stopped dead. The two screens were now divided into four separate feeds. They showed shaky button-cam footage of the same place with different aspects. She recognised the railings, red brickwork, kiddies' play area and billowing laundry. It was the Cally estate, and the ferals were darting in and out of view, fired up like she'd never seen them and going to war. In their little hands were machetes, tapped on the iron hand rails, making sinister music as they ascended the staircase three steps at a time and then ploughed along the balcony. In front of Flat 209, they hammered at the door with the blade handles. Granny B opened it, and they pushed inside, screaming and raising their weapons.

'No! No! Stop it! No!' Shev yelled, and she ran at al Shabah.

He tapped his keyboard. 'There, there—paused. Get your fat nose into this and it stops for good.' He held out the straw. 'Then you can go and pass on my good tidings to the King of England. A magnificent night awaits you.'

Something stirred deep inside her, deeper than any imagined dark well, awakening all her latent passions, combined and amplified—fear, anger, love, hate—into something beyond definition. Every slight and indignity, through the White Bear tear-up and all the rest, way back: *the forgotten dream, knee-high in the smoky flat, the music and hunger, tears and cries that no one could hear. The beautiful red-haired woman, the dread-locked black man, both asleep, who would not wake. So hungry, the acrid stench, sickly sweet, burnt foil and vomit and then the man came and opened the curtains. He stopped the music and used the phone holding a handkerchief; a red handkerchief. Her cries and those of the seagulls morphed into police sirens, and the man turned to leave, out the back. At last, she remembered the face—he turned before leaving, and she saw the kind eyes of a young Mr Snow.*

Shev approached the fiend, step by slow step, fists curled and clenched by her side, and drew breath from the soles of her feet. Then it came, louder than she'd ever yelled before; from deep beyond those depths and condensed memories, way back to times long before her own, the primordial tone and vibration preceded civilisation. All pain was distilled and sent forth as an unknowable sonic barbed projectile.

Like water on tissue, fear bloomed across al Shabah's face from a speck of concern to full-blown terror. He drew back in shock and recognition of overwhelming force, like a boxer caught flush on the chin. He grasped his throat and raised onto his tiptoes, his features contorting as his head smashed down into the transparent desktop, as if in a vain attempt to destroy it. A cloud of his powdered poison swelled into the air. He jerked bolt upright, still grasping his throat. His skull's impact repeated five more times, each with higher velocity, whip-lashing the ebony mane, as if some invisible strap behind his neck was attached to a massive weight plummeting down, deep beneath the concrete floor.

His nose was flattened into his face, and his features became a red pulp. Then, in silence, the limp body of Nadeem al Shabah slithered down to the ground. Shev stood stock-still as the rage dissipated, and she glanced back at the screen. The footage showed laughter and playful clips around the ear as the ferals left the flat, each with cupcakes as was the tradition but this time in exchange for the weapons. She caught sight of Granny B's fine beautiful features and thought she could discern a blown kiss. Then she darted down to her would-be saviour and took his hand.

'Mr Snow … how? Why? Hang on. Special Forces are coming. Hang on, Mr Snow.'

'Shev. No choice. My father … my father's father.' Snow's words were rattling and faint. 'Sworn, a spell, since … Always to protect … you.'

Shev could hear the clack and chop of the rotors above, the air pressure rattling the corrugated roof, further drowning out Snow's whispered words as the entrance door burst open, and the powdered air was sliced with a web of red laser sights.

Shev bent down until his lips touched her ear. ‘Always for the … last of you. Dora. Dora’s coming. Slipper … shell. Slippersh …’

Chapter 17

GLIMMER

Shev was hooded, cuffed and dragged backwards by crushing vices on each arm above the elbow. Her legs paddled in thin air, as if suspended above a too-fast treadmill, and she heard Bradley's voice shouting, 'Ours, ours, ours!'

She hit the ground, her right shoulder first, only to be yanked up again by the other arm. In the muffled darkness, she expected to take a nose-flattening punch that she couldn't see coming. More pushing, shoving, and voices filled with urgency and testosterone. Two-word orders were barked and acknowledged between Scots, Scousers, and a Cockney in the distance. Above them all, the overwhelming hack and downward push of the Merlin helicopter's rotors, which were held by the pilot a notch below take-off velocity.

The only jargon she understood was, 'Agent A

confirmed for exit. Two X down.' The Scotsman was nearest; the response was inaudible.

A flash of blinding daylight as the hood was whipped off, followed by her cuffs and a thump in the back, straight into the arms of Bradley's embrace. Then came a heavy slap on her aggrieved shoulder and a shove further into Bradley's chest, sending them both backwards.

She glanced back to the hanger as Bradley half-carried her away from the action and towards the waiting Range Rover. There, a squad of troops kitted to the nines, their helmets topped by the totem-like stalks of visual tech, were moving with the coordinated efficiency and drive of an ant colony. They had guns covering all angles, as the workers stripped the joint of its booty like camouflaged termites, back and forth, to and from the chopper. In the midst of the raid, two occupied stretchers were carried from the hanger, one attached to a drip.

'The back. I'll go in the back!' screamed Shev above the racket. Bradley obliged and opened the door.

'Bloody right you will!' He pushed her in, and they were off with a screech. Shev was flung against the window as they cornered out of the car park with a squirt of acceleration, and she looked back to catch the undercarriage of the Merlin roaring away, low and fast over the beach and out to sea.

'They left that bit out of the pop-up ad: clean underwear and change of clothes required following operations … Or a peg for your nose,' said Shev.

Her voice wobbled and was raised by an octave, and she began the task of cleaning and changing. The bag was there for the wipes and clothing, as she addressed the unholy mess she'd become, soiled with her own fear and Snow's clotting plasma.

They passed the harbour and raced away into the Icelandic wild that sat between civilisations.

'Clingfilm's effective,' Bradley said at last, in response to her comment. 'Contacts with the enemy and Para wings have something in common: brown trousers are compulsory. A rite of passage. Welcome to the club.' He met her eyes in the rear view mirror. 'There's foil, blankets and a flask on the floor to your left.'

Shev began cocooning herself with the blankets. 'They had a drip on NaS. My God. They need to bind that fucker tight, and I mean really tight.'

'I caught a glimpse behind Heavy Lift, as we got to you. You totalled him.'

'I don't know what the fuck happened, sir. Well … actually I do. The cunt killed Mr Snow. Point-blank, in cold blood.' She dropped back down to her typical pitch. 'The fucker.'

'The man down? This Mr Snow—you knew him?'

'This is a whole new world of crazy. He was my next-door neighbour. You should have seen it on the deep trawl screening or whatever you call it. Mr Snow. I trained with him in Krav Maga, and then he flitted just after I joined, as it goes. I couldn't make this up. I heard nothing from UT4.'

'I had a visual all that time. I didn't see him go in,' said Bradley, exonerating himself from the crime of non-intervention. He released a chuckle that was a blend of relief and disbelief. 'You did it. I'd just parked up and saw your feed was on and off. I called in Heavy Lift straight away. Anyway, I've seen more than my fill of what you'd call mad shit but carry on … if you want to.'

'I spotted Mr Snow in Nice, but I couldn't get to him. Then we're here, and he's in there with a fucking machine gun pointed at NaS, telling me to get out. I told you what happened next. As for mashing NaS, I didn't touch him; you'll see that on the cam. I was at least eight metres away. I didn't touch him, and neither did Mr Snow.' Shev dropped her head against the window and took in the landscape. Bradley let silence reign, except for the purr of the tyres on the tarmac, and she soon drifted off.

A moment later, she snapped back awake. 'You'll see it all on the TAVS feed. NaS ID'd me and Mr Snow using FRS, and he got to Gran in no time, sir. It's over—they're so powerful, so fast. "Actions on order, just like a cab." Those were his words. Something insidious.'

'Insidious? It looks that way. Whatever happened in there today—and something did indeed happen—Al Shabah's out of action and under lock and key. Max security, en route to Blighty.'

'I'm deadly serious. He's got to be bound, gagged and then some. I've never been as angry, and

I remembered something bad that happened yonks back; it all flooded over me. Snow was there at the Brighton flat twenty years ago, I'm sure of it, but it was like a forgotten dream. NaS said his real name and that he was ex-Mossad.'

'Did you catch anything from Snow before he went?'

'He garbled something about protection, like he'd always been there. He mentioned his dad … Adore. He kept saying "adore". A dying man, losing his mind … maybe.'

Bradley took a call on the holographic channel; the ultra appeared on the windscreen head-up. *'UT4 back on the net. Footage from GLIMMER cam uploaded. Heavy Lift stripped the site of all tech and chemical evidence. Porton have confirmed The NNT content of the drug. Revolutionary nano technology allowing temporary control of neural stimulators via an XG network signal. Making its users highly suggestable. The signal itself an erratic pulse originating via the LINX, that's why we couldn't detect it but we can now track along with the distribution network of the drug. The anaesthetic content of the drug prevents an initial allergic reaction. Observations have found the euphoria of the hit is followed by actions suggested within the XG signal. In line with our evidence. Physical symptoms include damage to nasal lining and extreme dilation of the pupils. That's all for now. See you back here. Out.'*

'There we have it, GLIMMER,' said Bradley. 'She'll sift it. Best book your flights back now.'

'Are they gonna stop it? The signal, I mean?'

He was silent for a moment, then sighed. 'No,

GLIMMER. Like she said, they're going to follow it, like a marked five-pound note, to see where it all leads.'

They were alone on the road, fast and silent, cleaving through a rich verdant dish of Húnavatnshreppur. The sun was lost to the peak of Jörundarfell, its rays shedding a memory of gold and teal as it set.

'*Autumn Stone*, please,' Shev piped up, like a child requesting a bedtime story. 'I'd like *Autumn Stone*.' Bradley said nothing and obliged in selected the song.

The passing show of outstanding natural beauty and air fresher than ice, combined with the lilting rhythm and flautist's touch, was the magic antidote to offset the vision and sensations of ultra-violence, cold-blooded murder and the loss of bodily control.

'There's a hell of a night ahead,' said Bradley. 'If you're still up for it. The roads are clear. We'll be back at the hotel for 2200 hrs.'

There was no answer. She was fast asleep once more.

'Enjoy yourself, it's later than you think,' sang Bradley as she exited the lift on her floor.

Upon entry to the room, she was greeted by the debris, but not the perpetrator. The Do Not Disturb tag on the door handle had deterred the housekeepers. According to Shev's itinerary, Biff would be at the *Kaffibarinn*.

'Sweet Jesus,' she uttered, reviewing all the telltale signs of a Biff jolly-up: sweet wrappers, crisp packets and empties strewn in every direction.

She retrieved the laptop from the safe, thankful that her 'boyf' had retained some basic common sense. She checked the blog posts and was pleased to see he'd done his work well. A clanging headache had bloomed to maturity between her temples, requiring instant medication. A Kombucha from the mini bar washed the bitter taste of paracetamol from her tongue. She pulled off the tracksuit to incredible relief. Green tea, and ordered well-done steak-wich from Room Service with all trimmings to follow a volcanic jacuzzi—that was what was needed, really needed. Robin Biffta Clifton could wait; she'd texted and called, he wasn't responding, but Find My Phone still placed him at *Kaffibarinn*. Unless, of course, he'd lost it.

10:45 pm. Her belly full, now clean and scrubbed up, the complimentary dressing gown seeming beyond snug, Shev awaited Biff's return. The app showed he was on his way back. A quick blow-dry, and she'd be all set.

Granny B was the forefront of her mind, but she resisted calling, as she was technically still on an operation. Intuition told her all was well; there had never been a concern until she saw what was unfolding on those screens.

Shev was sitting on the bed, drying her hair, when the door opened and Biff's frame mooched through. She switched off and grabbed a handful of mousse, working it into her corkscrew curls for a big-hair night. 'Thanks for the pigsty, hon. I'll be ready in ten. Whatchya think of it so far?'

She turned as he ambled over for his usual bear hug and was braced for a blast of beery breath, always icky when she was stone-cold sober, but she wrapped her arms around his love handles to receive him nonetheless.

The large, soft hands grasped her neck, and she was lifted up and off the floor, the grip instantly tightening. Nails and fingers dug deep into her flesh, crushing her circulation and breathing. She caught sight of the eyes, those of a doll's, set in Biff's pudgy, tanned face. Seconds seemed like minutes. He turned and carried her, kicking and scratching for a short distance, before drawing her close. Then there was a new agony as the back of her head impacted against the wardrobe. Her jabs to his ribs, body and arms had no effect. Blinded by tears and pain, the shape in front of her grew distant, the darkness hemmed in, and her arms felt like lead. No! Shev landed another ineffective kick below his ribs, and from the fulcrum of her wrist, her back-fist *uraken* snapped down onto his nose like a medieval mace smashing an apple, over and over, as the tide of silent darkness rose and engulfed her.

She heard her own rasp of inhalation, like the inversion of a punctured balloon. Her lungs were in survival reflex to intake maximum oxygen through a narrow passage. On the third attempt, she managed to lift a half-ton arm to clear her eyes.

'Mmmmmm.' The moan came from above. She was at his feet, foetal, sandwiched between him and the wardrobe. He loomed above her like a tracksuited shard. Both hands were at his face, and he moaned again, as if stirring from a deep slumber. With the fourth rasping breath, she drew strength enough to crawl free.

The distance was everything, the flesh either side of her windpipe screaming. She touched wetness and saw bright red on the soft white sleeves of the dressing gown; a combination of hers and Biff's. She was now on the far side, away behind the bed. She'd been overwhelmed in the shock of the attack, the old adage of 'the first strike wins on the street' proving to be grimly true. Now, she was ready for a full-throttle domestic, and she was angry—furious, in fact—at the violation and perversion of gentle Biff and the attack itself. Struggling to kettle the emotion, she clambered to her feet.

Biff turned to face her. He was a hot mess of scratches and a pulped face. A thick crimson stripe ran from his nose down past his navel, but his doll-like eyes were unblinking. Biff lumbered forward like an Egyptian mummy, intent on completing his task.

There was only one technique that came to the top of Shev's unarmed combat index: Combination 4b—the front kick and one-legged-punch. Her right foot kicked and carried through with the secondary twist of the hip, and her left-hand was open in a counterbalanced guard. As the technique reached terminal velocity, she raised onto the toes of her left supporting leg, and the ball of her right foot tore into Biff's torso above the hip and carried on forwards, taking in the internal organs, diaphragm and lower ribs.

The speed of the impact kept his feet stationary, jack-knifing his body forwards. Shev's kicking leg pulled back behind her, and she met Biff's approaching head, substituting a *jun-zuki* punch for a *hiji-ate* elbow strike. The impact of the pointed bone of her arm behind his ear, combined with the applied physics of their colliding bodies, rendered him instantly unconscious.

As he went down, Shev tucked in with her momentum and rolled back-to-back across his shoulders and to her feet with *zanshin.* What was once harmless Robin 'DJ Biffta' Clifton was laid face down, spark-out unconscious on the ash wood floor. His breathing was steady but laboured. Wary of another recovery and attack, she pulled off the dressing gown belt and lashed his arms behind his back, then pulled him upright against the bed and repeated the process with his legs. Then she called Bradley.

'Pulse is fine. Eyes are fine. Nice egg behind his ear. Internals—nothing frightening on the surface; we'll see when he comes round. Breathing is no issue, so no punctured lung. No doubt a cracked rib or two.'

'Or three,' said Shev, without remorse.

'Let's get him on the bed and into recovery.'

They struggled with Biff's eighteen stone deadweight and rearranged the ties.

'"A magnificent night awaits you,"'—that's what that maniac al Shabah said back there. No doubt sorting out his booby trap/goodbye present while I was standing there.' Her eyes welled. 'Poor Biff.'

'Poor you,' said Bradley in genuine sympathy.

'Poor us. Biff's toss-up: heads, he's the *Shevalogue* Culture Night strangler of Reykjavik with me stone dead at his feet or tails, he's battered mess and I'm stood here with a ragged neck, weeping about it.'

'Thank God it fell on tails. I'm going to get out and get everything I need to clean and patch you both up. Don't open the door to anyone but me.'

'Ohhh babe, what happened? What happened?'

Biff repeated the question over and over, like a scratched CD. The plea turned into a weeping whine. Shev looked deep into his eyes; those of Robin Clifton, blue-grey and bloodshot, bore no resemblance now to those of a child's toy. She cut him loose. He winced as he breathed, holding his side, then touched the plasters and dressings on his face and his flattened nose, wincing again.

'I was a bit late back, Biff. You went down that Blur pub and got totally fuckin' shitfaced. Did you start tooting with some wrong 'uns?'

His eyes began to dart left and right as they did when he was at a loss, then much more to the left, which the Hive had stipulated indicated fabrication. 'Nahhh. Oh, nahhh, babe. Just beers and optics with the locals. Tooting? Chisel? Disgusting. That's disgusting shit. You know me.'

Unfortunately, she did. Shev's eyes narrowed before she feigned sympathy.

'I do, babe … I got there, and some neo-Nazi Vikings took exception to us and off it went. You got a shoeing and one got me from behind and did this.' She pointed to the dressings on the sides of her neck. 'Then I did 'em both. Mr B got us back here and patched us up; he was an Army medic when he was young, you know. No real harm done, but you were off your nut. You wanted to go back and kill 'em, so we lashed you up for your own safety.'

Biff pulled the meanest face his injuries would allow. 'Fucking right I did! Fucking … 'slandic slags!' His eyes flicked to the left once again, and Shev stifled a giggle. 'You'll mend, babe; we both will. It was all too good to be true, wasn't it; there had to be some rough in it.' Biff shrugged and gave a meek nod.

'Your posts are great, though, Biff. Total likes-ville.' There was a crackle and fizz audible from outside. 'It almost midnight. Shall we go and see the fireworks from the roof, mate?' suggested Shev.

'And the Northern Lights!' added Biff, with a painful smile as the Eighth Day drew to a close.

Chapter 18

TAKING X

2320 hrs August 12th 202?

Ellesborough, UK

The shockwaves emanating from Dewhurst's intelligence report had crystallised into physical action.

Two of the four vehicles passed through the village nose to tail, and bared down hard on their destination through the unlit country roads of Buckinghamshire. It was precisely one hour and ten minutes since they had set off from New Scotland Yard and, as planned to the second, their blue pulse began from the dash, sidelights and radiator grill bracketed by the drystone walls.

Back in the capital, their sisters headed over Embankment Bridge towards South London. It was an ominous sight: twin blacked-out Range Rovers with blue lights, no sirens.

*

'I'm going up,' said the Chief's long suffering wife, Emily. 'My eyes are going, and my legs are jumping. No point fighting it.'

She pulled herself up from a reclining position on the sofa, dislodging their Russian blue cat, who nonchalantly leapt onto the lap of his other mistress.

The lounge was furnished with taste and decorated in Farrow and Ball neutrals. Its focal point was the Victorian tiled fireplace crowned with a curved screen TV that exceeded the width of the chimney breast. On the side wall hung a broad red and black Rothko of similar dimension. The remaining wall space was finely balanced with Naval oils and memorabilia, career highs and presentations and chrome-framed blow-ups of Emily's children and grandchildren. All were clustered around a print of a teenage girl and an old man embracing, pulled close either side of a young soldier in a maroon beret.

'I'm expecting someone. Can you hang on for the door?' said Dewhurst.

'What? At this time?'

'It's work, and they're due any minute. I'm sorry.' She rose to embrace, disturbing the cat once again, but Emily pulled away.

'Work, of course! Half ele … sorry, 2347 hrs on a Saturday night? Bollocks, you deal with it.'

Dewhurst grasped her arms and wrapped a

desperate clinging embrace, pushing her head hard to her wife's, causing her to flinch with its intensity. 'I'm so, so sorry. Please just do this.'

'Whoa, whoa, honey. Settle down, chill, OK? No bother. OK?' She reciprocated the hug, and their mouths met, expressing affection as they'd rarely done over the last week. Dewhurst's face was streaked with tears, a rare show of such emotion, even behind closed doors.

'I do …' Fifteen years together, and Dewhurst still struggled to say it.

'Sure, I know,' yawned Emily. After fifteen years with Charlie, she also knew not to ask if everything was OK, because it never was. Her wife had been on eggshells all week, and there was nothing she could do about it, only be there for her whenever the shit settled. 'And *I know*,' she added. That completed the private saying between them since Dewhurst moved into Naval Intelligence; it had been rested for a whole year of retirement before the Soon went rogue and SIS came calling.

Dewhurst straightened up. 'I'll be in the study, not the office.' She slid past, went to the front of the house, opened the blinds a crack and switched on the reading light by the window.

*

The first two range rovers were through were through the country house's three perimeter checkpoints with little argument, all docs checked, the emergency code for the day exchanged, phones and radios of those manning them confiscated. They drove straight up the gravel drive, and eight men disembarked and swept aside the external security with the same ease. They were in.

The visitors could deal with any internal resistance, even from their own, but the security here were much lower down the Special Branch food chain, and stood aside with a deferential nod as the SO20 men entered the building. They swept through the party like they were storming into a yacht, filtering through the guests like large deft ghost hounds, on the trail of their objective. A couple of junior ministers, merry with champagne and fuelled by the fatal combination of misplaced loyalty, pathological ambition pink powder tried to intervene and were swatted to one side, spewing toothless threats.

The pack had the scent and moved on to the scullery.

*

Dewhurst had settled in when she saw the first flicker of blue light, in perfect tick-tock rhythm as the vehicles rounded the corner and approached.

They took her back to Coventry, gazing down from her bedroom window all those years ago, the deathly pale policewoman with the worst of tasks and all that followed. The *Coventry Evening Telegraph* had printed the antithesis of a headline, bottom corner, page six: Local Private Marcus Derek Dewhurst of 2nd Battalion Parachute Regiment died in police custody after an arrest for drunk and disorderly in the town centre. A few more paltry lines, then 'more to follow'.

Only it never did. It said nothing of Grandad's broken heart or Derek's absence and permanent silence. Their line was that he'd resisted arrest and they didn't deviate. After the funeral, it was the unspoken rule: we don't talk about it. For it was as buried as he was. Only his pictures, the memories and his music remained.

The revenge taken from that day forth was for Charlotte Dewhurst to win. Win and pass every test, break every door, ceiling and jaw if necessary, to get there and prevail. Win for Derek. Forty years of it until this, brother and sister finally joined in fate. The pulsing blues were still and at full strength. She cradled the preselected hardback edition of Kerry Hudson's *Lowborn* as a suitable shield; the last purpose its author could have intended. The SIG P365 sub-compact pistol fitted her hand like the proverbial glove.

A triumph in ergonomics, ideal for the female operative. She chuckled to herself, the snub-nose tight against the central binding of the pages, completing its perfect utility. Ten rounds, ten headshots. Ambitious, even for a Bisley veteran. The second clip for afters was snug in her dressing gown pocket, should it come to that. Rear Admiral Charlotte Dewhurst, DBE, and Chief of the Secret Intelligence Service will not die at the hands of the Others, she told herself, shrugging her shoulders to shed tension as the doorbell went.

She estimated ten seconds. The first entered the

study in eight. The cluster of black-clad SO20 heathens fanned out as they approached, arms down, their Glocks remaining holstered. She didn't move a muscle and took the breath with which she would exhale as she moved and squeezed the trigger. The lead man continued his approach and raised his right hand as she settled on a firing sequence. Held in the black leather glove now extended towards her, she could see a thin black rectangle.

'May I, ma'am?'

She nodded and smiled. Behind the book, her thumb disabled the safety. Any second now, it's goodnight from me and it's goodnight from him, she thought as her trigger finger limbered to squeeze and she released and recharged her breath deep into her diaphragm.

The leader opened the rectangle, revealing a Surface and projected eight holographic screens. He checked his watch against the digits displayed in each corner as all nine people in the study observed the live footage. Entry into a room, one by one, eight separate feeds.

A semi-naked concubine was slumped on the sofa; a bouffanted head attached to a squat, bare-chested torso ran its tongue along the length of her leg from knee to the top of her thigh, making porcine snorts and grunts. It momentarily nuzzled deeper into the crotch, as oblivious to the eight observers as the giggling lady-friend as she spread her legs as far as they would go. The giver looked up, the rosy powdered nose and glassy doll's eyes mismatched by the shameless smirk so familiar and repellent to all.

The closest officer dictated the Caution, words that the listener had ridiculed before the nation's media on more than one occasion, which prompted him to flop back on the sofa and let out a long roar of maniacal, hysterical laughter. The concubine's braying created a bizarre, debauched duet. From eight vantage points, Dewhurst saw the same scene, each with date and time, which she constantly checked against her watch in vigilance of Deep Fake deception.

The submission of the report and its findings two hours before had been a massive gamble; a hellish test. Equivalent of calling heads before a tossed coin fell, was covered and then revealed beyond sight, whilst she was face down on a guillotine with its pull-cord and her life in the Director General of the Others—the domestic security service.

She imagined the carnage that Emily would find in the study, had the gamble gone the other way. Her imminent reunion with Derek appeared to be postponed, for the time being

.

'All is in hand now, I trust?' enquired Dewhurst. The lead officer gave a purposeful nod and folded the tablet. 'Then thank you, gentlemen.'

As she spoke, her phone rang. She was not surprised by the identity of the caller, but more what appeared to be their loyalty in the face of relentless corruption at almost the highest level. 'I must take this. Will that be all? Good evening, do show yourselves out.'

She maintained her grip on the pistol and its position and heard the slam of the door to the street and the two vehicles starting up and pulling away.

She answered the phone with her left hand. 'Good evening, Minister … thank you. Yes, indeed … yes. Yes!'

A second call came in and was placed on hold. It was her erstwhile executioner, rival, and saviour, the DGO, and she would have to wait. 'I must congratulate you, Acting Prime Minister,' continued the Chief, 'despite these unfortunate circumstances. Indeed, God Save the King. Goodnight and God bless.'

She sighed the tension away, sank further into the chair for a moment of silent reflection and then blinked away the stress. At last, she clicked the safety back in place, snapped the book closed and stroked the Sig's cold, snub barrel along the length of her high, fine cheekbone. She went up to Emily, who was dead to the world, and administered the antidote to ensure the condition was temporary. Finally, she took the Director General's call and discussed the taking of Subject X.

*

It was a Monday morning at Vauxhall Cross like no other; the fallout had been dealt with around the clock, with exhaustion only kept at bay with industrial strength coffee. After a final burst of incandescent madness, at last it was time to close. The jousting was over.

The Chief spoke.'BREAKSPEAR, where the hell do I begin? Everything we required, a different level. But for our loss, the casualty; a terrible blow. There really aren't any words.'

Bradley bowed his head in sombre acknowledgement. 'She was the price. The alternative was the end of everything. That close.' He pinched his fingers together. 'Within a margin of seconds, we would never have known.'

An hour earlier, they had sat in the same space with UT4 to the left and Shev to the right. All were before the Chief and under the gaze of her oil-on-canvas inquisitor, Sir Francis Walsingham, whose eyes seemed, for the first time, to have exchanged suspicion for warmth and possibly even pride.

From the Chief came cliched terms such as 'baptism of lightning in this Invisible Storm' and acknowledgement of 'meeting the challenge of an ever-evolving and mutable threat as you have done, and as we as a Service must continue to do so without relent.' It was all delivered with balanced force. 'NaS is being held here. Completely securely in our *special* facility downstairs.' She made the emphasis due to the threat he posed to both young women. 'He's recovered well enough for interrogation but has remained silent so far. But the Others are very persistent in their methods.' She paused for a moment, then gestured to the Ultra. 'UT4, you have the floor. Your presentation, please.'

Amira remained seated and brought up the

holographic screen from her Surface:

'This is Miss Isla Jónsdóttir. Icelandic national, elementary computer science ingénue and a graduate of the American Nanotech Institute. There has been no direct communication with her by friends, family or colleagues for a year. This was six months after she left Reykjavik and arrived in Australia, last seen in the vicinity of Pine Gap. This footage was posted the first week she got there, at a party. Look here.'

She zoomed in on a man sharing an intimate embrace with Isla and showed the couple becoming ever closely acquainted throughout the night. His were the rugged, unmistakable features of Nadeem al Shabah.

'But in June this year, Isla started posting on FaceBook, same time, same day, weekly from various locations. Just touristy stuff, steady flow. The posts continued even yesterday, look—but it's all from a sophisticated bot. Deep Fake.'

'This is *the* Isla?' asked Bradley.

UT4 nodded. 'The technology was beyond anything we've seen and existed only in theory. In the footage from GLIMMER's TAVS feed, al Shabah stated it was, "Isla's architecture and she had to go."'

'We have to wonder at the level of coercion and control she was under,' Dewhurst considered. 'Possibly she was a willing accomplice at first, until she realised what she was dealing with in that creature. Used, abused, collected and discarded.'

UT4 went on. 'Exactly, ma'am. Things changed. She left us a present.' Her eyes narrowed, and her forehead crumpled to a scowl in momentary recollection. 'A present of a dormant cyber pathogen, a tech-ping, subtle enough not to alert him but enough to red flag us.

'A message in the ether. Spouted by three disparate individuals hooked on Pink and the *Eighth Day* promise: a star in the shape of d'Orly, a somebody in Rub-a-dub and a nobody in Distance the plasterer. Isla Jónsdóttir alerted us to her creation from beyond the grave by spotlighting al Shabah's puppets. A very subtle ripple effect of a disruption within the algorithm. Not too implicit or too vague, enough for him to miss but for us to pick up.'

Bradley added, 'I have to say the Icelandic hub location was ingenious. Isla's home, North of Europe. The lab plotted up on the far side of the island, effectively with their back to the world, and from there, they could facilitate manufacture, export and the dissemination of Pink from street level up, through county lines beyond the capital. So, it seems, after testing in the UK from June, they were about to expand the distribution of Pink across Europe, with the imminent new XG network agreement signed off and active on the Eighth Day.'

'Chaos for sale. Mag-fi gone massive,' added Shev.

'Mag-fi?' Dewhurst asked what the others were thinking.

'It's when someone on your doorstep cracks your broadband for criminal activity, opening the bill payer to blackmail and incriminations.'

They were all impressed. 'The Hive?' asked the Chief.

Shev shook her head. 'The Cally, ma'am.'

UT4 explained, 'Just to clarify, GLIMMER is absolutely right, the mag-fi she described at street level was achieved by Eighth Day's compromising of the LINX.'

'Well, there we have it,' said the Chief. 'From the pavement up and up, to the very–' She broke off and addressed those gathered directly and sincerely. 'I appreciate the … personal complexities, but we have him. It's closed.'

'The forensic analysis from the Heavy Lift is almost complete,' UT4 said. 'I'll have it in before midnight.'

The Chief smiled, a most endangered and brilliant smile that even took Bradley aback. 'Thank you, UT4.' There was pause for thought. 'And thank you, GLIMMER,' said the Chief, without making eye contact.

Shev understood the dismissal. 'Thank you, ma'am,' she said and rose to leave on the heels of her colleague.

'I'll see you downstairs in the Bay. Wait there,' added Bradley.

They were alone, apart from Walsingham, Mother Seacole and the safety-pinned Queen.

'Maximus Lane was picked up from his toy by Heavy Lift off Gibraltar and the DGO has assured me he is singing like a butterball canary. D'Orly arrived today for the LINX meeting as planned and is being voluntarily interviewed, with the coordination and cooperation of DGSE. Beyond her, we haven't traced any evidence of conspiracy theories yet.'

'Not yet,' mused Bradley.

'Exactly,' the Chief agreed, 'but the deep sifting's just begun. The LINX is now secure—for the moment. But, as we've found, what is a moment in our world?'

'It's normally something that's already passed,' Bradley added with no hint of sarcasm.

'I want GLIMMER's final debrief, medical and evaluation concluded by EOP. Thenceforth, BARBELL will be deactivated.'

'The end of play will be fine, ma'am. There may be further information to glean from GLIMMER in addition to all we have.' He rose and buttoned his suit jacket. 'By the method of an old-fashioned brew.'

The dissipation of tension had moved them somewhere close to the realm of an ordinary conversation, the last in a week of firsts.

'This has to be the closest equivalent we've ever had to a narco-tech Gunpowder Plot, and the country is completely oblivious,' said the Chief. 'Even your most lurid War Gaming couldn't see this far.'

'If it hadn't happened, you'd laugh me out the room and into an asylum.' Bradley took a moment to sip his D&B. 'All those BARBELL reports, *The Stasi Changeling, The Malefici, Afgolem, Jiin, Dragaur* and the other assorted goodies.' He realised he was becoming animated, so he sat back and crossed his legs again.

'They're exactly where they should be,' Dewhurst cut in. 'Bought, paid for and boxed away in Registry, safely away from those of a nervous disposition.'

'Indeed, but now it's physically here with us. Right here! Sitting downstairs with a cup of tea.' With that he headed down to the Bay.

The old spy passed the crested leather coaster, all Trojan helmet heraldry, followed by a mug of latte printed with the same. 'Good, aren't they?' he commented as Shev showed her enchantment with the design.

He took his seat. 'I think C will wrap this today, so listen out for *meows*.'

Shev nodded in silent affirmation, checked her phone and lightly touched the fresh dressings on her neck. 'It's bloody itching. It means it's healing, according to Gran.'

'Did she get over that "episode?"' asked Bradley.

'Sure, nothing fazes her. It freaked me out, but trust me, I'd be more worried for those little sods.'

'So how's Biff?'

'He's over it,' said Shev flicking the coaster. 'It was an amazing experience, despite our little straightener. When we got home he swallowed everything I told him; that his back's perfectly fine, that he should get out polishing, that the *Shevalogue*'s old news now, and that he should work on his *Biff Cast* and … and that he should find someone else.' She looked crushed with sadness for a milli-second before blooming into a wide smile. 'As he's a Z-leb now!'

They sipped in silence for a moment.

'Something's still bugging you?' asked Bradley.

'There was something that NaS said, clear as day, about the family that I can't shake, and another thing about collecting that made no sense at the time, but it chimes with what C said about Isla. About her being collected and discarded.'

'Let me check the transcript. One moment.' Bradley pulled out his phone, demonstrating the godlike capability of maximum clearance on the operation, and read the passage of transcript aloud.

'See what I mean?' Shev said.

Bradley stiffened; he rose, walked out of earshot and made a call. 'Lab, BREAKSPEAR. This is imperative to be actioned immediately- I'm requesting immediate DNA comparison samples, historical and current, from Nadeem al Shabah to be cross-checked for comparisons to the Service personnel database. Send results direct to my device. Straight back. I'm waiting.'

He returned to his seat, attempting a reassuring smile, which was unnoticed by Shev as she stared wistfully out onto the Thames. Bradley's phone buzzed, and as he examined the message, his face drained of colour.

'What's the matter?' asked Shev.

He speed-dialed another number. 'Only everything,' he answered, with his phone to his ear. 'UT4, Call me straight back when you get this.'

'What's her button-cam showing?'

'Brilliant. Of course.' He brought up the hologram, and it took him further down into the depths of dread: NaS was across the interrogation table, eyes rolling, his head tilted and convulsing. 'Down to the basement straight away, you've got to stop this!' shouted Bradley. 'I'll follow!'

Shev vaulted down the core staircase reached the holding cell and met the armed resistance, a six-foot-four lump whom she was not going to reason with. A combination *yon-ken* knuckle strike to the throat and *fumikomi* stamping kick to the inside knee laced with an ear bursting *kiai* totalled him. She pulled his sidearm and swipe and was in.

UT4 was sat mirroring NaS's convulsions and position exactly. On the floor, either side of her chair, were the bodies of the interrogators, still and lifeless. As Shev took aim, Nadeem's eyes blinked open. She felt like she was immersed in ice water, unable to swim free from the familiar dreadful feeling of clammy tentacles coiling around her neck, while others violated every orifice and seemed to crush her inner organs.

With every ounce of strength, she tried to move, only succeeding in loosening the grip on the Glock, which now dangled from her trigger finger. Her breathing was reduced to shallow gasps. The ceiling panel lights began to flash in sync with the alarm bathing the room in red.

The darkness was coming again, last seen at the hands of Biff; on its edge, she saw the slim platinum-topped form enter the room. It reached out, took the gun from her hand and levelled it at the seated, quivering man, as she had moments before.

With the last of her strength, she managed to force a whisper through gritted teeth, 'Her … stop! It's … *her*!'

Bradley saw the pain and desperation and heard the words, then he smashed the butt of the Glock into the nape of UT4's neck. She slumped forwards, and the kinetic energy that held Shev released her to the floor and diverted straight to Bradley, slamming him against the back wall.

The Tree. It was her gift to Nadeem al Shabah four months early. No tinsel or baubles. Just the tree. She delivered its shape in bullet holes with instinctive accuracy.

It was her heartfelt present in return for all he'd given and taken over the last week, and indeed the last twenty years, all told: international terrorism, murder, the abduction and abuse of a minor and a direct threat to butcher her grandmother—two rounds to the forehead, two more to either side of the sternum. The head dropped back with a long gargling exhalation, and the beautiful, blank eyes stared up at the ceiling. She put a group of four in and around the larynx, shattering the vertebrae, on exit. 'Merry fucking Christmas.'

Shev checked on UT4; she was spark-out but breathing. Bradley was getting to his feet. She passed the gun. He loosened the clip, pulled back the slide and then placed it on the table. He was still breathless; her ears still rang from the shots and the shrieking alarm, but she read his lips as he said, 'Copy me. It'll be fine.' He struggled back down onto his knees and placed his hands on his head. Shev followed suit. The security burst in, and despite the mayhem, she focused on her slumped slain target and considered that she'd never noticed the gold amid the shark-like teeth or the redness of his hair.

*

'I can't deny your theory any more than anything within those BARBELL reports,' said Dewhurst as she tried to reconcile the morning's events. 'That NaS was attempting some kind of mind-transfer seems as feasible as anything else.'

'That was his long game. He caught us, not the other way round,' mused Bradley. 'We brought him to our table; that was his mission, to be in proximity to UT4, gambling that her curiosity and desire for revenge would overcome her professionalism, exposing herself to him. It paid off. He was moments away from absolute victory. We'd have been left with a catatonic NaS, and UT4 walks away to carry on his good work.'

Dewhurst was in agreement. 'On that basis, his sting partially succeeded by taking her out. She's safely sedated now. We can't know right now the degree of psychological damage or contamination. We'll watch, listen, analyse, and she won't know she's a prisoner. She got herself out of Iraq, away from that monster at eighteen, achieved all she has and compromised our maximum-security holding cell to get to cousin NaS, so we'll certainly have our work cut out.'

'Well, that's the thing, ma'am, the issue that alerted me. The DNA results showed a distant match to UT4, only three percent, that's way below a first or second cousin and inconsistent with the original samples of Nadeem al Shabah obtained in 2003 and 2014.'

'Explain.'

'I mean, that thing down there that looked like NaS, sounded like NaS and had the intellect and memories of NaS, was not, according to the latest sample, NaS. In the transcript, he said, "Did the ghost-al Shabah become al Jamie-the collector, or the other way round?" I think it was some kind of ab-human fucking snowball, rolling along, collecting minds, bodies and memories. Pardon my French.'

'Ab-human snowball? Well, this is real BARBELL stuff. The footage is insane; we don't have a body, just a pile of dried foliage; and it's inexplicable, like everything you touch. "Between DNA and technology, our prayers may find answers."'

'Very good. Who's that from?'

The Chief rebuffed his question. 'Finish your drink, Captain St John Bradley, and leave me with my rogue states, poly-criminals, terrorists, maritime piracy, and foreign technological sabotage. Leave me with normality. Please.'

He did as he was asked and made for the crimson padded door. As he reached for the handle, he turned back towards the Chief. 'For what it's worth, ma'am, there was a superior thirty-three percent match identified.'

'Where?'

'Very close to home.'

'Who?'

'Siobhan Uhuru-Behan, 808, code-name GLIMMER.' He opened the door.

'And what the hell am I to do with her?' Dewhurst ranted, thumping both fists down on the ebony.

Bradley looked over his shoulder to see her standing, leaning with her knuckles on the desk, her face etched with incredulity. As he crossed the threshold, he nodded above her to the man in the seventeenth century nest of black. 'Ask him, Admiral.'

The door clicked shut.

Chapter 19

SHAPE, SHADOW, SILHOUETTE

All debriefs and assessments complete, the emoji code had finally landed on Halloween. They'd said goodbye at Cardinal Place, the perfect nook, BREAKSPEAR said, for a live drop, a central blind spot existing in plain sight. But it was an exchange of gifts not intelligence, or so she thought, and it was over in seconds. From him to her the Walkman to keep and a new mix tape to enjoy, and from her to him a white label record. The crafty old sod was giving TAVS the finger, and now she had to decrypt his parting words: 'Listen carefully to track 13; the answer may be in the mirror in more ways than one.'

There was no track 13. The mix tape finished with track 12, a nod to her old career, a live version of *If I Were a Carpenter* by the Small Faces, so she'd raised the volume and listened back very carefully. The tape hiss was broken, interspersed with staggered silences. It amounted to a barely discernible looped message in Morse code.

She had a destination.

At 4 am, the black figure vaulted the gates and rolled into a run with animalistic power and grace. Weaving forwards, she blended with the forms of shape, shadow and silhouette that the environment presented. All senses fully attuned to the darkness, she headed into the pitch envelope, surging silently down the river path and under the bridge. She squatted and took time to be silent, studying the tree line across the Serpentine against the eternal luminescence thrown up from the city.

Her stillness let the nocturnal sounds of an urban park chatter to life again. She approached the bronze horn blower in a crouch, retrieved the finger-torch from the pocket of her hoodie, swept the halo of light down and located the leveret, then struck a line from the direction of its hind leg until it met the base of the silver birch tree. She slid her daysack off her shoulders, took out and unfolded a square of corec protection followed by a garden trowel.

An earlier downpour had softened the grateful soil, which she cleaved apart with ease. She worked down in a steady rhythm, assembling a mound of mud and displaced earth worms. Suddenly she was alerted by that preternatural sensation hardwired in humans since apes first walked upright; that of being watched. Crouching lower, she slowly and smoothly looked to her left.

The retinas and vertical pupils glinted and ambient light allowed the watcher's identification. Its white chest and black nose were low to the soil, where, at its rear, the flare of a brush moved gently, without a sound. They regarded one another silently for uncountable heartbeats until Shev smoothly and slowly returned to the dig and found resistance at the point of the trowel. She pulled out the polythene-wrapped prize and replaced the earth with care. The observing fox rose and silently exited into the last knockings of darkness.

Shev remained kneeling on the corec. Torch in mouth, she tore open the black polythene. It contained a second transparent bag. The torch's halo revealed what appeared to be a copied manuscript in hieroglyphic code. She turned it over and found a pink post-it note inside, handwritten in biro: 'Homework. B. x'

November 5th 202?
Ocho Rios
Jamaica

What's twenty-four hours among friends? Bradley asked himself as he rose from the wicker chair on the veranda. He rotated the ice in the glass tumbler as the tropical breeze came on a little stronger than was comfortable, moving his hair back and flickering the lantern's candle. He downed the last of his pleasure and took in the swelling sunset as it bloomed above the sea's horizon. An immediate refill was called for, and, of course, the gift.

Inside, he unsheathed the 9 oz vinyl and inspected the white label's felt-tipped scrawl. '*Sampa the Great*. Final Form. Hmm.'

He padded over to the turntable and did the honours, raising the volume to counter the north coast's crashing tide, pulled on by the full moonrise. Bradley nodded to the looped beats, and as he recharged the tumbler, he took a step back to survey the array of photos pinned to the corkboard. Allowing a moment's sentiment, he studied the young man briefing the gathered group of Saracen Firquat, Dhofar '75. Then a primitive Polaroid selfie of himself, Wallace and a bemused Oldfield. In amongst the array of pins, photos and tickets, he found what he was looking for.

She still made his heart leap. The ballpoint on the white border, written in her hand said: *Great Ormond Street Hospital, 2003*. He kissed his fingers and gently laid them on the surface, touching the heart of Janice in uniform, caught in action doing what she did best, her hands on the shoulders of a grinning little brown girl with almond eyes and natty hair, about to blow out three green flamed candles on top of the small iced cake.

§

EPILOGUE

1755 hrs, June 23rd, 1923

1 Melbury Road, Kensington,

London, W1.

It had been a wonderful afternoon that had stretched out from a dinner for two into the early evening. Valentine and his host had relished the retelling of stories, each filling in the blanks lost to memory with truths and outcomes unknown or untold. Each revelation was topped with hoots of laughter as the brandy flowed. Those were the fledgling days of the Bureau, but old habits die hard, so C kept strictly within the borders of Valentine's sphere of operations and experience. If only he knew about BARBELL, thought C. I'd either be in the ground, a millionaire or a resident of Bedlam.

His guest's secondary career, as a writer of espionage novels, had been particularly successful, and he'd often tried to pump C for spicy plot material, like a child with its nose pushed up to the glass of a toy shop window, but he'd had little success over the years and Valentine generally found himself deflected by C into ever more smoke and mirrors.

The grandfather clock in the corner chimed out six times.

'Is that the time? I really must be making tracks,' said Valentine. 'But straight up, old man, I have to ask, and you can blame my forthrightness on the brandy, but it's the middle of June and we've got the windows open. Why the blazes do you still have a log on the fire?'

C snuggled himself into the sofa and smiled thinly. 'I will forgive you for starters. Since the accident,' C explained, tapping his wooden foot with his cane, 'I've always been susceptible to chills. Malaria, the quacks say. The shivers come and go, so the little fire helps keep them at bay, even between June and August.'

C would soon be out of this for good. Old Val was always good for sport, keeping C's old wheels of deception lightly oiled, for a bit of harmless light sparring.

'Hmmm, I wish I'd never asked,' said Valentine, unconvinced, as he edged forwards on his seat, making his exit little by little. In reality, he was dragging himself away from the enigma that had changed his life.

'Convince yourself you didn't,' laughed C, before adding, 'Ask what?' His monocled eye winked.

Ann, C's secretary, knocked and entered as she'd been briefed to at the strike of six. 'Can I pour you more tea, sirs?' she asked.

Valentine waved no, but C nodded. Neither man lowered themselves to the point of eye contact with the girl. Ann poured C's tea, then left the room as Valentine rose to his feet.

'Is there anything we haven't covered today, old friend? What it is the life we've lived.' Valentine donned and straightened his trilby.

Looking wistful, C said, 'It's the reckoning, old boy.' It was an expression that Valentine had rarely, if ever, seen in his former master. The stick tapped the wooden foot again. 'The cost.' There was a momentary silence as the two men's eyes met.

'I'll bring my blasted abacus next time!' Valentine's axe-like interjection achieved its purpose with typical levity, smashing the ice of the spy master's reflection and returning the pair back to the present. C remained seated as the two men shook hands with enough vigour to dislodge the older man's monocle.

'Steady on, old man!' exclaimed C.

'I'll see myself out, sir, and do take care of that gold watch the PM's been saving for.' Valentine headed for the door. 'Until next time.'

'Until then, Val,' added C as the door closed. He drained the china cup and placed it back on its saucer. The old Chief heard Valentine bid Ann good evening, jump goat-like down the stairs, clearing three at a time, and finally the muffled thump of the street door closing behind him. Something in C's peripheral vision drew his gaze directly to the burning log in the hearth. Was it a flicker of green among the black, red and grey ash on the coals? It was gone; just a figment. His eyes were heavy. It's been a long game indeed, he thought. The reckoning at last … the final cost.

C leant back as his heart slowed and he closed his eyes for the last time.

Tilly, the flower girl, stood at her usual pitch on the corner of Napier Road, opposite the Crown and Sceptre. At the last moment, she saw a potential sale from a regular customer passing in front of her. 'Primrose, violets and pinks, Miss Ann?' she called out.

The figure stopped and turned. The evening sunlight glinted on the gold tooth revealed by the broad grin. 'Miss?'

Tilly drew back, startled. There before her stood a tall, handsome man with sandy reddish hair, longer than most, dressed in a bottle green suit. His eyes, of one blue iris and the other brown, almost black, met hers.

'I'm so sorry, sir! It must be these high summer days!' exclaimed Tilly, her face flushed red with embarrassment and her mind full of confusion.

The man cocked his head to one side and leaned forward. 'Tis midsummer, too, eh? St John's Eve, I do believe,' he said in a soft sing-song brogue, taking a violet from the tray and crossing the girl's palm. He grinned and walked on. Tilly looked down to see a small sprig of willow in the centre of her hand.

'And they'll be believin' in faeries next …' the man said to himself as he turned the corner.

'Oi!' called Tilly as she chased the scoundrel to collar him for a coin. She touched the green tweed of his sleeve.

The tray of flowers clattered onto the pavement, a blackbird sang to no one and the primrose petals began to dry out in the last of the evening's sun.

ACKNOWLEDGMENTS

I'd like to thank the following authors and podcasters whose sterling factual work was invaluable in my research for this book:

Naseem Nicholas Taleb, Alan Judd, Martin Pearce,

Thomas Cleary (quote translation)

Jonny Dillon and Claire Doohan -*Blúiríní Béaloidis*

Ulick O'Connor, Tim Pat Coogan, Denis Lenihan,

James Bridle, Shane Whaley, and the great Eddie Lenihan.

Badges: Retro Cards, Brighton

Editor: Debi Alper

Magnificent Betas: Mick Talbot, Captain RUJ, Secret Moona, Bob and Laura Peach.

Finally, my thanks go to my wife, as ever for her care, patience and tolerance as the world of the BARBELL series took form.

ABOUT THE AUTHOR

Andy Onyx was born in West Yorkshire in 1969 and grew up in Skegness, Lincolnshire.

He has lived, amongst other things, as a painter, martial artist, musician and educator and has enjoyed adventures in London and beyond since 1998.

His other works are ***dadless- a memoir*** and the ongoing ***BARBELL*** series of spy-fi novels.

@AndyOnyx1 | andyonyx.co.uk

GLIMMER

will

return

Thank you for reading.

To get clearance for classified BARBELL dossier material (and join the Microdot Books mailing list),

please subscribe on the link below:

https://expert-thinker-1881.ck.page/9ee2eb59da

Printed in Great Britain
by Amazon

69721178R00203